Don't Forget
To Die

Books by Margaret Chittenden

DYING TO SING

DEAD MEN DON'T DANCE

DEAD BEAT AND DEADLY

DON'T FORGET TO DIE

Published by Kensington Books

Don't Forget To Die

Margaret Chittenden

Kensington Publishing Corp.

http://www.kensingtonbooks.com

KENSINGTON BOOKS are published by

Kensington Publishing Corp.
850 Third Avenue
New York, NY 10022

Library of Congress Card Catalogue Number: 98-075338
ISBN 1-57566-435-6

First Printing: July, 1999
10 9 8 7 6 5 4 3 2 1

Printed in the United States of America

This book is dedicated to the F & H gang,
with undying affection.

This book is dedicated to the F & H gang,
with undying affection.

ACKNOWLEDGMENTS

Writers try to get their facts straight. Sometimes they need help. My undying gratitude to the following experts for their advice and information. Any errors of fact in this novel are mine, not theirs.

Detective III Paul Bishop, LAPD, Major Assault Crimes Investigations: author of the Fey Croaker mysteries

Dale Furutani: author of the Ken Tanaka Mystery Series and the Samurai Mystery Trilogy

John Giacobbe: Forensic Anthropologist (at large)

Teresa Loftin, Web designer and doctoral candidate in sociology at Emory University, Atlanta, GA.

Raymond Moeller, M.D.

Rick Stevenson, Educational Administrator

CHAPTER 1

"I don't want to be a *matron*," I complained to Savanna. "Why can't I be called your *maid* of honor?"

Savanna's lustrous dark eyes widened comically as she paused in her struggles with the hooks of the bustier she'd picked to wear under her wedding gown. She wanted to downplay her figure, she'd said, so she'd bought a size smaller than she should have, which had the double effect of pushing her bosom up higher and making her handspan waist look even tinier. This was downplaying? The white satin against her wonderfully smooth brown skin was something to see.

"Accept it, Charlie," she said. "There's no way your virginity can be reinstalled."

"But I'm only thirty-something," I reminded her. "Just like you. Would *you* want to be called a matron?"

Truth is, I was thirty-two, which made me six years younger than Savanna, but we'd both decided thirty-something was a convenient description whose use could be prolonged well into our forties. This was self-preservation rather than vanity—women are judged useless past a "certain" age, and we'd started fighting back early.

"Qualifying for maid of honor has nothing to do with age," Savanna said. "It has everything to do with virginity."

She and her little daughter Jacqueline and I were getting ready for Savanna's wedding in my apartment, a rectangular, multipurpose, minimally furnished loft above CHAPS, the country-western tavern on the San Francisco peninsula that Savanna and I each owned a sixth of.

"What's virginity, Mama?" Jacqueline asked.

She was sitting stiff and straight on my thrift-store sofa, looking like a miniature Degas dancer, the skirt of her white organdy dress pouffed out around her like a tutu. Her yellowish-brown hair, which was normally as frizzy as mine—we often commiserated with each other—was temporarily tamed into half a dozen fat braids laced with white rosebuds. There was an unusually solemn expression on her little gamine café au lait face.

Benny, my Netherland dwarf rabbit, sat just as stiff and straight on a towel on Jacqueline's lap, his usually smooth brown fur sticking out like the bristles on a bottle brush. His whiskers and ears were twitching rhythmically.

"Benny's nervous around little kids, isn't he?" Savanna commented.

"To tell the truth, he's not all that fond of women, either. He likes men with big hands best."

"Who doesn't?" Savanna said, with a wicked grin. "Virginity is something you have when you're a *good* girl," she added to her daughter, earning herself an exasperated glance from me.

"That child's going to grow up with some kind of complex," I said. "Besides which, I *am* a good girl. Since I divorced Rob, I've been completely celibate."

"What's celibate?" Jacqueline asked.

I looked at her mother.

"It's what you do at a birthday party," Savanna said. Then started in on me again. "Are you trying to tell me you and Zack haven't"—she paused delicately, with a sideways glance at Jacqueline—"done it yet?"

"Don't insult my intelligence, girlfriend."

"Yeah, sure," she said.

I could hardly blame her for being suspicious. It had become apparent to several people, including Savanna, that Zack used to have a serious effect upon my hormone quota whenever he ambled into my field of vision. (It's maybe not too well known that the word hormone comes from a Greek word that means "to urge on." Which is what hormones surely do.)

Zack, of course, was Zack Hunter, the immensely popular TV star slash sex symbol who was our senior partner in CHAPS. Fortunately, so far, my brain had managed to control the lustful urges of my inclined-to-be-traitorous body, thus keeping me off the long, long list of Zack's conquests, which Savanna and I had nicknamed his "doll brigade."

"Swear to God," I said.

I switched on my portable TV to get the local news and weather forecast as well as to get Savanna off my back. It was going to be warm and sunny all day, our perky local announcer said. Words to make a bride smile.

Without any change in expression or tone of voice,

Ms. Perky went on to announce that a dead body had been discovered in Herb's Budget Storage Facility in Bellamy Park. "Details when we return," she added before her smile faded and the commercial began.

My ears perked up. Since I became a partner in CHAPS, I've had a couple of unexpected encounters with corpses. I've also developed a morbid interest in any hint of murder in the neighborhood.

Savanna wasn't paying attention to the TV set, I realized. "Why don't you just nail Zack and get it over with, Charlie?" she asked. "P.J. thinks you should, too."

P.J. was Patty Jenkins, one of our CHAPS regulars. Not noted for her success with men.

"Gina Giacomini put it a little differently," Savanna went on, chuckling. " 'Charlie ought to just *do* it,' she said. 'She'll have the memory of it forever.' She looked real wistful, poor thing. She's probably regretting she let Angel get away."

I shook my head at Savanna. "Anyone with an ounce of sense agrees with me that my self-esteem is more important than some passing sexual satisfaction. 'Get away from that man,' they say. 'Sleep with him and you'll never forgive yourself.' I happen to think *they* are right."

"You sure you're not just afraid that if you did it, Zack would lose interest?"

"All women are afraid of that with every man they contemplate boffing," I said.

"What's boffing, Aunt Charlie?" Jacqueline asked.

"Some kind of polish," I said.

Savanna looked smug.

I sighed. "Okay, so you were confident about Taylor

Bristow. But wouldn't you agree that most women hesitate to do it with a guy the first time because they're afraid he won't respect them in the morning?"

She shrugged, which I took as agreement. "The biggest problem with most men is that they're men," I said. "Unfortunately, that's also their greatest asset."

Savanna laughed. "That's good, Charlie. You ought to get it printed on a refrigerator magnet."

Obviously she wasn't taking me seriously.

"We're all victims of the Madonna/Whore complex men have," I went on. "We're either up on a pedestal as a model of purity, or we're in the gutter because we gave in to base passion."

"Your passion for Zack is base?" Savanna asked with a grin.

"My passion for Zack no longer exists except in your lurid imagination," I said. "I'm over it. He doesn't affect me anymore."

"Uh-huh," she said. "And when, may I ask, did this transformation take place?"

I shrugged. "A while back."

It was shortly after the conclusion of a murder mystery that Zack and I had solved together. He took me to some fancy restaurant in Bellamy Park that was so trendy only Zack could have gotten a reservation at such short notice. We ate Crab Louis, we drank Veuve Clicquot, we made brooding eye contact. He took my hand and folded it into his. When I was totally mellow, ready to lie down and let him do whatever he wanted to do with me, and do it right back to him, he took me home to my loft, came in, petted Benny, took me in his arms, kissed me better than anyone ever kissed me in my whole life—and broke out in hives.

Turned out, he'd suddenly become allergic to crab. It was two days before he stopped itching.

By then I'd decided his reaction was a message from the gods directly to me to hang on to my original vow. *Don't do it, Charlie,* they had said, loud and clear.

And with that message firmly in my mind, I was able to finally grow up and calm down and stop reacting to Zack like one of Pavlov's female dogs in estrus. (You could look it up.)

"What's passion, Mama?" Jacqueline asked.

"Some kind of fruit, honey," her mother said.

Matron or maid, I was happy to be standing up for Savanna Seabrook at her wedding, though I was never thrilled at the prospect of prettying myself up. This lengthy process involved darkening my orange eyebrows with brow groomer, layering black mascara on my orange eyelashes, and spreading Elizabeth Arden's Final Finish mousse over the orange freckles on my nose. Not to mention the arduous task of raking through my long orange hair with a wide-toothed comb and Frizz-Free until it looked like a bundle of corkscrews instead of a long-neglected floor mop. One of the reasons I liked being part owner of a country-western tavern was that most of the time I could just slap on a cowboy hat and go.

About the time I got through prettifying, the commercials and station break finally came to an end and Ms. Perky came back to talk about the dead body.

Somebody who preferred to remain nameless had bought the contents of an apparently abandoned storage locker in a sealed-bid auction, and had discovered the body in among the lawnmowers and tools and garden furniture. The corpse had evidently been hidden on the premises for some time.

"Eeeuw!" I exclaimed. Once you've been exposed to it, the smell of a neglected dead body lives on, so to speak. Though I was immediately interested, it occurred to me that a dead body in a storage locker was not something my best friend should be hearing about on the morning of her wedding, so I reached over to switch off the television set.

"Hold it," Savanna said, raising her hand, her gaze fixed on the small screen. She chewed on her full lower lip. "You don't suppose Taylor would get called out today of all days, do you?"

Detective Sergeant Taylor Bristow was one of Bellamy Park's finest. He was also the bridegroom, so it was kind of important that he show up.

We watched the report in tense silence for a few minutes while the announcer presented a few more meager bits of information, then breathed twin sighs of relief when Detective Sergeant Reggie Timpkin appeared at the scene of the crime.

As always, Timpkin's chest was puffed out like a pouter pigeon's, his chin bunched down into his neck, his pale eyes narrowed to suspicious slits. His caterpillar mustache curled in disgust as he announced that the victim was a male. Would he have felt better if the body was female? "This is a dastardly crime," he proclaimed. Timpkin really did talk that way. Zack had said once that he'd watched too many episodes of *Masterpiece Theater*.

"The county medical examiner has determined that the victim died of several wounds caused by some type of cutting instrument," he went on. "Foul play is definitely suspected."

"Duh," I commented.

Sergeant Timpkin and I had crossed paths, and swords, a couple of times, and he was in no way my favorite law-enforcement officer, but far better him than Bridegroom Bristow for today's duty. I switched him off in midoration and stood up to retrieve Benny from Jacqueline's lap, then put the rabbit in his cage in the bathroom. He scuttled through the arch-shaped doorway I'd cut in the cardboard box he'd shown a liking for recently, turned around, hunkered down and stuck his head out of the opening, his head jerking as it drooped, his eyes blissfully closing. "East, west, home's best," I commented, and he twitched whiskers at me.

I glanced out of the window that overlooked CHAPS's parking lot and saw that the wedding guests were starting to assemble. It was time to get zipped into my long, dark blue matron-of-honor dress and button Savanna into her bead-encrusted and fringed wedding gown. Savanna never heard the expression "less is more."

"Hey, how you doin'?" the bride said in a low smoky purr as she joined her lanky bridegroom onstage in CHAPS's main corral.

Bristow's body visibly tightened and his amber-colored eyes glazed over as he looked at her. I was beginning to worry about Bristow's eyesight. How many clues would he miss as a detective if his eyes weren't properly focused? Maybe marriage would straighten him out. Marriage is one of the best cures for love. Trust me on this.

Angel Cervantes and I traded grins as the love-birds turned toward the minister. Savanna had asked Angel—our other partner—to give her away. She didn't have a father or any uncles living. She hadn't had much of a family at all until recently, even though her mother and aunts and cousins all lived in San Francisco. They'd ostracized her fourteen years ago when she married Teddy Seabrook, then a catering manager. He was a white man, twenty-five years her senior.

Teddy had turned out to be gay, though Savanna hadn't caught on to this little glitch in his personality until they'd been married ten years. She'd just thought he wasn't sexually interested in her. Not a good enough reason to leave a man, she'd told me solemnly.

After Savanna had divorced Teddy—now a restaurateur—so he could boff his sous-chef lover with a clear conscience, she'd figured it wasn't necessary to tell her family he was gay. So now they were all smugly convinced she'd just come to her senses, as they'd always suspected she would.

Now that Savanna was marrying an African-American, which, according to Savanna's mother and aunts, was what God had intended for her all along, her sins had been forgiven. The relatives, all female apparently, were in their places with smiles on their faces, sitting regally on the rented folding chairs that were lined up in rows on the dance floor.

"A police officer is a welcome addition to any family," Savanna's mother, Ofelia, had confided to me when we posed for photographs ahead of the ceremony. She'd also approved of Savanna wearing white, though the aunts had wondered if it wasn't a mite inappropriate. "That last wedding didn't count," Ofelia had explained to them, and they'd nodded solemnly.

I wasn't sure how she was going to explain Jacqueline in that case, but she seemed to have taken to her, so it probably didn't matter.

Savanna and Bristow were exchanging their vows, looking adoringly into each other's eyes, the groom lean in his tuxedo, his brown and elegant bald head gleaming under the wagon wheel light fixtures. He'd refused absolutely to wear tails.

Angel looked great, too. Straight out of *Gentlemen's Quarterly*. Although I'm not sure men with ponytails and drooping Pancho Villa mustaches are welcome in *GQ*. After handing over the bride, he'd stepped to the side of the stage. I noticed Gina Giacomini was sitting a few rows back, her spiky hair its usual mixture of colors. Her lipstick and nail polish appeared to be blue to match her thigh-high leather dress. Gina was punk but sweet-natured, the manager of Buttons & Bows, the Western concession in CHAPS's lobby. Her gaze was fixed yearningly on Angel. For a while we'd had high hopes of Gina and Angel connecting. They'd shown great interest in each other the previous year, but Angel had broken off with her a few months back. There was something he had to do, he'd said, something that prevented him from getting romantically involved with anyone until it was done.

A mystery man, our Angel. I watched him for a few

minutes and saw him glance at Gina a time or two from under hooded eyelids. *Something ought to be done to get those two together.* I filed the thought away for future action.

You may have noticed I haven't mentioned that Zack was among those present. I'd been trying to ignore him, which wasn't too easy for the matron-of-honor to do to the best man. It was the first time I'd seen him "all duded up," as he'd described himself. Apart from a couple of times when he'd been naked except for short shorts or that swimsuit that looked as if he'd painted it on especially for the Hawaiian Sunshine Soap commercial, and an occasional appearance in sweats, I was used to seeing him in the signature black cowboy garb he'd plagiarized from Johnny Cash.

As you might expect, he was no slouch in a tuxedo, either. He looked attractive, attentive, competent, and, of course, as camera ready as a TV star is supposed to be.

Did you ever see the comic strip *Dilbert* in which the main character walked around with a cloud of doom over his head and anyone who came near him immediately disintegrated into body parts?

Zack has a similar cloud that has a similar effect on women, except that his cloud contains chromosomes in heat. As far as I'm concerned, Zack's cloud also spells doom. Which is why I've learned to be unmoved by it.

He produced the rings smoothly on cue. Any second now someone would say, "The envelope, please," and award him an Emmy for playing the part of the best man so well.

After the vows, Bristow quoted Shakespeare. *Two Gentlemen of Verona*, Act IV, Scene II, according to the wedding program.

I may have mentioned before that when he wasn't chasing down crooks, or working a crime scene, Detective Sergeant Bristow did Shakespeare in the Park. He loved that his new mother-in-law was named Ofelia, even if she didn't spell it right.

He'd changed the name of the character in the quote he'd selected as his part of the ceremony, which brought yet another adoring smile to his bride's face.

"Who is Savanna? What is she, That all our swains commend her? Holy, fair and wise is she; The heavens such grace did lend her, That she might admired be."

His voice was deep, vibrant. If any of the enthralled guests had dropped a program when he hesitated for a breath to carry him through the rest of the quote, it would have been heard.

But then the phone rang.

My fault. I was in charge of the festivities. Why hadn't I thought to turn off the ringer or unplug the telephone? It kept on ringing. I visualized a telemarketer wanting desperately to sell us some aluminum siding, or to save us hundreds of dollars every time we made a phone call.

Zack leaped gracefully down from the stage to answer the phone, then signaled Angel that it was for him.

Angel's high cheekbones acquired the reddish tinge that meant he was embarrassed.

Bristow started in on Shakespeare again, but most of us were watching Angel. He'd turned his back to the crowd and was speaking in the lowest of voices, a bare murmur running beneath Bristow's monologue. But his hand was gripping the phone so hard his knuckles showed yellow-white against his bronze skin. When he hung up and turned around, he looked as pale around the mouth and eyes as he had that time he fainted on top of the skeleton we found in CHAPS's flowerbed. If you missed that story you can probably find it at your local library.

Possibly aware that his audience was distracted, Bristow flubbed his last line, stumbling over the pronunciation of "garlands." Jacqueline giggled. The guests chuckled in response.

Obviously embarrassed, the little girl covered her mouth with her hand and looked as if she might burst into tears.

Bristow—dear wonderful Detective Sergeant Bristow—bent down from his great height and picked her up. From then on, he and Savanna held her between them while they finished their readings. By the time Savanna got through with a poem she'd written herself, and Lonnie Tremayne, backed up by the California Rangers, sang "Keeper of the Stars," there wasn't a dry eye in the house, and nobody was paying any attention to Angel.

Except me.

I'd hired Dorscheimer's, the restaurant in CHAPS's lobby, to cater the reception, even though I was always banging heads with them over the amount of fat in their food. I care about such things, which irritates a lot of people. "Who worries about fat content at a wedding feast?" the chef had countered. I'd conceded he had a point.

Angel got in line at the buffet in the bar area with everyone else, but he appeared to be absentmindedly helping himself to some of everything as if he were sleepwalking, ignoring the people who spoke to him, his dark gaze distant, his forehead furrowed. I think I already told you Angel is the other partner in CHAPS besides Zack, Savanna, and me. He's one of our bartenders, the bouncer, and the best dancer of us all. He and I teach most of the line-dancing and couples dancing at CHAPS, though Savanna lends us her feet from time to time as well as waiting on tables. Zack sort of hangs around, leaning against a railing or a bar. He does a very sexy lean.

Angel had told me he'd bought his share in the tavern because he'd reached a stage in his life when security looked pretty good to him. He'd inherited the money to buy his one-sixth share, he'd said, but he hadn't said who from and I'd never questioned him about it. Which was very restrained of me, considering I have what my late parents used to call "a mountain-size molehill of curiosity."

I went in search of Zack to see if he had any information to offer. He stood with his back to the far wall, clutching a plate of food, a hunted expression on his normally good-humored face. A gaunt bespectacled woman with gray hair pinned up in a loose knot on top of her head was haranguing him, holding a piled plate herself and waving her fork in his face.

"You don't *have* a favorite sexual fantasy?" she exclaimed as I pulled in alongside. "I don't believe you.

All men have sexual fantasies. Most commonly about making love to two women at the same time. Either dominating, or being dominated."

I'm always amazed at the intimate way some people talk to celebrities like Zack.

"I'm not like all men, ma'am," Zack said. From anyone else that would have sounded pompous, but Zack's green eyes have a teasing light in them and his smile is crooked and deliberately self-deprecating, so you always get the feeling he's inviting you to share a joke at his expense.

"All men say that," the woman said sternly.

She glanced at me. "Ms. Plato? Jane Arnett here. Terrific wedding. I understand you're responsible. Good job."

"Thank you." This woman hadn't been on any guest list I'd gone over. Surely no one would crash a wedding?

"This is a serious research project," she said severely to Zack. Then she hauled a business card from her jacket pocket, stuck it in the breast pocket of his tuxedo, patted it briskly and turned away. "Call me if you decide to participate," she said over her shoulder.

"Thanks for gallopin' to the rescue, Charlie," Zack said. A mischievous light appeared in the famous green eyes. "You're lookin' mighty pretty, darlin'. Don't know that I ever saw you in a dress before. You want to know about my favorite sexual fantasy? I wouldn't mind tellin' *you*. Doesn't have anythin' to do with two women."

"Forget it," I said.

His knowing grin said he thought I was probably turned on by the suggestion. He always thought women would be turned on by anything he did or said. Which was one of his more maddening traits—and the one that was mainly responsible for my being cured. "You suppose that lady has a cuckoo in her clock?" he asked. "What kind of research project do you reckon she had in mind?"

"Probably wants to shut you up in a room with some pubescent female and some sex toys and watch through a peephole to see what you'd do."

Any other man would have realized I was being sarcastic, but Zack looked interested.

"Who called Angel?" I asked.

Zack picked a chili pepper off his plate and bit into it, which caused my eyes to water and made me worry about the mascara I'd put on.

"Some guy," Zack said. "Didn't give a name."

"Did you tell him we were in the middle of a wedding?"

He nodded. "He said it was urgent. Talked with an accent."

"A foreign accent?"

"Nah. Had a drawl. Somethin' like Angel's, only more so."

"Angel used to live in Texas, remember? Said he worked on a ranch there. About the only thing he ever told us about his past."

"Uh-huh. Could've been Texas."

"Did you notice how pale Angel was when he hung up?"

"Nope."

He was regarding me with lofty amusement. He often teased me about being nosy. Which I freely admitted to. I was trying to grow beyond the habit, but at the moment I was too worried about Angel to work on improving my character.

Angel was standing with his back to the wall nearest the buffet. I walked over and stood next to him, but he didn't even notice me.

Angel is a year older than me, average height for a man, so he and I can talk face-to-face. He's not a big talker, though. He especially doesn't talk about his past.

When he forgets to look worried, he has a smile to die for. But he wasn't smiling now. He just stood there, holding his filled plate and the napkin with the bride and groom's names written in silver, lost in his own silence.

After several minutes, I moved into his field of vision. "Hey, Angel," I said as gently as I could. "You want to eat with us?"

"Sure," he said, but his liquid-brown eyes were still shadowed.

He followed me to the large round table I'd reserved for the partners and staff, nodded to our eccentric deejay, Sundancer Brown, and Patrick, our youngest bartender, then stood looking questioningly down at the plate he'd placed on the table.

"You going to sit down, Angel?" Zack asked, coming up behind us.

It took a minute for Angel to reply. Then he shook his head and looked at me as if he'd just this minute noticed who I was. "I have to go, Charlie," he said.

"You can't leave now," I protested. "You're standing in for father of the bride. You have to dance with Savanna, propose a toast."

He nodded, his expression bleak. I put a hand on his arm. Beneath the fine wool fabric of his tuxedo I thought I detected a faint tremor. "What's wrong, Angel?" I asked.

"I have family business needs attending to." Turning on his heel, he headed toward the exit.

"Angel has family?" Zack queried behind me.

My very question. As far as I could remember, Angel had never mentioned any relatives at all.

CHAPTER 2

Every once in a while I get twisted up in my sleep, wake up with a crick in my neck and take myself off to my chiropractor, who fixes me up in no time. Actually, I go even when I don't need to. Regular adjustments keep a person healthy.

Dr. Yarrow's clinic is conveniently situated on Cavenaugh Street, in one of those upscale medical malls that have huge skylights and a jungle of tall plants everywhere you look. The mall houses everything from a dentist to a physical therapist to a heart surgeon. It also features a great health food restaurant, and I usually manage to time my appointment so I can take advantage of it.

Feeling totally well adjusted as I climbed down from my Wrangler in CHAPS's parking lot, I was further relieved to see Angel sitting on the steps that led up to the tavern's streetside door. I'd been worried about our missing partner. He hadn't been seen or heard from since the wedding two days earlier. Judging by the either dejected or exhausted way he was sitting there—his shoulders slumped, hands dangling uselessly between his knees, head drooping so that his

straw cowboy hat shaded his face—he had not bene-
fited from taking Sunday off without notice.

As I lifted out the bag of grocery items from Lenny's
Market, and the daily newspaper I'd picked up after
seeing that there was a follow-up story on the body in
the storage facility, I noticed a new-looking though
dust-covered black Dualie parked a few slots over.
Cowboys love a Dualie, I'd learned since I'd 'gone country.' A Dualie's the cowboy's Cadillac.

"You get a new set of wheels, Angel?" I asked,
admiring the truck over my shoulder.

"Excuse me, ma'am?" he said.

That's when I realized he wasn't Angel. The voice
was deeper and throatier, and the Texas accent was
stronger.

I swung my head back around. He was around
Angel's height and had Angel's black hair and high
cheekbones. Now that he'd straightened out of his
slump and was standing, I could see that he didn't have
Angel's mustache or ponytail. Lean but sturdy, he was
wearing black jeans stacked over dusty black boots, a
T-shirt with a bucking bronc on it, a white straw cowboy hat that was a little grimy around the beaded
hatband. Angel always looked as if he'd just emerged
from a Western clothing store wearing the top of the
line. This man looked as if he'd been traveling on horse-
back through the desert. He also looked tough.

"Miguel Cervantes," he introduced himself, clasping
my hand with a solid grip that came close to mangling
my fingers. His hand was callused, hard. His eyes
flicked me over, not in an insulting way exactly—more

of an assessment. "If I was to guess, I'd say you had to be Charlie Plato."

"You're related to Angel?" Stupid question. He was the spitting image.

He appeared to examine the question for hidden traps before answering. "He's my little brother."

"I didn't even know Angel had a brother. I thought you were him. You really do . . ."

". . . look like him," he finished for me.

"Did you come to see Angel? He hasn't been around the last couple of days."

His eyes were even darker than Angel's. Almost black. Angel's eyes were gentle. Kind. Miguel's were expressionless, hard. As he studied my face, I was aware of tension in his body. "Since when?"

"Since Saturday, during the wedding. He had a phone call and took off. Was that you on the other end?"

He didn't answer. I supposed he figured it was none of my business.

I tried an indirect route. "You drove all the way from Texas since then?"

"Nope."

"Where then?" See how difficult it is to keep from being nosy sometimes? It's the only way to find out anything when you run into these closemouthed types.

His chin came up. There was a hard edge to this man that wasn't present in his brother. He seemed coiled and wary. I thought he would probably refuse to answer, but he surprised me.

"Seems like Angel mentioned a time or two you had an inquisitive nature, Miz Plato." He considered for a moment, then evidently decided to let loose some information. "I've been calling Salinas, California, my hometown for a while. 'Cept when I'm taking part in some other rodeo. At the California Rodeo in Salinas they call it ro*day*o, but what I do is *ro*deo. Had a rodeo going on last couple days. Couldn't get away. Drove up here this morning but Angel's not home. Thought he might be here at SHAPS."

I must have blinked.

"I guess you say it CHAPS, the way Angel does," he said. "SHAPS is the right way—as in chaparral."

"It's our tavern," I said mildly. "We can pronounce it fish if we want to."

His eyes narrowed the way Zack's do when he's putting on his "squintin' into a dust storm" look, but he didn't comment. "Do you know where Angel is?" he asked.

"Nope," I said. I could be monosyllabic, too, when I wanted to be. He gave me another hard look.

"You want to come in?" I asked. "We have a part-ners' meeting due to start in a few minutes. Angel hasn't missed one yet.

He seemed surprised when I took him into the office. "I heard you lived here," he said.

"Upstairs, yes."

Surely he hadn't thought I'd take some guy I didn't know into my loft, even if he was the older brother of my good friend and partner. I knew all about the major differences between Cain and Abel. I thought this man could quite easily pass for Cain.

"What seems to be the problem?" I asked as I dropped the groceries and newspaper onto the floor.

Sitting down at my desk, I waved Miguel to a seat opposite.

Instead of taking it, he walked over to the window, turned and hefted one hip onto the sill. It was a very sexy pose. Zack often assumed exactly the same position. It also meant I had to look at him against the light, which cast his eyes into shadow.

I got up and switched on the overhead light.

"What makes you think there's a problem?" he asked.

"Angel seemed—well, out of sorts, I guess, after he got your call—that call—whoever. He took off shortly after and hasn't been seen since. Looks like a problem to me."

His mouth tightened. I recognize negative body language when I see it.

I sat down again. "So you're a bull rider?" I said when a silence seemed to be setting in.

He inclined his head slightly.

"Why would anyone want to ride a bull?"

"It helps if you have an ornery disposition." A glint appeared in his dark eyes. "You'd have to look back at history, Ms. Plato. Cowboys on the ranch, on cattle drives, working hard, competition arising naturally out of the day-to-day business of ranch life. Roping, riding, horse-breaking. Who can ride the wildest horse, stay on longest, take the falls, get back up and do it again. Then, when you got really good, looking for a bigger challenge—hey, how about a bull. Bull or horse, the animal's instinct is to throw off anything gets on its back. The challenge for the cowboy is man against animal, man against himself, man against man. I ride bulls because that's what I want to do. And I want to do it better than anyone else."

"Must be a worry for your family, all the same."

He pushed himself off the windowsill and came over to take the seat I'd indicated earlier. "I don't have a family," he said, leaning forward to make strong eye contact. "I'm a loner. Best way for a bull rider to be. Best way for a rodeo cowboy to be—traveling most all the time—five rodeos a week spring and summer, three a week in the fall. I heard you're a loner your-self?"

He had turned the question around on me. Fair enough. It was a method I sometimes used myself. "My parents were killed in a plane crash when I was still in school," I said.

"I believe Angel told me you were divorced?"

I was surprised Angel had told him that much about me.

"Did he?" I didn't talk to just anyone about my marriage. I'd fallen in love with and married a fairly famous plastic surgeon about the time I graduated from the University of Washington. We'd had a few happy years together, and then I'd caught him in one of his treatment rooms with his pants down around his ankles, boisterously "examining" an even more famous photographic model named Trudi. Turned out it was his usual modus operandi.

"Would you like a beer?" I asked.

Miguel nodded, and I conducted him into the main corral, where we sat at the bar and talked awkward small talk about Zack's collection of microbrewery beers, each of which had its own weird and wonderful name, until Angel arrived.

The brothers went through a ritual that never ceased to entertain me. Two strong men gripping hands, jaws like steel, trying not to show the emotion that was vibrating between them. At some point in this display of machismo, Miguel lifted his eyebrows at Angel and Angel nodded ever so slightly. And Miguel's face tightened. With anger? Concern? I'm a student of body language, but with these two stone faces, it was difficult to tell what emotion was dominating.

Zack showed up about the time the brothers separated. He was carrying a small cooler, which he set down beside the bar. He, of course, had to go through the grip testing ritual, too. I love to watch male bonding.

"Zack got that scar on his face from a bull," I told Miguel.

Miguel raised an eyebrow.

Our man in black touched the zigzag scar on his left cheek and looked rueful. "An episode of *Prescott's Landin',*" he said.

Miguel nodded. "Angel told me you were on TV. Never did watch much."

"Bull was supposed to be tranquilized. Dose wasn't strong enough."

There really had been a bull? I was surprised. I'd always thought Zack's scar was much more likely to have been bestowed by a jealous husband.

"You get a ticket on the way up?" Angel asked his brother with a half-grin.

Miguel shook his head. "I drove like somebody's granmaw. Didn't want to attract any police interest."

That statement definitely attracted *my* interest.

Angel looked at me. "I'm forever razzing Miguel about his lead foot, Charlie. It's a habit of his to drive over the speed limit."

Miguel was not amused. "I get going from rodeo to rodeo, I don't have time to mess around. I figure what I make from getting to the next rodeo in time to compete more than pays for the tickets I pick up on the way."

"I haven't seen my brother in a few months," Angel said when Miguel excused himself to the restroom to freshen up. Probably he'd sensed the questions that were working their way from my inquiring mind to my mouth.

"He seems a bit tense," I said.

Angel took off his straw cowboy hat, studied the sweatband as if looking for the manufacturer's name, then resettled it on his head. "Miguel is always tense," he said. "High-strung. Always looking for action. Our mother used to say she should have called him Diablo instead of Miguel. El Diablo. The prince of darkness. The devil," he explained for Zack's benefit.

His brother's arrival seemed to have loosened Angel's tongue. This was more information than he had ever given us about anyone in his family. I searched my mind for a way to keep him going. "The action he looked for wasn't necessarily legal?"

Angel sighed. "Miguel was always in trouble. Mostly kid stuff. Shoplifting. Drinking too much. Borrowing cars without permission—going on joy rides."

"Is he in trouble now?" I asked.

Again it took him a while to answer. Then he muttered, "Maybe," and asked if he and Miguel could borrow the office for a few minutes, so they could talk in private.

Zack gave him permission before I could get around to it. So, okay, Zack was the senior partner, but I did more work in the office than anyone. About the only time Zack even went into the office was to use the phone to call one of his dollies, or to throw darts at the board we kept on the back of the office door. Occasionally he and Angel played computer golf, and Sundancer E-mailed with a bunch of people on country music loops and Web pages. But I kept the books and did all the computer-related business stuff. I thought of it as *my* office, and I also thought I might have found a way to persuade Angel to invite us into the office, too.

"What?" Zack asked when I scowled at him.

I let it go, opened a mineral water for each of us, and came around the bar to sit on a stool next to Zack. I was eager to discuss this unexpected and very interesting turn of events. "Something's going on," I said. "What do you suppose it is?"

He took a few seconds to answer. For some unknown reason, he was carefully peeling the label off his bottle of Pellegrino. "Goin' on where?"

I sighed and took a swig of water. Zack's a mite dense sometimes. To be fair, though he has ceased to discombobulate my hormones, I have to admit he makes up for that by being something special to look at. He's tall and lean, with more than a hint of muscle under the all-black cowboy clothing. He has great hair—thick, untidy black hair that tousles up attractively when he takes his hat off. I've already mentioned his green eyes and the wry smile that hovers around his mouth most of the time. Add to all of that a pair of quizzically slanted eyebrows and you have the reason why most women, regardless of age, find him well-nigh irresistible.

"Angel and Miguel," I said with uncommon patience. "They apparently have some kind of problem. I'm pretty sure Miguel was the one who called and talked to Angel at the wedding. Angel was all shook up, remember? So now Miguel Cervantes, who we've never even heard of in two years of knowing Angel, drives up here from Salinas a couple of days later. Why?"

"To visit Angel, I suppose. It's not that far, Charlie. Eighty-five miles tops." He handed me the label from the water bottle, making an actor's small drama of the presentation.

"I'm supposed to save this for you?" I asked. "You're suddenly collecting labels instead of dollies? What's next, stamps?"

His crooked grin was pure mischief. No, not pure. "Tradition says if a guy gives a gal the label off a bottle means he's invitin' her to sleep with him."

"That's one of the dumbest things I ever heard."

He shrugged. Gracefully. The way he did everything. "It's a bar game, Charlie. If the label rips when you try to get it off, it doesn't count. Mine never rip."

"Why am I not surprised?"

He grinned smugly, impervious, as always, to sarcasm. "Gal accepts it, she's sayin' yes."

I slapped the label onto the bar as if it was too hot to handle, which, symbolically speaking, it was. "What's in the cooler?" I asked to change the subject.

He reached down and hefted the container onto the bar, opened it and took out a glass jar full of dark gray blobs. "Leftover caviar from the weddin'. Seemed a pity to waste it."

Sliding off his stool, he went around the bar and rooted under it until he came up with a pack of crackers. "Should be toast points, but we'll make do," he said cheerfully, as he put the cooler back on the floor.

In some ways Zack is culturally challenged. He never heard of Plato, the philosopher my Greek father had always insisted was our ancestral relative; when Bristow quotes Shakespeare he goes blank; when I mentioned Agatha Christie's Hercule Poirot once, he said he thought that dude maybe had his own TV show sometime back. Most of Zack's references originate in TV or movies. But the aunt who took him in when he was seventeen had lived in Beverly Hills all of her adult years and she'd taught him about the niceties of life, such as wines and caviar and which knives and forks to use when.

With a small spoon, he piled caviar on a cracker, gave it a squirt of juice from a lemon wedge he'd brought along and held it to my mouth. "Here you go, darlin'."

A few months back I would have said there is surely nothing more weakening to the knees and the brain than a sexy green-eyed man gazing at your mouth and offering it food. A reversal of Eve and the apple.

Fortunately, I was immune now. Mind over matter really works. You should try it.

The salty beads exploded with ecstasy against the roof of my mouth. This stuff was Beluga, the rarest and costliest caviar in the world. Zack had provided a generous amount of it for the wedding. I remembered my father telling me that Picasso loved Beluga caviar and bought it with cash wrapped in one of his drawings. I almost shared that anecdote with Zack, but was afraid he'd say, "Who?"

Like a baby bird, I opened my mouth for more. Two more cracker loads later, I was feeling much more kindly toward Zack than I'd felt in a while.

Fortunately, Angel showed up in the entrance about then. "We're leaving now," he called. "Okay I take a couple more days off to get things settled?"

"Sure," Zack called back before I could ask what "things" and precisely how much time a "couple more days" meant.

Great, now there were only two of us to run CHAPS. Savanna, of course, was on her honeymoon in San Francisco with Bristow, Jacqueline safely stowed with her grandmother. "You'll have to help with the dance lessons on Wednesday," I told Zack.

"Happy to, darlin'." He looked thoughtful. "How about we start off with the Desperado Wrap? One of my favorites. Don't know that I've ever seen it done at CHAPS."

I shook my head. "I'm not familiar with that one." I lied. I had danced it several times before I ever came to CHAPS. I knew damn well it was one of the most intimate couples dances you could imagine.

"Real pretty dance." His voice was as casual as could be. "You wanna try it out now?" he asked, waving the caviar spoon at the shadowy main corral dance floor.

I slid off my stool and turned away. "I have to go work on the Web site," I said over my shoulder as I headed for the exit. "You might do an inventory of the bar, as long as Angel's not going to be here to do it."

"Yes, ma'am," he drawled, using exactly the intonation his TV character, Sheriff Lazarro, would have used in his heyday—before the writers of the incredibly popular, incredibly unbelievable show, *Prescott's Landing*, killed him off. That was one character who certainly deserved to die. He was far too noble to live.

Zack didn't usually need to approach a woman; he was forever being propositioned and hadn't learned how to say no. So he wasn't used to rejection, except from me. It intrigued him, I guess. The way I saw it, Zack had caught on to the fact that my inner parts no longer went Whomp! whenever I looked at him. So he'd started a campaign to prove he could conquer me if he had a mind to. Probably he was curious to know how long I could hold out. *Forever*, I could have told him, but he'd have interpreted that to mean I was really fighting to make it.

Which, of course, wasn't true.

Putting Zack out of my mind, I fixed my attention on business. With the help of some advice from my friend and computer guru, who was coincidentally named Macintosh, I was developing a site for CHAPS to go on the Worldwide Web. Today, I wanted to upload our lesson schedule. We were increasing it, trying to bring in more people through the week. We were charging for it, too. Our overhead was eating up income at an alarming rate. We'd already instituted a cover charge on weekends and Wednesdays and were considering renting out the premises during the day and on Monday nights for group meetings or parties.

I pulled up short as I was about to enter the office. The front door was opening. I eased back around the stairway to see who was coming in and saw Angel and Miguel enter.

"We talked things over in the parking lot and we reckon we need to talk to you and Zack, Charlie," Angel said. His voice was so heavy, I felt an answering sinking inside my stomach. Whatever the problem was, it was serious.

"I'm just heading into the office," I said. "Zack's in the main corral. Give him a shout."

When I entered the office, I saw that the newspaper I'd dropped on the floor with the grocery bag had been opened out on the desk. The story about the dead man in the storage unit was uppermost.

CHAPTER 3

"Have you read that?" Angel asked, indicating the newspaper.

I shook my head. "I heard about it on television. On Saturday, while Savanna and I were getting ready for the wedding."

Zack leaned over the desk and turned the paper around so he could read the headline. "Yeah, I saw somethin' about this on the local news station. Somebody bought whatever was stashed in the locker in an auction and found a body in amongst the loot. Weird."

"Read it," Angel suggested. Shadowed by his cowboy hat, the bronze skin covering the planes and angles of his rough-hewn face was drawn tight as shrink-wrap. He was obviously holding back strong emotions.

I edged in beside Zack and we read the story together. Detective Sergeant Reggie Timpkin was quoted extensively. A resident of Bellamy Park had rented the storage locker eight months previously. He had paid in cash, six months in advance. But then he had failed to make the next two payments and the owner of the storage facility had put the contents up for bid. The owner could give only a vague description of the person who had rented the locker using the name "Bill Bailey," which had turned out to be an assumed name. Duh! The man had paid in cash.

Detective Sergeant Timpkin had subsequently discovered (Reggie loved words like "subsequently") that the real name of the man who rented the locker was Sal Migliatore—a popular local building contractor. A heavy smoker, Sal had died in Bellamy Park Hospital of lung cancer four months prior. Which explained why the rent on the storage locker had not been renewed.

The investigation was progressing satisfactorily, Timpkin had told the reporter. Right at the end of the interview, he had conceded that the dead man in the storage locker had been identified. His name was Vic Smith and he was probably Hispanic.

"Doesn't sound Hispanic," Zack muttered.

We both turned to gaze inquiringly at Angel and Miguel. Miguel was standing by the office door, looking out toward CHAPS's foyer as if he'd rather be anywhere but here.

"We want to ask you for some help," Angel said. "But we don't want to hang around here while we explain."

"You think CHAPS is bugged?" Zack was reverting, as he often did, to his old TV role as Sheriff Lazarro. The previous fall he had taken off for La-La land to shoot some more episodes of the show. This had surprised me considering his character had been killed off at the end of the last episode. But nothing is impossible in Hollywood. In the first of the new dramas, Sheriff Lazarro had awakened from what had miraculously turned out to be not death but a coma, weak but wise as ever. After recounting his near-death experience and religious conversion, he had gone on to solve six unlikely crimes in weekly installments. Fan mail had poured in, accompanied by, according to the tabloids, renewed interest in Zack from his costar, the eternal ingenue Molly Carstairs, who had never owned an outfit, on- or offscreen, that didn't owe a lot to Wonderbra.

I had often felt confused about Molly Carstairs, as Zack used her name to refer to the character she played as well as the real person. Eventually I'd discovered that *Prescott's Landing*'s writers had thought her real name fit the character so well they had used it. Stuff like that makes the line between fiction and reality even harder to distinguish for someone like Zack.

Predictably, the February sweeps had shown out of sight ratings for the return of the series, and the money men had reacted with typical glee, showing all six episodes Zack had shot, then putting on a long string of reruns. So far no one seemed to have noticed that none of the reruns were in order. Actors aged and became young again overnight, the original cast gave way to later replacements, then miraculously showed up again.

Pretty soon, Zack would be getting the call from Hollywood he'd been waiting for and he'd waft off again. Which was possibly why he was keeping Sheriff Lazarro handy.

Angel finally broke the silence. "We're afraid we might be arrested if we hang around places I work at or go to often."

Zack and I both stared at him, but he didn't offer any more.

"We want to get out of here, talk somewhere private, somewhere safe, okay?" Angel went on. "Today's Monday, CHAPS is closed tonight—you have anything you absolutely have to do?"

Zack and I agreed there was nothing outstanding that was more urgent than helping a friend.

There's a salt marsh where a small area of Bellamy Park borders on San Francisco Bay. Not long ago, when Zack was running for City Council, his opponent wanted to pave over that land and build an exclusive residential development with apartment buildings, motels, a golf course, tennis courts.

You may remember that the guy who was in favor of all this came to a bad end. The proposal was defeated.

The salt marsh is a great bird-watching area—about seventy percent of all the birds migrating up or down the Pacific Flyway stop off in the southern arm of San Francisco Bay. It had remained a beautiful, natural area, and though I wasn't a fanatical bird-watcher I went there sometimes when I wanted to get away from people noise for a few hours, or minutes. So it was the first place to come into my head. Sometimes it was crowded with schoolkids accompanied by earnest parents or teachers who wanted them to learn about shorebirds, cord grass, and pickerelweed. Luckily, the place was deserted when we got there. Like CHAPS, the Interpretive Center was closed on Mondays.

The day's sunshine had produced an onshore flow of marine air that had given rise to some foggy patches in the area, though it was possible to see Mount Diablo poking up darkly in the northeast. Miguel and Angel looked nervously over their shoulders as I escorted our little group from the parking area to a small wooden pier that had railings I liked to lean on.

For a few minutes, we stood silently side by side, looking toward San Francisco Bay and the mist-shrouded hills of the Coastal Range. A marsh hawk floated lazily above us, riding a thermal, looking down as though wondering if we were edible prey. Orange stuff that looked like dirty cotton candy covered some of the pickerelweed to our left. Salt marsh dodder, I remembered reading in the Interpretive Center—a supposedly harmless virus.

"You and Miguel know something about the dead man who was found in the storage locker," I suggested to Angel when nobody seemed to know where to begin.

"He's our father," he blurted out.

For once I was speechless. A rare phenomenon. Even the usually imperturbable Zack was struck momentarily dumb.

"We've been looking for our father for twenty-three years," Miguel said heavily. "He left us when I was fifteen and Angel was ten. We were living a ways outside of Houston then."

I flashed on a memory of Angel asking me once how to go about finding someone who'd gone missing. I'd been caught up in a murder investigation at the time and obviously hadn't given his question the attention it deserved. "When you told me you were looking for an old friend," I said to Angel, "you were trying to find your father?"

"Your father's name was Vic Smith?" Zack queried.

Angel's mouth twitched under his Pancho Villa mustache. "That's the name he took after he left us."

"He changed his name to avoid child support?" Zack asked.

I looked at our senior partner with interest. He'd jumped to that conclusion without much to go on. Had *he* ever been dunned for child support? Considering the number and variety of his sexual conquests in the short time I'd been tracking his record, it seemed entirely possible.

"He was running for his life," Miguel said.

We stared at him. There had been a bitter note in his voice. I suddenly didn't want to know what was coming next, but of course there was no way I could avoid it.

Miguel had evidently shut down for the moment. I never saw a face so closed up and stern. It was up to Angel to enlighten us. It took him a couple of minutes to get to it. He spent the time watching traffic speeding over the bay via a distant causeway.

"Before our father took off—he killed our mother." Angel's voice was flat, but I could clearly hear the pain underlying the words. "Miguel and I came home from school and found her lying in her own blood on the kitchen floor—shot to death."

"Whoa!" Zack exclaimed, paling.

My stomach turned itself into a pretzel. I remembered how Angel had fainted when we discovered the skeleton of a foot in CHAPS's flowerbed. That was the first murder case Zack and I were involved in. Angel had explained that as a child he'd discovered the body of someone who had been murdered. But he hadn't told us it was his mother's body.

"So you started looking for your father," I prompted to get away from the horror of the image that had planted itself vividly in my mind. Two boys, one ten, one fifteen, sturdy and dark-haired. Coming home innocently from school. Finding their mother dead. Murdered. Lying in a pool of blood. I swallowed hard. "I think you'd better start at the beginning," I said.

The foggy patches were increasing and joining together, forming a blanket around us. In a way, that was helpful. As Angel and Miguel alternated in telling parts of their story, we weren't distracted by the view—which was rapidly disappearing—and it was unlikely we could be seen from the parking area if anyone else decided to come out to the marsh. All of which tended to make it easier for the two brothers to talk.

They were born in Mexico. Between them, there had been two other babies, both boys, both stillborn. Their father was a carpenter who, while very young, had gained a reputation for cabinetmaking and fine wood finishing. He had also loved playing baseball, which made their mother, Malena, very angry, because it was, in her opinion, a waste of time, which could be better used earning money.

And then one day a man named John Sterling heard about this terrific pitcher, came to see him play and persuaded him to move to the Houston area.

John Sterling was a major-league baseball player

who had just retired and was bored. He wanted to train the boys' father and become his agent.

"Long John Silver Sterling?" Zack exclaimed, so surprised he forgot to drop the "g." "I remember him. He was one of the great ones. What was your father's real name?"

The brothers exchanged a glance. "Vicenzo Cervantes," Miguel said.

Zack shook his head.

"It's okay, Zack," Miguel said. "*Nobody* ever heard of him."

Sterling found Vicenzo a job as a cabinetmaker and got him onto a local team. Sterling's wife, Yvonne, employed Malena on the Sterling ranch which was just outside of Houston. Everybody was content, including Vicenzo, who was a fun-loving guy. "Especially around women," Miguel added.

About the time Vicenzo was ready to break into the major leagues he decided to show off at a local tavern. Drunk, he rode the mechanical bull, something he'd never done before.

"Probably to impress some bimbo," Miguel said.

Vicenzo didn't stay on the bull long and he fell heavily, sustaining a fractured collarbone, his muscle pulled clean away from his shoulder. His right shoulder. His pitching arm.

The brothers were silent for a moment, both leaning on the pier rail, both squinting into the fog as if they could see that one stupid act being replayed just for them.

Vicenzo had never recovered from the disappointment, Miguel said. After that, he had turned on his wife, his children, on the world. And then one day Miguel and Angel came home from school to find Vicenzo and Malena shouting at each other. This was not unusual. What was unusual was that Malena had packed all her husband's belongings in garbage bags and ordered him out of her house.

"When she wouldn't stop cussing him, he punched her in the face, knocking her to the floor," Miguel said. "I jumped him and he flung me off, picked up the bags and left. Our mother shouted after him, very sarcastic, 'Good-bye, don't forget to write.' And he yelled back, 'Good-bye, don't forget to die.' "

Angel took up the story, his mouth set so tightly, it was difficult to understand him. "The next day, we came home from school and found our mother shot dead on the kitchen floor. The gun was beside her. A pistol. We thought at first she had shot herself, but some deputies came from the county sheriff and said somebody else had killed her. Probably our father, they said. They went looking for him, but he had skipped town. They said someone must have helped him disappear. They were pretty sure it would have been Long John, but he denied knowing anything about it. They had put out a warrant for his arrest, somebody said, but he got away. They said there probably wasn't enough evidence to convict him anyway. But we had seen him hit our mother. We had heard what he said to her. That was enough proof for us."

"And all of a sudden, you had no parents," I murmured.

Angel nodded, Miguel shrugged. "Long John was kind to us," Angel said. "He and Yvonne took us in to live with them on the ranch, but Miguel wore out early on ranch work and took off to Big D." He glanced sideways at me. "Dallas," he explained.

"Went to work for a ranching family that raised bucking bulls," Miguel commented.

"But you stayed?" I said to Angel.

"I was ten years old. What could I do? John was a good man. He sent me to college. Texas A&M."

"You're an Aggie?" Zack said.

Angel nodded.

"Little brother has a degree in rangeland management," Miguel contributed.

Angel shrugged. "I worked the ranch until Long John died of a heart attack."

He paused, shook his head and hitched a booted foot onto the lowest rail. "After John died, Yvonne decided to sell the ranch. She died soon after—she was lost without him, she said. But before she died she asked me to help her with John's papers and I came across letters from my father to John. Evidently John had known all along where he was. He asked about his boys and seemed to know everything we were doing, so I guess John had kept him up to date. The letters mentioned Bellamy Park."

He hesitated. Behind us there was the sound of a small plane descending toward a nearby airport. I hoped the pilot had better visibility than we did.

"I told Miguel about the letters and we came to California," Angel continued. "I looked for work in Bellamy Park. I saw Zack's ad and bought into CHAPS with the money John left me. Miguel transferred to

Salinas. Went into partnership in a company that provides bucking horses and bulls."

"It isn't clear to me why you are afraid of bein' arrested," Zack said.

Miguel's mouth had set in a grim line. "Maybe if I tell you that when our mother was murdered, I made a vow to the county sheriff that someday Angel and I would find our father and kill him for what he did?"

"Yeah, that would do it," Zack said.

"Bellamy Park police will find out about that vow eventually,'" Miguel said.

"Looking for our father, I tried some of the places you suggested," Angel told me. "I even followed up on a TV commercial that promised to find the missing person in my life. But I didn't turn up any trace of him. You also suggested a peoplefinder on the Internet, Charlie. A friend of Miguel's who had access was willing to try it for us. No luck. Then we hired a private investigator who showed photographs of our father around this area and found out where he was living and the name he was using."

"You knew where he was before he died?" Zack asked. He was back in Sheriff Lazarro mode, frowning importantly. "That's not good. Does anyone know you found that out?"

"The woman he has been living with," Miguel said. "We went to her house months ago and talked to her. Roxanne Smith. Wants to be called Roxy. Seems like . . ." He bit down on his lower lip and went silent, then started in again as if he'd changed his mind about what he wanted to say. "Seems like she and our father pretended to everyone they were married, but they never were."

"She's a real estate agent," Angel put in.

"Number-one agent company-wide, she told us," Miguel said, with a cynical twist to his mouth. "Very proud of that, she was."

Angel said, "She told us our father had left her for a younger woman and, though she was pretty sure he'd be coming back, she didn't know when."

"When was this?" Zack asked.

"Middle of October, last year."

Eight months ago.

According to the newspaper report, "Vic Smith" had been dead about eight months.

"Miguel got the woman to tell us where our father had been working," Angel added. "We went to see his boss."

Evidently sensing that I was vibrating, Angel looked at me. "I know, Charlie. You want to know who the boss was. His name is—was—Sal Migliatore."

"The man who rented the locker," I said on a long breath. "He was alive then."

"He was ill," Miguel said. "Had one of those oxygen tanks on wheels people drag around when they can't breathe on their own. Plastic tubes in his nose. He said our father was a fine cabinetmaker, did good finish work, and it was hard to find someone who could do that well."

He frowned. "I think he did not like my father even though he employed him. He said he had no knowledge of where 'Vic' had gone. He was very short with us."

"Crabby," Miguel contributed. "He said there was

no knowing what had persuaded 'Vic' to leave Roxy—
there had been no problem with his work and no one
had complained about anything he had done, and it
was for sure he and Roxy were very much in love and
very happy together from all he'd ever heard. They
were forever smooching, he said. He also said he
thought maybe our father had some kind of seizure
while he was away from home, or had an accident and
developed amnesia or something like that."

"Mr. Migliatore's aura was black," Angel said. "Black
is always negative. Nothing getting out. Sometimes
that means the person is hiding something. But of
course, in this case, the man was very sick, I could see
death all around him."

Angel had mentioned auras before. Some other time
I was going to have to question him about the mystical
side of his nature.

Angel contemplated a squirrel that had run up from
the floating dock at the end of the pier and was sitting
on the top rail, "washing" its face. "What it came down
to . . ." He stopped and started again. "Evidently, Mr.
Migliatore knew exactly where our father was, but he
wasn't about to tell us."

"You think Sal Migliatore might have killed your
father?"

"I think it is most likely, yes, but now Mr. Migliatore
is dead and we are alive and we were asking questions
about our father, not just of Roxy and Mr. Migliatore,
but the people who worked for Mr. Migliatore, and
people at the other place. So we think we will come
under suspicion."

What other place? I was about to ask, but Zack, the

expert in all things to do with law enforcement because of his advanced education in TV drama, nodded wisely and said, "You're right," and while I was working back to what that applied to, I lost the thread.

Miguel took up the story. "I hung around Bellamy Park awhile, but our father didn't show up, so I went back to Salinas."

"We had the detective continue to search," Angel said. "But there was no more news until Miguel heard the TV report about the body in the storage place in Bellamy Park."

"And called you at the wedding," I said, looking at Miguel.

After a pause long enough to indicate he was as reluctant as before to part with information, Miguel nodded.

"Did you kill your father?" Zack suddenly shot out—some technique from *Prescott's Landing*, no doubt. Quite often, Zack was about as subtle as a branding iron.

I scowled at him, but he had his green eagle eyes fixed on Miguel's face and didn't notice.

I realized Miguel hadn't yet answered, and turned to look at him myself. He was gazing out into the fog, expressionless.

"I always planned to," he said.

"But he didn't do it," Angel said quickly. "He never even saw our father."

"Miguel?" Zack asked.

Miguel shook his head as though he were just waking up. "I spent a good part of my life bent on killing that man." Leaning over the pier rail, he gazed down at the mud below us. "I guess I'll never know now if I would have done it."

Angel jumped in again. "But he didn't do it."

Miguel hadn't actually denied it himself, I noted. "Angel?" Zack asked.

"I never even wanted to kill him," Angel said. "I was a kid when he left. I hated my father for killing my mother. I wanted him to pay, but properly, in prison."

"You didn't kill him?" Zack persisted.

Angel's cheekbones acquired the red streak that meant he was either embarrassed or angry. "I didn't kill him."

Zack nodded, evidently satisfied.

I was pretty sure Angel wouldn't kill anyone. I wasn't so sure about Miguel. He did have that hard edge. I sighed. "You should get in touch with the Bellamy Park police right away," I advised. "They're going to know who Vic Smith really is as soon as they check out his fingerprints."

It occurred to me to wonder if the corpse would *have* any fingerprints. I remembered Dr. Martin Trenckman, the county coroner/medical examiner, saying about the skeleton that had popped up in CHAPS's flowerbed a couple of years back, "All that rain . . . the flesh had slid off the bones."

I swallowed. Hard. It wouldn't have rained in that storage locker, I reminded myself. "It will look a lot better if you go into the station voluntarily," I said.

"I'm not so sure that's a great idea, Charlie," Zack said. "Reggie Timpkin is in charge of the investigation, remember." He adjusted his cowboy hat to its best angle and did his famous squint. "Give me a minute, here. Seems to me I should be rememberin' somethin'."

One of the clichéd plot lines from *Prescott's Landing*, no doubt. In the past, Zack had offered up one or two of them for consideration. To Zack, art didn't copy life, or vice versa, art *was* life. If you could call *Prescott's Landing* art. I sure wouldn't.

"Going to the police would be committing suicide," Miguel said emphatically. "We are the most likely suspects." He paused. "I haven't always had the best of relations with the police."

"You have a record?" Zack asked.

He shrugged. "Minor stuff. Barroom brawls. Couple of knife fights."

That didn't sound too minor to me. "Vic Smith" had been stabbed with some kind of cutting instrument, according to Detective Sergeant Reggie Timpkin. I could imagine Miguel using a knife against someone.

"How about this then," I suggested. "How about I call Taylor Bristow?"

"You know where he's spendin' his honeymoon?" Zack said, sounding surprised. "I thought that was supposed to be a deep, dark secret."

"Are you going to stay at Angel's place?" I asked Miguel.

He shook his head. "We don't think that's such a great idea."

"*I'm* not even staying there," Angel commented.

I waited a couple of beats, but nobody offered any further information. "Probably best if I don't know where you are, in case Bristow asks," I said. "I'll call him and tell him your story, see what he says. Maybe

Zack and I can go see him tomorrow morning. You can call me tomorrow afternoon and we can discuss whatever he advises."

There was a silence while both brothers contemplated the mud, or maybe they were watching the long-legged heavy-billed California clapper rail that was strutting awkwardly along the edge of the channel.

Then Angel said, "Tell you what, Charlie. If you and Zack will agree to look into this whole mess the way you did for old man Stockton a while back, I'll agree to you calling Sergeant Bristow." He hesitated, looking at his brother, who was frowning. "Otherwise, I'm afraid we'll just be processed through the system and the police won't worry about looking for the person who really killed our father."

"Deal," I said.

"Sure," Zack agreed.

If this kind of thing kept up, I was going to have to apply for a private investigator's license and start charging clients for my services.

CHAPTER 4

Taylor Bristow was not pleased to have his honeymoon interrupted. "It's a matter of life and death," I said, after he'd eyed me balefully around the doorjamb for a couple of minutes.

"Sure it is, Charlie."

"I'm serious," I insisted.

He sighed and opened the door marginally wider. "Come on in then." He glanced at Zack, his wide mouth twitching into a half-smile. "Bring your sidekick with you."

Bristow and Savanna had picked out a charming little Victorian B&B for the week following their wedding. The only reason I'd been told where they were was that I was making daily telephone calls to check on Jacqueline's welfare and had promised to report in immediately if she evinced the slightest unhappiness.

Bristow led us into the cheerily wallpapered living room of a large suite and gestured us to a sofa with a cabbage rose slipcover.

"Savanna's in the shower," he explained. "We were . . . a little late getting up."

Zack grinned reminiscently. He was probably used to having a woman in his shower around midmorning.

"We came to ask what you know about this body that was found in a storage locker in Bellamy Park," I said, thinking it might be wise to start off objectively and get subjective later.

Bristow gave me a suspicious once-over as he sat down in an overstuffed armchair. As usual he was dressed in jeans and a polo shirt—a red one today. I'd never seen him wear red before. But it was Savanna's favorite color.

"And why, Ms. Plato, should I satisfy your notoriously avid curiosity?" he asked.

"Because we, in turn, will give you information about the victim. We'll even tell you who he is."

"We *know* who he is," he said.

"No, you don't," Zack put in.

I hate it when he jumps in with the punch line, but my only sign of irritation was a sigh.

"Well, give it to me with both barrels," Bristow said in a bemused fashion. That was a direct quote—one that had always nauseated me—from Sheriff Lazarro of *Prescott's Landing* fame.

Zack looked smug.

"Let's talk of graves, of worms, and epitaphs," Bristow murmured.

I was pretty sure the quote this time was from Shakespeare, though I didn't recognize it. It sure *sounded* like Shakespeare.

"The information I have is that the victim was a cabinetmaker named Vic Smith, late fifties, probably Mexican or Mexican American," Bristow said. "He was employed by one Sal Migliatore, building contractor, until he disappeared off the job first week in October. Rumor at the time was that he'd left town with some young chick."

He gave me his wide grin. "Woman," he amended before I had a chance to bristle.

"When Reggie Timpkin discovered Sal had rented the storage unit the victim was found in, he toddled right off to interview Sal's employees," he went on. "One of them—a guy named Otis Reeder—told him about the sudden disappearance of Vic Smith. And the reason for it. Mr. Reeder also identified the remains."

"There was enough left to identify?" I asked.

"You have a grisly turn of mind, Ms. Plato," he said. He waited for me to comment, but I just gave him my politely inquiring look, and after a moment he continued.

"We don't yet have laboratory confirmation, but we are quite positive on the identification. The deceased was wearing a Rolex watch inscribed as a gift from John and Yvonne Sterling. Around his neck was a religious medal. Our Lady of Guadalupe. Vic Smith had worn a Rolex watch with those names engraved upon it and a similar medal. Mr. Reeder had seen both on him. Second, the deceased had black hair with silver at the temples, Vic Smith had black hair, streaked with silver at the temples. Third, Vic Smith had a damaged right shoulder—there was evidence of a similar injury to the dead man. Vic Smith's widow was located and brought in and she vouched for the same identifying factors. She said she'd suspected for some time he was having an affair—wives always know, she said—so she hadn't been surprised when Vic told her he was taking off with the young chick."

He smirked mischievously at me. I let it pass. "It had never occurred to her, she said, that Vic had gone missing. In fact, she was expecting him to tire of his lady love and come home as he had frequently done before."

He hesitated. "X rays and/or dental records will of course establish the victim's identity beyond question."

"Did Sal Migliatore kill him?" I asked.

He drummed the fingers of one brown hand on the wide arm of his chair. "Mr. Migliatore is dead."

"We know that," I said.

"What else do you know?" Bristow demanded.

"Sergeant Timpkin said on TV that the victim had been stabbed with some kind of cuttin' instrument," Zack said. "What's that supposed to mean?"

"It was a knife. Reggie likes to befuddle people."

"Was the knife at the scene?" I asked. "Was Vic killed in the storage locker?"

Bristow shook his head. "He was moved after death. No knife has been found as yet. It had a narrow, tapering blade—that we know."

"Was the body . . . you said he was identified by his medal and hair color and so on—wasn't it possible to identify him by—well, you know, his features and so on? Does a body deteriorate that fast when it's indoors?"

He gave me a look. "Vic Smith had been stabbed several times. This caused draining and drying of the body tissues. The storage unit was relatively warm and dry. The body fluids had been absorbed into"—he hesitated before going on—"something that had been wrapped around him. All of which caused the body tissues to become hard and dry instead of decomposing. As a result, there was some mummification, rather than putrefaction. Mummification dramatically changes the shape of the individual. The face was not recognizable. Nor could fingerprints be obtained."

He raised an eyebrow. "Is that a tinge of green around your gills, Charlie? Have you heard enough?"

I *felt* green.

Bristow shook his head. "Doesn't matter how often I see what human beings can do to one another, or how tough or clinical I think I can be, seeing something like that makes me want to find some desert island somewhere and never have to look at another dead person."

We were all silent for a couple of minutes; then Bristow looked from Zack to me and back again. "You *are* going to tell me why you are interested in this case?"

Again we both nodded.

"Any information you can give us will be helpful," I added. "We do have a really good reason for asking. Honestly. And we have stuff we can tell you. For one thing, the woman who calls herself Vic Smith's widow was never married to him."

He pursed his mouth in a soundless whistle as he mulled that over, then waved his hand in a fanning motion as if to wave away his own objections to our inquisition.

"You know you can rely absolutely on our discretion," I said to help him along.

"Sure," Zack agreed.

Bristow hesitated a minute more, then leaned forward. "Okay, here's what I have heard so far. Sal Migliatore's fingerprints were found on the duct tape that was used to fasten the plastic tarp that had been wrapped around the body." He stopped, then went on. "Something else was wrapped around the body first, but we do prefer to keep that to ourselves for now."

He frowned and passed a hand over his smooth head. "Sal Migliatore also rented the storage locker. Seems pretty obvious he disposed of the body. However, this does not make him the murderer, and certain other evidence seems to point to someone else as the killer."

This was not good. If the police did not suspect Sal, then Angel and Miguel were not off the hook.

We waited. For a while it seemed Bristow wasn't going to elaborate, but then he sighed and said, "Okay, because of your previous assistance and discretion, and considering your promise to provide information, I will tell you something the media does not know and will not know until we are ready to tell them. When someone is stabbed, it is not always possible to know whether the victim has been stabbed by a right-handed or left-handed person. Most people don't stand still to be stabbed. As they turn, the knife might get them on the opposite side of the hand that is doing the stabbing, so it can look like a left-handed person did it."

He looked from me to Zack and back again to see if we were following. "In this case," he went on, evidently satisfied that we were keeping up, "the murderer hit the victim with a heavy object on the side of the head.

The victim fell to the floor, landing on his back. The murderer apparently straddled him and stabbed him several times. Given all this, the medical examiner has been able to come up with a pretty good case for the murderer being right-handed."

"And Sal Migliatore was *left*-handed," I guessed.

"Got it in one," Bristow said. Then he looked at me expectantly. I understood this was all we were going to get until we did a quid pro quo. I glanced at Zack and he made a chivalrous "you go first" gesture. Which probably meant he had no idea how to proceed.

"Vic Smith was a false name, an alias," I said. "The man's real name was Vicenzo Cervantes."

"Cervantes!" Bristow repeated, his eyebrows climbing.

"The dead man is Angel's father."

Zack and I took turns telling Angel and Miguel's story. Bristow made notes in an official-looking little notebook he'd pulled from his pants pocket. I wondered why he was carrying it around on his honeymoon. Habit, I supposed.

Bristow was a superb listener, giving us his full attention, interrupting only to elicit extra details.

About halfway through, Savanna wafted out of the bathroom, dark skin gleaming through a sheer white negligee, her perfume—Obsession?—almost a visible presence. Surprised, but not a bit put out to see visitors, she hugged all three of us and drifted into the bedroom, leaving Zack and Bristow looking dazed.

" 'She's beautiful and therefore to be woo'd. She is a woman, therefore to be won,' " Bristow murmured, and we gave him a minute before going on.

When Zack and I were finally through talking, Bristow tucked his notebook back into his jeans pocket, leaned back in his overstuffed chair, hands clasped behind his head, and whistled irritatingly under his breath for a few minutes.

Finally, he straightened up and nodded. "The Cervantes brothers will have to report in to Bellamy Park and make statements. No help for it. Obviously it isn't going to take Reggie Timpkin long to find out who Vic Smith really is. And it's only a short step from there to finding out he has two sons in the neighborhood who have a dandy motive for killing him."

"I don't think Angel would have hesitated to come in right away if you were in charge instead of Detective Sergeant Timpkin," I said.

"Angel's afraid he and Miguel will get railroaded," Zack said. "Knowin' Timpkin I'd say he's probably not too far off the mark."

Bristow didn't comment on that. "You need to understand that Detective Sergeant Timpkin is the primary detective in this case," he said, then sighed. "I do have a lot of respect for Angel. And Savanna is certainly fond of him. I would not like to see him—" He broke off and tapped on the chair arm some more. "I'm probably going to regret this, but here's what I can do. It *is* good timing, because Detective Sergeant Timpkin will be in court all day tomorrow."

He allowed himself a half-smile. "Savanna and I will just happen to come in to CHAPS tomorrow for a little visit. While on the premises, I will just happen to stumble into Angel and his brother, who will then volunteer to accompany me to the station to make true and lengthy statements."

He fixed us with a glance. "I'd *better* run into them," he said softly. Maybe even menacingly.

When he's in a kindly mood, Bristow's eyes shine with a clear amber light, but they were not amber now. They were a hard brown, with no light shining in them at all.

I could see Bristow taking Miguel's measure the following evening when the two brothers presented themselves. Bristow's eyes were still hard, though he did shake hands with Miguel when Angel introduced him.

At my suggestion, Bristow had timed his arrival to coincide with the break between dance lessons and open dancing. He was wearing his usual polo shirt-and-jeans getup, ready for action with his gun in its holster, which, along with a spare clip, pager, and his badge was fastened to his belt.

Zack suggested the office for privacy and Bristow nodded without cracking a smile.

Zack, Savanna, and I followed, which surprised Bristow when he turned to seat himself on the edge of my desk and surveyed us all. "I'm not sure it is necessary for the entire staff to be here," he said bluntly.

"Angel's our friend, our partner," Savanna protested. "Miguel's his brother. This is not just police business as usual. This is friendship. This is showing support."

"I will never act officiously or permit personal feelings, prejudices, animosities, or friendships to influence my decisions," Bristow intoned. "That's part of the Law Enforcement Code of Ethics. Which I swore to uphold when I graduated from the academy."

Savanna gazed at him lovingly. He continued to eye her sternly for a few more minutes; then the amber light returned to his eyes and he smiled and showed both palms in surrender. Savanna smiled back and pulled out my swivel chair. The air pressure in the room returned to normal.

I leaned back against the windowsill next to Zack, feeling admiration for Savanna. She obviously had her new husband's training program going along just fine.

"Savanna's cranky because my beeper went off in the middle of lunch and I had to leave her in the restaurant," Bristow said.

"It's going to be hell being a police officer's wife," Savanna commented, deadpan.

"I thought you were off duty for your honeymoon," I said.

Bristow sighed. "Tell that to the chief."

He looked at Angel and Miguel, who were both standing with their backs to the wall, either side of the closed door. Very symbolic, I thought.

"You did a wise thing showing up here as requested," he said evenly. "Detective Sergeant Timpkin had already discovered your father's true identity before I spoke to him. Your stepmother told him. She also told him she and Vicenzo Cervantes left Texas because he was afraid of being falsely accused of murdering your mother."

Angel swallowed visibly. Miguel's eyes narrowed.

This limited body language didn't show a whole lot of emotion, but I could feel the strength of the feelings the two men were clamping down on.

"She's not our stepmother," Miguel said. "She never legally married our father."

"My apologies," Bristow said. "I did know that, but I forgot." He hesitated, still looking directly at Miguel. "I understand there were threats made at the time of your mother's death."

"We were kids," Miguel said.

Bristow nodded, but didn't say anything. He looked silently from Miguel to Angel. I was about to remind Angel of the deal that had been made when I saw the memory register on his face. He reached up to stroke his mustache into place, then stood very straight. "My brother and I wish to come into Bellamy Park police station to make a statement about our mother's death and our actions since then," he said in a very formal tone.

Bristow switched his gaze to Miguel. Miguel looked for a minute as if he was going to protest; then he nodded resignedly.

"Let's go," Bristow said.

Savanna, Zack, and I stood in CHAPS's entryway watching as Angel and Miguel climbed into Bristow's automobile. Savanna was going to wait at CHAPS until Bristow came back for her.

By the time he did, just past closing time, Angel and Miguel had made their statements and had been warned not to leave town. We all breathed a sigh of relief that the brothers hadn't been arrested; then

Savanna and her husband went back to San Francisco to resume their interrupted honeymoon.

Bristow showed up at CHAPS again the following Sunday evening, before closing this time. The tavern was crowded, and noisy. Usually Sunday was fairly slow, but we'd been working on changing that by including special events. This particular Sunday, we had a live band in and a female vocal contest going on. Used to be Zack and his buddies, including my friend Macintosh, played poker on Sunday nights, but since we got more crowded and needed Zack's help, the poker game had been shifted to an afternoon.

Sundancer was in charge of the contest and wouldn't let the rest of us get involved with the judging, so Angel, Zack, and I left the Patty Loveless and Mary Chapin Carpenter wannabes to it and trooped into the office one more time. Miguel was not among those present.

"A report has come in from Texas," Bristow said. I sat down on my office chair, Zack lounged against the windowsill, Angel stood near the door again, arms folded, face closed.

"Whoever killed Malena Cervantes more than twenty years ago tried to make her death look like suicide," Bristow told us, his voice and face stern in a way that indicated to me he was just going to give us the facts as though they didn't pertain to anyone present. None of us wanted to look at Angel.

"It was definitely *not* suicide," he said bluntly. "Malena Cervantes was shot in the neck, but there was no gunpowder tattooing of her skin, which means she was shot from a distance of more than fifteen feet. There was no powder residue on her hands. All of this," he added, with a quick glance at Angel, "indicated homicide rather than suicide."

"Fingerprints on the gun?" Zack asked in full Sheriff Lazarro mode.

Bristow's smile was wry. "In real life, Zack old buddy, we don't always find prints on guns. Fuming sometimes shows them up, but the finish doesn't always lend itself to good prints."

He shook his head. "Also, someone had clumsily wiped this particular gun before setting it near the victim's—Mrs. Cervantes's—hand. Not the work of an expert murderer, I would say."

I dared to glance at Angel. His mouth was clenched tightly. His face looked blotchy under the bronze.

Bristow talked on. "Vicenzo Cervantes, otherwise known as Vic Smith, was the number-one suspect. There wasn't any physical evidence at the scene to link him to the killing. But he had disappeared. The sheriff at the time, since deceased of a heart attack, was convinced that Vicenzo was the killer. There was not, however, any determined effort made to track him down."

"Why not?" I wondered aloud. "Vicenzo could surely have been hauled in as a possible witness, or a person of interest, or whatever it's called, couldn't he?"

"According to the current sheriff, a warrant for Vicenzo's arrest was issued, but there were rumors of pressure being brought to bear not to find him."

"Long John Silver Sterling," Angel contributed through tight lips.

Bristow gave him a keen, but sympathetic glance. "Possibly."

After CHAPS cleared out—a process that always required some personal persuasion for the last hangers-on and the one or two drunks who had to be poured into taxi cabs—Savanna, Bristow, Angel, and Sundancer Brown went home. Zack divided one of his special microbrews between two glasses and we hoisted ourselves onto barstools. We had about an hour before the janitorial crew would show up.

Reverting to his Lazarro role, Zack explained the situation to me. "It seems as if the crime scene investigation is done with, Charlie, as well as the ME's report and the lab workup. Doesn't seem as if they've come up with anythin' earth-shatterin' about Vic—like who might have done him in—though I suppose the officers are probably still knockin' on doors and talkin' to people. And, like Bristow says, they're waitin' on X rays and dental records."

"*We* have to get out there and meet people and uncover things," I said. "I know that as we aren't police officers people might call us nosy . . ." Catching the way his quick wry smile dented one corner of his mouth, I made a face at him. "But it's the only way to find out what really happened."

I lifted my glass and thoughtfully swigged a mouthful of beer. "We need to start looking right away," I suggested. "If Timpkin's got two suspects, why would he bother to look further? If you don't solve a murder PDQ it gets more and more difficult to figure out.

Besides, we did promise Angel and Miguel we'd investigate."

"*You* promised," Zack pointed out.

"Angel's your friend as well as mine," I protested.

"That he is." His eyebrows slanted up. "Where should we begin?

"How about where the body was found? The storage locker?"

Zack pondered, then nodded. "Not a bad idea," he said graciously. And we agreed to start out at noon the following day.

CHAPTER 5

The long lines of flat-roofed storage lockers covered half an acre of ground at the end of a cul-de-sac behind some neglected-looking office buildings. Judging by the height and variety of weeds growing between the rows, the lockers had been there a long time.

"If this was Georgia, those buildings would be covered up in kudzu," Zack commented as we headed toward a squat construction that had an office sign sticking out above its doorway. "Some kind of weird climbing plant. I saw it around Atlanta, on location for *Prescott's Landin'* one time. Humongous humps at the side of the road. Trees and bushes covered all over in kudzu. An abandoned car. A telephone pole even. Cover over an army tank if it stood still long enough. Now *there* would be a place made for hidin' a body—in the kudzu. Nobody'd ever find it!"

He grinned at me sideways. "The way you and I are goin', Charlie, doin' all this investigatin' and such, we're on the way to bein' experts in body disposal."

"The only body I ever get to feeling I'd like to dispose of is yours," I informed him.

This comment elicited a meaningful glance from the

green eyes. "My body turns you on, doesn't it, darlin'? Where'd you like to dispose of my body? You got a place in mind? My place or yours?"

I ignored him.

The woman in the office at Herb's Budget Storage recognized Zack the instant she turned her attention away from the portable TV she was watching. She introduced herself as Gloria Blatt. Her face was as browned and wrinkled as a carved apple doll's and her bony body looked as if she'd been actively practicing bulimia for the last forty years. Her very short gray hair had been tightly permed into those wash-and-wear curls so many older women seem to favor, but her blue eyes were young as she beamed up at Zack.

I didn't have to say a word. I don't think she even knew I was there. I often become invisible when I hang around Zack.

Within five minutes, Zack had pulled out a small notebook from his black Western-style shirt pocket and was writing the name and address of the man who had bought the contents of the unit and discovered Vicenzo Cervantes's body.

The notebook was similar to the one Bristow owned. I guessed Zack was used to preparing for his role down to the last detail.

Gloria offered to drive him to the man's apartment.

"Got my pickup outside," he assured her.

"Wish I knew more about this mess, honey," she said, after pausing to flick a lighter at a long brown cigarette. "My dhh handled everything."

"Dhh?" Zack queried, ballpoint poised.

"Dumb hubby Herb. He was the one talked to the first lot of police."

It always amazed me when people accepted Zack as a real law-enforcement officer. TV has blurred the lines between fiction and reality. Zack never pretends to be a police officer, but the mistake is often useful.

"Dumb Herb told your buddies he couldn't recall who rented that locker," Gloria said. She had a gravelly voice that seemed marinated in nicotine and sarcasm. "Like we didn't know Bill Bailey was really Sal Migliatore. Everyone in this whole neighborhood knows Sal Migliatore. We were both right here when Sal came in and made the arrangements. Didn't look too well even then. Musta knowed he had the Big C. Real subdued he was. Couldn't hardly breathe."

She looked thoughtfully at her cigarette, then sucked in a mouthful of smoke and let it stream out through her nostrils like dragon fire.

"When did he rent the locker?" Zack asked.

"Jeez, don't cops ever talk to each other?" Gloria said. "It was October fourth. I told Sergeant Timpkin that. Sal said he wanted a pseudonym on there for tax purposes. No skin off our noses. I got back from grocery shopping the day Herb pleaded ignorance. I told the police exactly what was what. I do believe in cooperating with the law."

She gave Zack what might have been a saucy grin, but the effect was somewhat spoiled by her nicotine-yellowed teeth. "Paid six months in advance, Sal did. Cash on the barrelhead. I'd a charged Sal double I'd a knowed what he was gonna put in that damn unit. Just shows you never really know a person. Who'd a thunk old Sal would up and murder someone! 'Specially the state he was in."

She leaned forward over the counter that separated her from Zack. "I was in Florida helping my youngest with my new grandbaby when Herb put Sal's things up for auction. I'd never have allowed Herb to do it just because Sal was dead and nobody came to claim them. Has to have every unit rented, Herb has. Couldn't stand it when the rent stopped. Up to me, the body would have rotted away to nothing 'fore I did anything about that locker. Just look at the fuss Herb got us into! Police, newspapers, television cameras all over."

The relish with which she named the various intruders belied the complaint she was making. I had an idea Gloria Blatt had enjoyed "the fuss."

"Must have been powerful aggravatin'," Zack drawled sympathetically and she melted into a puddle of estrogen and gave him her yellow smile again.

"Always willin' to help out Sheriff Lazarro," she drawled in turn.

"That's right nice of you," Zack said politely. Zack was always polite to women. Any age. Any kind of appearance. He *liked* women. *All* women. This trait might have been endearing if it wasn't so irritating. "You've been mighty helpful, ma'am. I'm obliged."

He bestowed his trademark crooked smile and she dropped her cigarette into a nearby coffee cup. It sizzled. "Wait till I tell the gals at Dusty's," she said. "Imagine, Sheriff Lazarro hisself coming to my office and . . ."

Zack touched two fingers to the brim of his cowboy hat and backed out of the doorway.

On the way to the pickup we stopped and looked at the storage unit in question, blinking at the sunlight on the white aluminum siding. Yellow crime-scene tape still fluttered across the wide door. I shivered. There's something about a place that has been visited by a violent death. It's as though the ground or walls or atmosphere retain the memory of the violence. Violence is a hot thing, but the memory of it causes coldness.

After that skeleton popped up in our flowerbed at CHAPS, I felt a chill grab my spine every time I passed the place. It affected me that way until a man from Hoshizaki, the gardening syndicate that looked after Adobe Plaza, took out the old soil and put in new and planted a vigorous bottlebrush tree in it.

Same way with the body we found in Zack's Acura. He replaced the car with a pickup even before the police released it. Gave him chills to even think about driving that car again, he'd said.

I decided it wasn't constructive to dwell on the deaths I'd run into in the last couple of years, one way or another. At least CHAPS wasn't connected with this one, except through Angel.

Dill Eisenhardt, the man who had bid on the locker contents and discovered "Vic Smith's" body, was not overjoyed to find our man in black on his apartment doorstep. Some men are as awed by Zack as the women; others take a more jaundiced view of celebrity and affect a hostile stance immediately. Dill was a short man and had to tip his head back to look at Zack's face, which apparently added to his irritability.

I asked him about finding the body. "No comment," he said, tight-lipped, holding up a hand to shield his face as if we were a TV crew with a candid camera pointed at him.

"We just wondered why you bid on that particular—" I broke off, searching for a word. "That particular lot." I'd used my most soothing voice but it didn't do much good. Dill's granite face stayed uptight.

"I'm on Herb's list of bidders," he said curtly. "We all get notified automatically when there's something for sale."

Gloria hadn't told us that. I wondered why. She'd said she wasn't home when Herb put the locker contents up for auction. But surely she'd known about the list of potential bidders. Probably she'd just wanted us to believe she had no involvement whatsoever.

"I have a valid business license," Dill added, then shut the door in our faces.

"What now?" Zack asked as he turned on the truck's ignition. Apparently none of his TV shows had provided a similar plot line for him to follow.

"Hang on," I told him, and reached for his cell phone to call Angel. Zack always had a phone handy in case his agent, or one of his former producers, or some famous director, or talk show host, or one of his doll brigade should call. It must be gratifying, I thought, to always be in demand.

A few minutes later, we were on our way to where Bellamy Park meets the neighboring town of Dennison,

Angel having given me the address where "Vic Smith" had lived with his significant other.

There was a long line of vehicles parked at the side of the residential street. "Is this where Vic's wake is?" a man in a black Jeep Cherokee asked me after I stepped down from Zack's pickup.

The question gave me pause. Maybe this wasn't a good time to intrude, but on the other hand . . . "This could be the right time to be here," I told Zack as we walked up the front steps of the small two-story house. "If this is really a wake, his friends should be among those present. We might be able to get some information out of them. Let's play it cool, okay?"

He gave me a look that said cool was the only way Zack Hunter knew to play. "Sorry," I said with a smirk. He put his sunglasses on. Evidently he was traveling incognito.

The entryway opened onto a fair-size living room that was unoccupied. A kitchen behind it had a huge central island laden with all kinds of food on platters—a potluck assortment. The usual raw vegetables were arranged around some kind of creamy dip. I wrinkled my nose. Why didn't people at least blanch the veggies? They tasted so much better and didn't get stuck so firmly in your teeth. And what was the point of even eating fresh vegetables if you were going to put some fat-laden gunk on them?

I perked up when I saw some real sliced turkey and sandwich makings. Not deli turkey made up of pressed bits taken from who knew what area of the turkey carcass, you understand, but the real, and increasingly rare, white and tender-looking breast meat. Beside the platter was a wooden serving board holding dense-looking whole wheat bread that had sprouts sticking out of it. And there was a bowl of mesclun, too—that wonderful salad made of exotic leaves like arugula, mache, red oak leaf, sorrel, friseé, and radicchio. I had died and gone to heaven.

"Help yourselves," a tall, exceedingly thin man with wispy hair said as he wandered in from the backyard. Evidently the wake was being held outside. I could hear voices—male and female—and an odd bopping sound I had yet to identify. The man was dressed in shorts and a T, so evidently the wake wasn't too formal; Zack and I would be okay in our Western gear.

My stomach was already rumbling. It had been a while since breakfast, so I put together a sandwich that could have been used as a doorstop. Zack followed suit and we both accepted the beer bottles the thin man pulled out of the refrigerator. Henry's dark. One of my favorites. We carried our plates through the kitchen doorway. They were real plates, china plates, not paper. I liked it here.

Two large picnic benches were occupied by casually dressed people, most of them in our thirty-something age group. The strange sound turned out to be a game of badminton in progress. I hadn't seen badminton played since I was a kid in Sacramento and our next-door neighbors set up a net for visiting grandkids. If I'd thought about it, I would have assumed the game was long gone, along with croquet and horseshoes, but, evidently, in this house at least, there was a revival going on. Seemed a bit out of place at a wake, all the same.

"Vic loved badminton," the tall man said in a mournful voice as he indicated a couple of spaces at one end of a picnic bench. Then he looked hard at Zack. "You must be a friend of Vic's. You sure look familiar."

Zack looked pleased, but muttered something noncommittal as we sat down side by side.

A minute or two later, a woman approached Zack with her hand out and a stunned but delighted expression on her face. She was a tall woman with a boyish figure and honey-blond hair cut in very short layers that accented her well-shaped head. She had an air of self-confidence about her. She was dressed in a very attractive black silk jumpsuit. Her posture was terrific. Zack scrambled to his feet and shook her hand.

"Zack Hunter," the woman said in tones of awe. "I cannot *believe* you came to Vic's wake. I'm so glad to meet you. I'm Roxy Smith. You are very welcome."

Roxy. The sort of widow. My first response was surprise that she wasn't Hispanic. My second that she was younger than I expected. I was immediately annoyed with myself for unconsciously forming such expectations.

In the bright sunlight, it was obvious she was no more than forty, which made her only two or three years older than Miguel, and twenty years younger than his father. Interesting.

She smiled up at Zack. "You have that wonderful house up in Paragon Hills. Great location. Location is everything. You ever decide to sell, let me know. I could get you a really, really good price for it—that location's in great demand. I could do a walk-through sometime, maybe?"

I thought for a minute she was coming on to Zack. Most women do, single, married, widowed—it doesn't seem to make any difference. But then I realized her voice was brisk and businesslike. It really was the house she was interested in. I decided I liked her.

"I'm not figurin' on movin' in the near future, ma'am," Zack told her. "But you're welcome to come look at my house anytime you like."

I poked him in the ribs. He evidently took the action for a reminder rather than an annoyance and he introduced me. To her credit, from my point of view, Roxy Smith seemed just as pleased to see me as she had been to see him. "You're one of *them*, aren't you?" she said with a very pleasant smile. "At CHAPS? Angel mentioned you."

"Maybe this wasn't a good time for us to come," I said. "We didn't know about the wake; we just wanted to . . ."

She shook her head. "The more the merrier, Vic always said. That's why we're saying good-bye to him this way. You don't think it's out of place, I hope. That man of mine surely did love a party."

Her eyes filled with tears, which she dashed away in an attractive fashion with her fingertips. I've never learned how to do that. I always have to mop up with half a box of tissues and blow my nose seven or eight times until it gets cherry red. There's always something a little wrong with my picture.

Roxy waved at us to carry on eating and went to greet more newcomers. For the first time, I noticed a group of people sitting around in deck chairs beyond the badminton court. I was amazed to see a couple of familiar faces. One was the veterinarian who'd taken care of Benny a time or two—Dr. Brian Andersen. He'd seemed sort of interested in me a while back, but I'd been occupied with looking into the murder of the owner of one of his other patients and had put him off. I'd said I might call later, but I hadn't. Too much going on.

I might find my way over there later and see how the vibes were doing, I thought, perking up at the prospect.

The other familiar face, which sported a fuzzy brown beard and kind brown eyes behind bifocals, was that of Macintosh, whom I've already mentioned. Macintosh is sixtyish and what my Scottish mother used to call roly-poly. Macintosh is a Scot, too, and I love hearing his accent, which of course reminds me of my mom. As well as becoming my computer guru, he had become my good friend. I nudged Zack into seeing him, too—he's one of Zack's poker pals and fishing buddies.

Zack raised his eyebrows at me after silently contemplating Macintosh and the man next to him for a few minutes. I knew what he meant. Macintosh was engaged in a very intense conversation with his friend David.

"Friend" didn't quite cover the situation in this case. Macintosh and David were life partners. Because Macintosh produced and starred in *Spreading Circles*—a wonderful TV show for children that was much praised by librarians and the PTA—he kept his sexual orientation a secret. The fact that David was here with him meant he was among friends he could feel safe with. Which must be a great relief to both of them, I thought.

So here were people I knew at a seriously unusual wake for the man who had been the missing father of one of my partners—my good friend Angel. Life moved in spreading circles, just as Macintosh's show implied. Surprisingly often, the circles intersected.

I remembered that Macintosh's partner was a wood-carver, which perhaps explained his and David's connection with fine wood finisher Vic alias Vicenzo.

As usual, it wasn't too long before Zack became surrounded by admiring women; sunglasses aren't much of a disguise when you're well over six feet, wearing all black cowboy gear, and radiating charm.

When I was through eating my wonderful sandwich, I picked up my beer and went off to test the Brian Andersen waters.

The veterinarian was behaving in character, petting a beefy, tough-looking cat that had some alley and a lot of Siamese in him. "Sumatra—Charlie," Brian introduced us as I sat down in the neighboring deck chair.

I put out a hand to touch Sumatra's velvety paw and he promptly bit my finger. "He's not terribly sociable, Charlie," Brian said. The flirtatious grin on his nice open face said *he* was.

The vibes were still there.

Question was, did I want to do anything about them? I might be cured of lusting after Zack Hunter, but I still wasn't sure I wanted to give up on celibacy. On the other hand, every once in a while I felt the need of a lube job.

Brian Andersen was no hunk, but he was reasonably attractive, as Scandinavian as his name. One strike against him was that he was a veterinarian and I'd been pretty well turned off by any kind of medical professional when I caught my husband the doctor practicing extracurricular medicine on top of one of his patients.

Brian was an animal doctor, however, thus hardly likely to have sex with his patients. Though the blissful way Sumatra was responding to the tummy rub Brian was giving him might cause you wonder.

"Is this how you know Roxy?" I asked, gesturing at the cat.

He grinned, hefting the cat to his shoulder, where he clung, purring and kneading. "Roxy and I go jogging together three times a week," he said, and cocked an eyebrow at me. "I was Vic's friend first. He wasn't into exercising for the sake of exercising. He did enough physical labor he didn't need to. You a friend of the family, Charlie?"

"I came with Zack," I said, fudging just a little.

"So I saw." He glanced across to where Zack was gracefully leaning against the wall of the house. Several female faces were turned up to him like flowers toward the sun. "He going to do more *Prescott's Landing* episodes?"

"I sincerely hope not," I said, and he grinned.

I jumped as some music came on fairly loud, then blinked in amazement as a bunch of people started doing the macarena, which always looks to me as though the participants are trying to scratch an itch they can't quite reach. A good-looking young black guy was doing Michael Jackson's old moon walk.

"Vic had some weird friends," I commented. "What kind of man was he?"

Brian thought about it for a few minutes, a frown on his clean-cut face. "Well, he was a good-looking guy. Women seemed to think so anyway. He liked to party."

I remembered that Miguel had similarly character-ized his father, but had said he'd changed after damag-ing his pitching arm and losing his chance at baseball greatness. Maybe Vic had recovered his sociable nature after murdering his wife.

"Vic's parties usually had a lot of young people present—and he always seemed to be having a good time."

"I heard he and Roxy did a lot of smooching."

His fair eyebrows pulled together even further. "Really? I can't say I paid that much attention. I do know that Roxy's devastated that Vic's gone." He grew thoughtful for a minute or two. "Vic had one big flaw. He couldn't resist women."

"Sounds like Zack," I said.

He lifted the cat down from his shoulder and put him down on the grass. Twitching his tail in obvious irritation, the cat stalked off in the direction of the house. Brian studied my face. "What exactly is your relationship with Zack?" he asked.

I thought of the answer I might have given a while back. *He makes my innards go whomp every time I see him.* How pathetic I had been.

My smile felt smug. "We don't have a relationship outside of business. He's the senior partner in CHAPS. He owns half of it. Savanna and Angel and I own the other half between us. That's it."

"Do you know where Angel is?" Roxy asked from beside me. "I wanted to invite him for today, but he doesn't answer his phone. I left a message on his answering machine, but he didn't call back."

"He's away, maybe," I said lamely. I noticed that she hadn't mentioned Miguel, so I didn't, either.

"I wanted to ask him to help me get Vic's body away from the police," Roxy went on. "They won't give him up."

"It takes time," Brian said soothingly. Then he stood up and walked over to the house, looking for food maybe, or not wanting to be parted from Sumatra.

"Can we talk?" I asked Roxy, abandoning any plans for Brian for the moment. This was more important.

She waved a hand vaguely at the crowded yard. "It's a little difficult . . ."

"Tomorrow?" I suggested. "Could we maybe do lunch? Do you know Casa Blanca? It's a Mexican restaurant—"

"In Adobe Plaza? Yes, I know it."

"Noon?" I pressed.

She hesitated. She was going to say no. "I might be able to talk to Detective Sergeant Bristow about Vic's body," I said. "He's with Bellamy Park Police Department." There was no way I could influence Taylor Bristow to release Vic's body, but I hadn't exactly said I could. I'd merely said I'd speak to him. I know. I was fudging again. It gets to be a habit when you start investigating crimes. How else are you going to make progress?

"Oh, okay then," she said, distracted by the arrival of a loosely built man with a sweaty pink face and a halo of blond curls surrounding a sunburned bald spot. He was clutching a plate that had traces of food on it.

"You got any more of that Green Goddess pie, Rox?" he asked. "That stuff is awesome." Looking at the plate, he picked up the knife that was on it and licked green goo off it. "Awesome," he repeated.

"In the fridge," Roxy said. "Help yourself, baby. I'm so glad you got off work for the wake."

The man had rather protuberant eyes that were the same pale green as Roxy's, so I guessed he was related a moment before she introduced him as her "baby" brother, Hank Spangler. He worked in research and development for a plumbing company in Palo Alto, she said.

Spangler sounded familiar to me but I couldn't place it.

I could place *him*, though. File him under *S* for sleaze. He was one of those people who get right in your face, invading your space. I could smell onion on his breath, and more than a hint of b.o.

"Hey," he said, with a look that was more like a leer. Roxy's green eyes were attractive; his looked more like the gooseberries my restaurant-owning parents used to put in one of *their* dessert specialties. Gooseberry fool. Was Hank a fool? I wondered.

Being a polite sort of person, I held out my hand as soon as he held out his. I expected soft and sweaty and wasn't disappointed.

"Pleasure to meet you, Charlie," he said in just the right kind of voice for a sleazy person. Sort of oozing. "P'raps we c'n do dinner sometime, 'kay?"

I managed not to say, "Over my dead body," which

wouldn't have been too tactful considering we were at his sister's significant other's wake. So I just sort of mumbled something about CHAPS keeping me busy.

"We c'd have a real good time," he persisted. And then he stuck a finger in my palm and wiggled it around.

"Hank's lived with me for almost a year now," Roxy said as I wiped my hand on my jeans. "He came to us when Vic was still . . . here. They were great pals."

Hank's lip curled. I wasn't sure what in Roxy's statement had caused the reaction. Maybe he was just doing Clint Eastwood.

While I was trying to figure out how to get away from Hank and find somewhere to wash my hands, the tall, skinny man who had first greeted Zack and me stood up and announced it was time to eulogize the dear departed.

Several people took turns telling anecdotes about Vic, making him sound more and more like a good-time type. Keeping an eye on the Sleaze in case he launched any more maneuvers, I noticed the curling lip seemed to coincide with Vic's name, like an automatic twitch. Dislike? I wondered, ruling out grief without really thinking about it.

Vic's party reputation began to come clear as more people took center stage beyond the badminton court. Apparently Vic had tended bar on weekends and some evenings at an East Dennison bar named Grumpy's and most of the guests present had met him in that capacity.

Roxy talked tearfully about being with Vic for twenty-three years, since she was seventeen years old. I did some rapid mathematics. Vic/Vicenzo had left

Texas, probably immediately after murdering Malena, when Miguel was fifteen and Angel ten. Twenty-three years ago.

Had Vic met Roxy here right away?

Roxy was only seventeen years old when they met? Vic had to have been in his late thirties.

So?

Macintosh got up to talk next.

Hank's lip curled.

Maybe it was just a habitual twitch.

Macintosh talked about how he'd met Vic when Vic made kitchen cabinets for Macintosh's kitchen and how they'd become friends after that. I had seen those cabinets. Vic had been a *very* fine wood finisher.

I made a mental note to talk to Macintosh at a more appropriate time.

And I'd have another visit with Brian Andersen, too, I thought. And yes, I did concede I had an ulterior motive where he was concerned.

CHAPTER 6

Casa Blanca was owned and managed by Jorge and Maria Blanca. The outstanding chef they had hired a couple of years ago had instituted a low-fat menu that wasn't bad at all. Fortunately it didn't include nonfat tortillas. I may have an interest in healthy food, but there are some things I draw the line at.

Zack accompanied me to my lunch date with Roxy. When interviewing a woman, I've found it pays to have Zack along. Women answer any question he asks. (Especially if it requires a "yes" answer.)

A Lincoln Town Car drove into a parking slot in front of the restaurant when we were halfway across Adobe Plaza. Roxy stepped out of it. I could not imagine ever wanting to drive a big car like that, even if I could afford it, but I supposed Roxy needed something impressive and large when she took clients around.

Evidently not noticing us, she went on into the restaurant. She was already seated in a booth when we entered.

It was immediately clear that everyone in Casa Blanca was thrilled to see Zack. Thirty plus people, all taking in a deep breath, cause a certain atmospheric condition to form.

Zack slid in next to Roxy, which was good thinking on his part. She'd probably respond more easily to him, and I could keep an eye on her facial expressions.

I wasn't quite sure Zack's motives were all that pure, however. Roxy was a very attractive woman.

Right after we sat down flashbulbs started popping. Apparently, some people carry cameras around all the time in case a photo opportunity presents itself. Witness all those videotapes that turn up after someone bops someone, or robs a bank, or sets fire to a building.

To Zack's credit, he never turns his profile to make a better photograph, he just carries on as though no one is paying attention.

Roxy was wearing a sage-green heavy silk pantsuit that matched her eyes. Her short blond hair was crisp perfection—like overlapping petals. Color me green, too—with envy.

It was a little awkward while we were scanning the oversize menu and ordering—Roxy didn't have anything to say—but once our burritos and salads were served, she relaxed enough to smile nervously at Zack.

I seized the moment. "Have you heard anything more from the police?"

She turned her attention to me immediately. I found myself warming to her again. I don't enjoy being invisible, Zack or no Zack. "Detective Sergeant Timpkin, you mean?" she asked, making a face.

Reggie Timpkin puts a sour expression on more faces . . .

"He still says I absolutely cannot have Vic's body,"

she went on. "I called him less than an hour ago. He says the ME's department will let me know when they are finished with it and I must be patient."

"That's too bad," Zack said soothingly.

"I'm sure they'll release Vic soon," I added, though I had no idea how long such things took. "I really will talk to Sergeant Bristow about it."

A frown crinkled the skin above her nice straight nose. Evidently she hadn't heard of Taylor Bristow, even though he was often in the local newspapers, either for some benefit he'd helped put on, or for courageous duty, or for one of his Shakespeare in the Park performances.

I searched my brain for something that would convince her to talk.

"We'd appreciate any information you can give us about your husband," Zack said solemnly, turning to make eye contact with Roxy.

She returned his gaze, but her mouth had set in a stubborn line. "It would save us having to do a search on the Internet," I put in.

She looked at me in a surprised sort of way. "The Internet?" she queried. "Vic never did anything on the Internet. He didn't even own a computer. Me, neither. I've never wanted to."

"You don't use a computer at work?" I asked, surprised.

She gave a mock shudder. "I'm technology phobic, Charlie. I won't go near a computer. Other people in the office handle computer stuff as necessary and the agency is on the Internet. Our Web page is handled by . . ." She broke off, rubbing with her fingers at the frown that had appeared on her forehead. "Well, I forget the name, but it's not important." She shrugged. "No, I don't use a computer," she finished.

"Everybody's information is on the Internet, whether they own a computer or not." I had no idea if this was true. I made a mental note to find out. "You can find almost anything you want to know on the Internet," I said. "It just takes time."

She mulled that over for a minute or two, then sighed and did a surrendering gesture with her left hand. "Well, ask away. I don't have anything to hide."

Zack was looking at me with admiration. For my devious mind, probably. "You know about Vic's real name?" Roxy asked.

"We know most of the story," Zack said solemnly.

Way to go, Zack. Stop her from talking, why don't you? If we know most of the story, why are we interrogating her?

I jumped in again. "I guess you must have met Vic—Vicenzo—soon after his wife died. Did you meet him here, in Bellamy Park, after he came west?"

Her eyebrows shot up again. Evidently this question had surprised her, too.

"Zack and I promised Angel and Miguel we'd try to find out who killed Vicenzo," I said. "The more you can tell us, the more help we can be to them. I'm sure none of us wants them to be arrested."

Her eyes widened. "Angel and Miguel are suspects?"

"Sort of," I said.

She grew thoughtful for quite a while. "I can't imagine Angel killing anyone," she said at last.

I couldn't either, and said so. "What about Miguel?" I asked.

She hesitated for an even longer time. "I've thought about Miguel a lot," she said finally. "But he is Vic's son. It's hard for me to imagine a son killing his father." She sighed. "I suppose it does happen."

"There was a story on *Prescott's Landin'*," Zack began, but Roxy talked over top of him. Thank God.

"Miguel's tough enough, I guess," she said. "And he's not what you'd call stable. He was angry as a rabid dog when he first came to my house looking for Vic. Yelling about him killing his mother and then running away. Hit-and-run Daddy, he called him. Along with some Spanish words I didn't understand but which sounded pretty violent. Spanish is a great language to cuss in. Vic used to do it all the time."

A fond look crossed her face and she was silent again for a minute.

"I thought Miguel was going to attack me when I said his father wasn't there," she went on. "He tore through the house looking for signs and, of course, Vic's clothes were still there—he'd left them behind, which was one of the things that convinced me he was coming back."

She paused, delicately stirring her salad with her fork as if to coat it with dressing. "Miguel is very bitter," she said finally. "But I got the impression all along that he didn't really expect his father to be there, that he was just making a lot of noise to impress me and maybe Angel."

I supposed it was possible that Miguel *had* killed his father, but I didn't see how he could have persuaded

Sal Migliatore to wrap up the body and rent a storage unit to put it in, especially as, by the time Miguel arrived on the scene, Sal was already sick. But sick or not, Sal *had* wrapped the body, rented the storage locker and put the body in it.

I wondered how much Timpkin had told Roxy. I was pretty sure it wouldn't have included anything about Sal's fingerprints being on the wrappings.

"I guess I'd rather get the third degree from you than that Sergeant Timpkin," Roxy said to Zack while I was still mulling things over. "He's weird, isn't he?"

"Strange dude," Zack agreed.

She took a sip of the diet soda she'd ordered. "He and Vic got in an argument one time. At Grumpy's— the bar. Vic told me Sergeant Timpkin came in off duty one time and got in on some pool. One of the regulars accused him of cheating—something about accidentally hitting the cue ball into a pocket and lifting it out when he thought nobody was looking. Timpkin threw a punch at the guy and the guy wrestled him down to the floor. Vic tried to throw them both out, didn't know who Timpkin was. Timpkin told him. Made Vic very nervous. He was always very careful around police officers, didn't want anyone looking into his past, you know?"

She sighed and thought some more. "I guess Angel didn't tell you I met Vicenzo at a church-sponsored party in Houston, a few months before Malena . . ." She let her voice trail away.

I've noticed before that once people get started talking about personal stuff they tend to go on. It's as if they think once they've told you some of it, they're almost obliged to give you the rest.

"I was the other woman," she said after a moment, a note of pride in her voice. "I was the woman Vicenzo and Malena were quarreling about before she died. My name was Roxanne Spangler then."

The name Spangler chimed in my memory again, but before I could wrap my mind around it, Roxy went on. "I was seventeen years old when I met Vicenzo. Still struggling through Saint Joseph's High School. God, I hated school."

She bit down on her lower lip. She had the kind of teeth granted only to those whose parents can afford to provide them with braces in their youth. Maybe she'd been wearing braces when she ran off with Vicenzo Cervantes. Some men get off on teenage kids with braces and school uniforms.

"I told Angel and Miguel I was the other woman when they first came to see me," she added.

I must have shown my surprise.

"They didn't tell you?" she asked.

"They told me they'd met you and that you'd lived with their father. They didn't tell me you'd been with Vic all along. I thought Miguel was going to tell Zack and me something one time and then he seemed to change his mind. I guess he didn't think I needed to know that."

Or else he hadn't wanted me to know he and Angel *knew* Roxy was the other woman. Or that they'd known there *was* another woman.

"I thought they had a right to know I was the woman their parents had quarreled about." Roxy shuddered.

"I thought for a few minutes Miguel was going to hit me. He scared me half to death! He said it was all my fault Malena died."

Her eyes were suddenly glazed with fear. "If Miguel did kill his daddy, what's to stop him deciding he ought to kill me, too?" She half rose in her chair as though to bolt.

"What was it like when you met Vicenzo?" I asked hastily, and she slumped down again. After a minute, she straightened herself up and gave a half-smile.

"When I met Vicenzo he was soooo handsome, and soooo . . . different. He looked a lot like Angel does now. Dark and sort of exotic, you know? Those cheek-bones! Oh, yes, Vicenzo was quick-tempered, like I think maybe Miguel is, too, but if you don't have a temper, what are you, some kind of limp thing with the personality of a lettuce?"

I thought this was an interesting observation. I'll admit I have an attitude, but I rarely lose my temper and then only when there's a good cause at stake. Did that make me a limp sort of person? I flashed on an image of a lanky Raggedy Ann doll, woolly red hair, thin arms and legs hanging loose. My imagination put a cowboy hat on her. Yep, could be me.

"You don't sound Texan," I observed.

"It's been twenty-three years since I was even *there*," she said. "And my daddy was always after me to talk proper English like a little lady."

"You said Vicenzo had a quick temper. Do you mean that he abused you?" Zack asked.

"Oh my goodness, no," Roxy said, her eyes widening. "He'd never have gotten away with that. I didn't ever have a bad temper like Vic said Malena had. Hey, I'm a business woman—a real estate agent. I can't be getting mad at people. Besides, I loved Vic, though I wasn't some kind of Stepford wife."

"He abused Malena?" I asked.

"I didn't say that," she said crossly.

"So you fell in love with him," I prompted when she seemed ready to zip her lip.

"I always liked older men," she said with a reminiscent smile. "Boys my own age seemed very boring to me. And Vic fell for me like a ton of bricks. It didn't seem to make much difference to him that he was married, or that he was twenty years older than me. So I didn't worry about those things, either. But then Malena found out. Turned out she'd heard about me right after that party. She'd had a cold and couldn't go. So after she heard gossip, she spied on us. Vic was really mad when she did that."

She stopped suddenly and put her head to one side, as if she'd just heard what she'd said. "But not mad enough to kill her," she added quickly. Too quickly? "He'd never have done that. He did tell Malena he'd break up with me, but he didn't, never intended to. He was crazy about me, and she found out we were still seeing each other and she got mad and packed up all his stuff. They had a big fight, he told me, and the boys came home in the middle. Angel was upset. Miguel pretended he was too tough to be upset. He was angry, though—he tried to punch out Vicenzo. And they heard their father say he was leaving. Angel told me about that stuff Vicenzo said, that "Good-bye, don't forget to die . . ."

She rolled her eyes. "I told Angel that was just Vicenzo being dramatic. Grandstanding. He was like that."

"Angel and Miguel said Vicenzo hit their mother,.' Zack said.

She shrugged. "I already told you Vicenzo had a quick temper. Malena probably didn't know how to handle him."

The implication was that Roxy did.

"Vicenzo did *not* tell me he'd hit Malena that time," she said after a moment's silence. "Nor did Angel, when he and Miguel came looking for Vic. Miguel didn't want to tell me anything."

She shrugged. "Vic spoke of his sons often. He called them 'my boys.' He really, really missed them. I tried to tell them that, and Angel seemed pleased, but Miguel said he didn't believe me."

She sighed over that for a moment. "I still get mixed up between the names. I got used to saying Vic, but after the boys came looking for their daddy, I started thinking of him as Vicenzo again. So now when I think of the time before we came to Bellamy Park—well, *that* was Vicenzo. Since then, whatever happened was with Vic. But anyway, all Vicenzo told me was that he and Malena had this big fight and she'd thrown everything he owned into garbage bags, so he left. He went back the next day to get something, he said, a watch that meant a lot to him. She wasn't home, so he went in and got it. Everything looked all right then, he said. We left Houston, and Texas, that same day."

"He didn't have any blood on him, did he?" I asked,

thinking of what Angel had said about blood in the kitchen.

She gave me a worried look. "I didn't see any blood on him," she said, her jaw going crooked as if she was trying not to cry.

I felt like some kind of really mean person and mentally kicked myself, but after a minute, she went on. "He told me Malena might try to get revenge on me for him leaving her, and she had some mean friends, so we should go somewhere else to live. I was surprised he'd leave his boys like that, but he seemed to think it was better to make a clean break. I don't mind telling you, I sure didn't want them coming with us. I mean, after all, Miguel was only two years younger than me—Angel seven years younger. What would I have done with them!"

She had stopped eating some time ago. Zack and I were both through. Her large eyes looked very sad. "I swear to you, Vicenzo didn't know Malena was dead. It was a week or so later that he called Mr. Sterling—Long John—and found out she'd been murdered the day we left the state. Long John told Vic there was a warrant out for his arrest and he should get himself a new name and not come back to Texas ever again."

Roxy was still sitting up very straight. How did she maintain that posture? It was very attractive. Not many people do that. I resolved to remember not to slump in the future. A work in progress—that's me.

"Vicenzo always insisted he didn't kill Malena," she said. "He told me over and over many, many times that he didn't shoot her. He would get mad and punch the wall in the living room of our house and he would keep saying, 'I *didn't* kill her, I *didn't*, I *didn't*.' "

"Did you believe him?" Zack asked.

"Of course I believed him. Completely. Always. Why else would I have stayed with him? You think I would have stayed with him if I thought he'd killed his wife?"

Was she protesting a bit too much?

"Who do you think did kill her, if Vic didn't?" I asked.

"John Sterling told Vic Sheriff Grigsby said who-ever killed her tried to make it look like a suicide. But I think maybe it *was* a suicide. Maybe she couldn't bear to live without Vicenzo. I can understand that now that I've lost him."

She looked down at her clasped hands on the table. Her lips were trembling. I thought for a minute she was going to break down and cry. Zack evidently thought so, too.

He passed her a napkin from the holder on the table and she pressed it to her eyes and was silent for a moment. Then she put it down and swallowed visibly. "I'm okay," she said. "Hank, my baby brother, says I'm like a rock. But even rocks fall apart sometimes. Especially if they get hit with a hammer."

She cocked her head a little to one side. "Sometimes I think maybe someone Malena knew killed her. Maybe *she* was having an affair. Who knows? I don't think the police looked for anyone else but Vic."

She sighed. "Vic hated not ever being able to go home again. Having to live with a false name and iden-tity."

"How did he establish that identity?" Sheriff Zack asked.

"He had a friend who had been in and out of jail. Vic said this guy knew his way around such situations. He got all kinds of papers for us. Drivers' licenses. Birth certificates. A marriage certificate. Stuff like that. It cost a lot of money."

"Was the friend Sal Migliatore?" I asked.

"No. This was a man in Sacramento. I never got to meet him. I think his name was Harry something. Vic didn't know Sal until he went to work for him."

I had the feeling I was running out of questions, but also that I'd missed something, something that might be important. I couldn't think what it might be.

"Who was the woman Vic was supposed to be going off with when he left you?" Zack asked.

That was probably the question that had eluded me. I almost looked at Zack with admiration. But then I thought, Hey, this is Zack. He does the *cherchez la femme* thing every time. Nothing brilliant about that.

Roxy laughed in a dry sort of way that ended with a choking sound. "He told me he'd fallen in love with a girl named Bambi, a teenager, used to come into Grumpy's—where he worked, you know?—with a fake ID. A teenager!" she repeated. "Can you imagine how Malena must have laughed in heaven? History repeating itself."

"Did you ever meet Bambi?" I asked.

She shook her head. "Sal did, though. I called him up and asked him after Vic left. Sal said Bambi had come to see Vic at work a couple of times, which he hadn't liked a bit. He said she was a perky little thing.

Wore too much makeup. Smudgy stuff around the eyes. Blusher on her cheekbones."

"Did you tell Sergeant Timpkin about Bambi?" Zack asked.

She nodded. "Sure. What do you think? No reason to protect *her!*" She sighed. "I don't even know her last name. Sal didn't know it, either. I thought maybe one of the people who used to go to Grumpy's knew her. I asked the guys and gals who came to the wake, but none of them would admit to remembering her. I guess they were trying to protect me. Or maybe Vic was more discreet than usual."

She paused to think. "I don't know now if he did take off with Bambi before he got killed, or if he got killed before they could go away together. I guess we'll have to wait for Bambi to tell us that." She swallowed again. "It upsets me that I didn't know he was dead. I just kept thinking he'd come back when he was through with Bambi. He'd have been bound to get tired of her— he always did get tired. I just kept waiting for him to come back."

She put the napkin to use again as her voice broke.

"Did he take all his clothes with him?" Zack asked.

She'd already said he'd left them behind, so I guessed the sheriff who lived inside Zack was being tricky.

Roxy sniffed. "He took only what he was wearing. I sure wasn't going to pack his stuff up in garbage bags, the way Malena did. I'm not like that. He left his old pickup truck, too. He must have rented a car, or else Bambi had one."

"Miguel said you and Vic never got married," I said.

She shook her head, looking mournful again. "Vic wouldn't risk it. All our papers were forgeries, you know? What if someone had found out? But it didn't bother me. We had twenty-three years together. I sure felt like I was his wife."

"But I guess you don't inherit anything?" Zack said.

I guessed Zack was eliminating motives. "Though you could claim palimony, I suppose," he went on. "We had a case on *Prescott's Landing* . . ."

She interrupted him. I liked this woman. "There wasn't anything to inherit. Vic was a hard worker and a good husband, except for his going after other women from time to time. Especially at that bar. Grumpy's. I put up with it because that's the way he was and there was no changing him. He always came back to me. Always. But he wasn't much of a provider. I mean, I probably brought in more than he did most years."

Her voice trailed away. For a couple of minutes, she dropped her head and shredded the napkin Zack had given her. "Vic wanted to be young again, you know. When he met me, he was going on forty. When Bambi showed up, he was almost sixty. He hated the idea of getting old. It happens to men, you know? More than to women even. Men think a younger woman will make them young again. It's like they're dipping their wick in the fountain of youth."

Zack was looking at her sympathetically. Evidently he hadn't seen any reflection of himself and his doll brigade in Vic's behavior. "So, you didn't report Vic missing," he said.

Duh.

"Why would Roxy even think Vic was missing?" I

said, exasperated. "He told her he was leaving. She even knew who he'd gone off with, even if she didn't know where."

Roxy smiled tearfully but gratefully. I rolled my eyes to indicate "Men!"

I had become aware of a middle-aged woman who was sitting at the next table, facing Zack. She had dyed black hair and long sparkling earrings that looked out of place in daylight. She had been watching our little group for some time.

Every once in a while when Zack glanced her way, she'd give him a flirtatious glance. The kind where you look at a man's mouth and then at his eyes, then back again. Demurely. Well, sure I've done it. What woman hasn't?

Zack of course had been flirting right back at her. Flirting is second nature to our man in black.

All of a sudden, the woman showed up at Zack's elbow with a paperback novel and an uncapped ballpoint. "Would you?" she asked eagerly.

Zack smiled, took the pen and signed boldly on the title page of the novel. It was a mystery novel, I noticed, by a writer I admired. There was a sword on the cover. If the author discovered some TV actor was signing his book, he was liable to come after my partner with that sword. If an outraged husband didn't get to Zack first.

Had Bambi had a significant other who might have taken umbrage at Vic Smith for seducing his girl? I wondered. But then why would Sal Migliatore dispose of the body for him?

Sal had known Bambi, Roxy had said.

"Tell me some more about Sal Migliatore," I suggested.

She seemed reluctant, but then Zack said, "Please, Roxy, it's very important," and she responded at once. Nobody ever refused Zack.

"The police think Sal probably killed Vic," she said, all resistance gone.

I shot a quelling glance at Zack, who had opened his mouth to speak. I didn't think he'd tell Roxy that the police were discounting Sal as a murderer because of the physical evidence, but you could never be sure what would come out of his mouth.

He evidently got the message. He closed his mouth and gave me his wry smile.

"Vic always said Sal didn't like him," Roxy continued. "They were always fighting. Not with fists, not anything like that. But quarreling. Arguing. Vic was often late getting to the job because of being up until all hours working the bar. And Sal was like, if he could have installed a time clock at every house Vic worked in, he would have been happy. Vic kept saying it was the workmanship that mattered, not the time he put in, but Sal hated when he didn't show up when Sal wanted him to."

It hardly seemed possible that two men who didn't like each other could have put up with each other for twenty-three years, even for their mutual financial benefit. But then, men are seriously strange. Once in a while a fight will break out at CHAPS. Angel will throw the guys out and they'll have a knock-down-drag-out fight in the parking lot. Next thing you know they come staggering back in with their arms around each other's shoulders, buying each other a beer, the best of buds.

So, how come Sal got involved in the packaging of the body anyway? And where did Bambi fit in? Had Sal had some prurient interest in seventeen-year-old girls, too? Had Bambi killed Vic and gone to Sal for help?

Roxy's next statement made that seem unlikely. "Sometimes I wondered if maybe Sal was gay. He never did marry and he didn't seem to like me much, either. He didn't seem to think much of women, period, Vic said. He said Sal was a—whatever that word is that means a guy doesn't like women."

"Mysogynist," Zack supplied.

I looked at him, surprised.

"We had a guy like that on *Prescott's Landing*," he said. "Thurber Oakley. Sheriff had to run him in for foul-mouthin' the ladies. Hated women. Hadn't ever been married, so nobody knew the reason for it, but there it was."

"This was an actor?" I asked. "Or a character?"

"A character," he said after a few seconds thought.

"If Sal was gay, it might be that he made a pass at Vic, sometime," Roxy said slowly. "Vic wouldn't be polite about that. Though he did have tolerance for gay people . . ."

She glanced at me. "Macintosh told me you and he are friends. You know about him?"

I nodded.

"Vic was okay with homosexuals as long as they didn't do anything out in the open. Couldn't understand why anyone would want someone of the same sex, though. Because he liked women so much, I guess it was hard for him to imagine. He used to tease Macintosh all the time, but in a good-natured way."

"About what?" Zack asked.

She smiled. "Oh, he'd talk about outing him. But he'd never have done it." The smile gave way to a frown. "At least I don't think he would. It used to upset Macintosh. You know how he loves that TV program of his—probably wouldn't sit well with people in charge, it being a children's program and all."

Zack pursued the subject. I couldn't imagine why. "You say Vic razzed Macintosh a lot?"

She nodded. "It didn't mean anything."

"Uh-huh." The wise sheriff took to ponderin'.

"Does it seem odd Vic and Sal would work together for twenty-three years if they didn't like each other?" I suggested, bringing everyone back on topic.

Roxy thought about it for a minute. "I suppose. But the kind of work Vic did, he wasn't around Sal that much. And Vic was so good at what he did, Sal would never fire him. Fine wood finishers are hard to find."

She hesitated as a little boy appeared at Zack's elbow and silently presented an autograph book. I didn't know autograph books were still being manufactured. Badminton and autograph books. Obviously I wasn't keeping up with retro fads.

Zack obliged and the child returned to his mother, who snatched the book from his little hand so eagerly, it was clear whose idea it had been in the first place.

"What was Sal like?" Zack asked.

Another good question. I shot him an approving glance and he gave me the smile that used to make my innards go whomp until I boosted my immune system with self-talk.

"Tall," she said, after thinking about it. "Taller than Vic, so maybe six feet two or so. Gray-haired, very light eyes. Gray eyes? Lined face. He was an old man," she added with a dismissive shrug.

I seemed to recall from the newspaper report I'd seen that Sal was only five years older than Vic. Maybe sixty was a cutoff age for Roxy.

"I hardly knew him," she went on. "I met him formally when Vic went to work for him and I saw him maybe two or three times over the years when Vic's truck was in the shop and I was picking him up. He wasn't the kind of boss who had annual picnics and Christmas parties for his employees and their spouses. We didn't go to his house; he didn't come to ours. A cold man, Sal Migliatore. Not a bit like Italian men are supposed to be."

"That was interestin' about Macintosh," Zack said as we walked across Adobe Plaza after saying good-bye to Roxy. A light breeze was cooling the historic pavers, ruffling the leaves of the California live oaks, catching the pizza smell from Casa Blanca and following us with it.

I had no idea what Zack meant.

"That stuff about Vic razzin' Macintosh about outin' him," he said after a minute or so. "There was a story on *Prescott's Landin'* like that."

"Here we go again," I said. "Do we have to judge everything by how it would play on *Prescott's Landing?*"

"It's all part of the package that makes up Zack Hunter, Charlie," he said.

Rob used to say that whenever I criticized some aspect of his personality. "It's all part of the package."

In other words, accept me as I am.

It really makes me mad when a man says that. It would make me mad if a woman said it. But I've never heard a woman do that. Most women would say, "You don't like me the way I am? Wait a minute, I'll change."

Come to think of it, that makes me mad, too.

Zack's face was solemn. "I think it might have been Molly Carstairs who threatened to out someone," he said in a musing tone. "The banker, I think—Lawrence somethin'. Lawrence Post. Old Lawrence tried to run her down with his BMW. The episode was rerun a couple weeks ago. You missed it?"

"I have better things to do with my time than watch you strutting your stuff on that dumb show." Evidently he watched the reruns of his old shows himself. Which didn't surprise me.

I suddenly caught on to what he was talking about. "You're surely not suggesting Macintosh killed Vic?"

His jaw assumed its Dick Tracy slant. "It's not unheard of, Charlie. It means a lot to Macintosh to have his secret kept secret. If Vic threatened him . . ."

"Roxy said Vic teased him, Zack—that's not exactly synonymous with threatened. Macintosh is your friend; how could you possibly think—"

"I was just explainin' an analogy," he said. "Voicin' a theory, you might say."

I was impressed. I wouldn't have thought he would have recognized an analogy if it sat up and nipped him on the nose, but I was still mad that he could apply it to Macintosh.

"Apart from the fact that Macintosh is your friend, and mine," I said, "he's the gentlest, nicest human being who ever walked the earth." My voice was heating up. We stopped on the steps leading up to CHAPS's entry. "This may surprise you, Hunter, but *Prescott's Landing* is not real life."

He put a hand on my shoulder, and to my dismay a tendril of something or other zigzagged around my innards like a misplaced section of forked lightning—an echo of my past sexual response to him. "Did anyone ever tell you you're amazin'ly beautiful when you're angry, Ms. Plato?" he asked solemnly.

I was tempted to kick his shins, but was afraid he'd mistake it for an attempt to jump his bones, so I contented myself with stomping up the steps and slamming the door in his face. Yes, I know that's childish behavior. But it felt good.

CHAPTER 7

It was a slow night at CHAPS. Tuesdays were often that way. Angel and Miguel didn't show. Zack left early. I was glad when Sundancer closed out the final dance in his usual manner. "Farewell from CHAPS, where it's always hot, hip, and country!"

After checking the building and locking up, I resisted going into the office to work on the computer and went on up to my loft, thinking about some of the stuff Roxy had told us.

The phone rang while I was brushing Benny down with this glove I bought that has little rubbery nubs on it. It takes off the excess hair so he doesn't get hairballs in his throat. He loves that glove and was vibrating with pleasure. I almost let the phone go to the answering machine, but on the third ring I put Ben down on the floor and picked up the phone.

"Charlie?" a familiar male voice said.

My ex-husband Rob. The plastic surgeon with the bedside manner to lie down for.

"Hey," I said.

"Hey?" He sounded amused. "You've really gone

country, Charlie. I take it you're still working at that bar?"

I had told him a dozen times I was a partner in CHAPS, and that it was an upscale country-western dance hall and tavern, but he insisted on pretending he thought I worked in some tacky saloon. I was tired of arguing the point.

"What can I do for you?" I asked.

"I read this item in the *Seattle Times* about a body showing up in Bellamy Park. In a storage locker? Seemed the sort of caper you'd be mixed up in, so I thought I'd better check up on you."

"Very kind of you," I said without trying to disguise the insincerity.

"So, are you? Mixed up in it?"

"You think I have nothing better to do than to go around stumbling over bodies?" I asked.

Engaged in washing himself—he does it the same way a cat does—Benny stopped to look at me as if he knew I was lying. But he didn't look disapproving. Of course, that's not an easy expression for a rabbit to assume. Mostly Ben just looks as if he's awake or asleep, unless he is eating or yawning.

"Well, you've done it a couple of times," Rob said. "I thought maybe you were making a career of it."

"I already have a career," I said. "How's *your* career going? Boffed anybody famous recently?"

"Charlie!"

I relented. "How are you, Rob?"

"Fine." I heard the smile in his voice and pictured it. He had a wonderful smile. "And you?"

"Doing great, thank you."

There was a short silence; then he said, "Well, then, as long as you aren't keeping company with corpses, I guess I'll leave you to it."

"Nice of you to check up on me," I said. Yes, insincerely again—what did you think?

"I still miss you, Charlie," he said.

After I hung up, I waited for the little tug of nostalgia that always came after Rob called me. Not that he called often. Only when a dead body showed up in Bellamy Park. I wondered why he bothered, then realized I didn't care. The tug of nostalgia hadn't appeared. My marriage was totally, finally, over.

There was some sadness to that, but it wasn't overwhelming. I was free. Single.

But still celibate.

Would that change now that I felt nothing for Rob? I had no idea.

I played tag with Benny for a few minutes. He always starts it by hopping up to me and bumping my ankle with his head, then haring across the room. When he finally gave up and sat yawning at my feet, showing me his cute little buckteeth, I tucked him into his cage for the night, turned out the lights and did my usual last check through the slats of the miniblinds that covered all the windows, examining the plaza and the parking lot for any foreign bodies. Earning my keep as security guard.

I was just turning away from the window that overlooked the walkway between CHAPS and the bank next door when I thought I saw a movement at the corner where the walkway opened up into the parking lot. There was a public phone booth at that corner.

There seemed to be a shadow either inside it or just beyond it. It was hard to tell from that angle. I moved to the next window and held the slats apart with two fingers as I peered out.

Nothing seemed to be moving. But as I turned away, I again caught the sensation of movement, this time directly below. I reached the farthest window just in time to see a man—a young man judging by the way he walked and the general look of him—disappearing around the corner of the bank, which jutted out just enough beyond CHAPS that I couldn't follow the person any longer. I waited and finally saw a slender man of average height, wearing a ball cap and sweats, emerge into the street beyond and walk briskly across it and into the all-night convenience store that was located there.

False alarm. Someone looking for a carton of milk for his breakfast cereal, or a pack of cigarettes. I laughed. When you get involved in murder, however peripherally, you tend to get suspicious about every incident that occurs.

Feeling relieved, though still a little on edge, I went around closing all the blinds, then took a mystery novel to bed. The one I was reading had a subplot that involved a woman in jeopardy—not a good choice for nighttime serenity—but it was gripping and held me until I discovered I was "reading" with my eyes closed.

In the morning I brought Benny down from my loft in his cage, and took him into the office for company while I did some work on CHAPS's Web site.

It has always been my custom to check CHAPS's E-mail when I boot up the computer. There was the usual cluster of letters and ads, and I opened them and answered or deleted them as I went. Until I came to one addressed to "CPlato@CHAPS.com." In the "Who" line, it said, "anon311."

My mind moves in odd ways sometimes. Seeing the "anon," I made a connection to Taylor Bristow, who quoted Shakespeare from time to time: "As hush of death, *anon* the dreadful thunder." I'd read a lot of Shakespeare in school and my head was full of such tidbits.

I opened up the letter and had read the whole thing before I realized it wasn't from Bristow.

"You're sticking your nose into other people's business, Charlie Plato. Don't you think you'd better quit while you've a head?"

Clever play on words there.

This wasn't the first time in my life I'd been threatened, but that didn't make it any easier to accept.

The E-mail wasn't signed, of course. Be a pretty stupid person to sign a threatening letter. I ran my mind around the people I'd talked to in the last few days. Which of them owned a computer? I wondered.

I looked at the "From" line more closely.

anon311@moonstorm.com

Moonstorm sounded like one of the bands that had performed at CHAPS recently. But why would a band send me threatening letters? Oh, no, that was Moonstone.

It had to be a joke. Whoever heard of someone sending threatening letters by E-mail? The sender was probably one of the many people who were always teasing me about being too nosy.

I shot back a terse reply telling anon his joke wasn't funny, and went on to CHAPS's new Web site to check where I'd left off the previous day. But just about the time the page finished loading, my server returned my response to anon311@moonstorm.com—courtesy of the Mailer Daemon—with the addition of a lot of gob- bledygook about unavailable service, autogenerated failure, and a permanent fatal error.

Those last couple of words gave me pause, until I remembered I'd seen it before on undeliverable E- mail.

Alongside my desk, Benny suddenly chewed on his cage wire, startling me. It's a horrendous sound that always sets my teeth on edge. I realized I felt the same sort of unease I'd felt the night before over the man in the walkway. That had turned out to be an innocent stranger on his way to buy supplies, but maybe the letter wasn't a joke after all.

I reached for the phone to call Macintosh, who had been my computer guru ever since I came to CHAPS.

And paused.

And felt guilty for even thinking . . .

No, of course it wasn't Macintosh who'd sent that weird letter.

He answered on the second ring, sounding breath- less.

"Is this a bad time?" I asked.

"Charlie lass, it's never a bad time when I hear your lovely voice. No, I just came in through the door. I'm so insecure I cannot bear to miss a phone call." The Scottish accent that put a burr on every "r" was reas- suring. It brought his image to my mind. Roly-poly body, fuzzy brown beard and hair, gentle brown eyes. No way would Macintosh threaten me.

"Someone sent me a funny letter," I said.

"Och, zap it into cyberspace," he said at once. "Those lists of jokes or supposedly true headlines from newspapers or church bulletins are the work of people who have no proper job to keep them occupied. Pay them no heed, Charlie."

"Not that kind of funny. Funny peculiar." I explained.

"I'll be right over and take a look," he said.

He arrived in a little under a half hour. He had two hours to spare before he had to tape his TV show for tomorrow, he said.

He had to visit with Benny first. Everyone loved Benny. And it was a novelty to visitors to have a chance to pet a rabbit instead of a cat or a dog. Macintosh held him cradled in his hands when he came to look over my shoulder at the computer screen. Benny is a dwarf rabbit, remember, so he's not very big, just a little round brown fuzzy body, a smaller round brown fuzzy head, and relatively short ears for a bunny. He liked nibbling gently on Macintosh's beard, which was similar in texture to his own hair. Maybe he thought Macintosh was a relative.

Macintosh had his head tilted back so he could see through the lower part of his steel-rimmed bifocals. "A dummy address, you may be sure," he said. "I take it you've not heard of a remailer?"

"You take it right."

"Well, lassie, a remailer is a person who sets up a free computerized service for people who don't want to leave any footprints or fingerprints out there in cyberspace."

"Why would anyone want to provide a service like that?"

"Because they know how to do it, I suppose."

"So, who would want to use it?"

"Well, look at the fuss some people made over telephone ID, lassie. They didn't like the idea that the person on the other end would know who was calling before they announced themselves. Probably law-abiding people who worry about their right to privacy. They feel the same about E-mail, that you shouldn't have to put a return address on it every time. Or someone might want to express political views that might get him or her in trouble with an employer or with the police or some government agency."

"A whistle-blower like Deep Throat in the Nixon thing."

"Possibly. Or perhaps our mythical person might want to place personal ads, while keeping his or her own identity secret." He hesitated. "Suppose someone—let's call her Judy—is mad at a local politician named Skip and wants to tell him why, but doesn't want him knowing who she is because she's afraid it might affect her government job. Judy finds out about an anonymous remailer run by a Mr. Sunbeam (which is, of course, a fictitious name itself) and is given instructions on what to do. She sends her letter to him, he replaces Judy's address with the dummy—in this case anon@sunbeam.com—and sends it on to Skip."

"I tried to respond to anon311@moonstorm.com and it came winging back," I told him.

"Aye, lass, this is just one of many wrinkles, you see. The return address does not really exist."

"So there's nothing I can do about it?"

He took a few seconds to put Benny back in his cage, then straightened and looked down at me. "Well, Charlie, you can report it to your friend Detective Sergeant Bristow, I suppose. What I'm thinking here is that someone might have set up this bogus domain just long enough to send this message and then shut it down. Because no responsible remailer administrator would tolerate someone sending a death threat, which is what this one implies. If someone did set this up just for this purpose, then your anonymous person must have a fair degree of computer know-how."

"Could you do it?" I asked.

He hesitated and looked away for a minute, then tilted his head back a little to look at me. He still didn't have the hang of his bifocals. His spaniel-friendly eyes, magnified through his close-up lenses, were not quite as mild as usual. "I suppose I could, if I wanted to," he said. "But it's not anything I could ever contemplate doing."

I had the horrible feeling he could see right into me and knew why I'd asked him that question. I squirmed a little on my chair.

"This is not much to go on," I said, looking back at the computer screen. "Probably it's just someone's idea of a prank."

He made a doubtful sound.

"If I get another one I'll take it to Bristow," I promised.

"Well, lass, you've a mind of your own, I've noticed.

So I'll do this. If you'll print out the letter, I'll try to trace a remailer and report this incident and see if I can find out who sent it. Is that all right?"

"I guess so," I said.

"There are quite a few remailers—more than two dozen last time I counted."

Quite evidently he *had* looked into remailing at some time or other. And he did *know* about it.

While I printed out the letter, he pulled up a chair to the other side of my desk, sat down and looked over the top of his glasses at me. "You're looking into Vic Smith's murder, I suppose," he said when the printer quit.

My innards tightened in response. "What makes you think that?"

He gave me the same warm and friendly smile he bestowed on the children who visited his TV show, and again I thought—No, Macintosh could not possibly have anything to do with this murder. "I deduced as much from your apprehensive reaction to the letter. It accuses you of sticking your nose into others' affairs. I gather that part of the message speaks true."

"Oh, well, I am *interested* in the case. What did you think of Vic?" I asked, seizing the opening.

"Well now, lassie, I thought he was a fine cabinet-maker, as did David. My partner didn't care overmuch for Vic himself, I'm afraid. David's a bit low-key, as you may have noticed. He's a thinking man's companion—quiet and bookish and a wonderful artist—the way he brings out the soul of the wood he's carving never fails to ... well, enough of digression. David thought Vic was too eager to impress, too hail-fellow-well-met, too much the extrovert. I liked him, however. He was a vigorous man and good-looking and full of life. I'm truly saddened that he's gone."

"You have any ideas about who might have killed him?"

He shook his head. "I didn't know him or Roxy all that well, and I didn't know any of the people they socialized with. Hadn't met most of them until that strange wake." He looked at me over his glasses. "I wondered what you were doing at Vic's wake. I'm glad to have my curiosity satisfied. I could not quite imagine you being a friend of his. I thought perhaps he might have patronized CHAPS."

"Never met the man," I said.

"This is a purely clinical interest then, is it?"

"Sure," I said. I hate telling lies, but I could hardly tell him Angel and Miguel were well on the way to being suspects in their father's death.

CHAPTER 8

If I had thought about it, I would have imagined that Zack had forgotten mentioning the dance called the Desperado Wrap during our caviar-tasting the day Miguel Cervantes arrived in town.

But then halfway through our regular Wednesday-night session of line-dancing lessons, while I was drinking a well-deserved mineral water, Sundancer Brown announced in his adenoidal voice that the next lesson would feature a couples dance—the Desperado Wrap. Startled, I glanced up to see our man in black coming through the crowd in my direction. Sundancer was already playing the music. And wouldn't you know it was one of my favorite singers—Doug Stone—with one of his best songs, "A Different Light."

"A Different Light" is about a man seeing his female coworker coming into the office dressed in her business suit, with her hair pinned up, after making love to her the night before.

I was sitting on a stool next to Savanna at the main corral bar. "How about you doing this dance with Zack?" I suggested to Savanna as casually as I could manage.

"Not on your life." She dimpled at me. "I'm a respectable married lady now. I've *seen* that dance." Her killer smile widened. "There's no need for you to worry about dancing with Zack, is there? Zack Hunter doesn't affect you, right? You're cured. Over him. End of story. *Finis.* Wasn't that what you *tried* to tell me?"

I ignored her. She wasn't being any help at all. Zack had been stopped by a vivacious redhead in a denim miniskirt and the tightest tank top I had ever seen, giving me a few seconds' grace. "Quick, Angel," I said. "Can you do the Desperado Wrap?"

He shook his head. "Sorry, Charlie, I don't know that one."

A minute later, Zack took me by the hand, hauled me off my stool and chivvied me ahead of him to the dance floor.

This is how the desperado dance goes: visualize it, okay? Here's this long-legged hunk of terminally horny male. Put him together with an orange-haired female who hasn't had sex in more than two years. We're both facing in the same direction, him behind me. He joins his hands over my shoulders and we do a few simple side steps and foot touches in position. So far, not so bad.

Then I bring my arms up above my head and he puts his hands over mine, forming a cone shape that I can turn in, and we do a sort of turning, rolling grapevine, then drop our arms down to our sides, still holding hands. About here, I decided somebody must have turned off the air-conditioning.

After a little more stepping around, we bring our arms up shoulder high, stretched out to each side, and we glide and sway in unison and his arms end up with mine, hands clasped together, wrapped around my body, his body curved suggestively behind mine.

I discovered later, reading a step chart about this dance, that you were supposed to allow a comfortable space between arms and bodies.

Zack didn't do that. What he did do was press me against his body spoon fashion and perform a hip grind that wasn't in any step chart ever written. It brought applause and whistles from our spectators.

"Whoa!" I said.

Zack gave me his low, lazy laugh and pulled our arms in tighter. My body seemed to have gone limp and boneless, but my brain was alert and it commanded me to kick backward, connecting the heel of my cowboy boot with Zack's right shin. While he was hopping around laughing and clutching his knee to his chest, I propelled myself out of harm's way.

There was more applause.

I noticed that Miguel was leaning against a pillar, watching us. Watching me. He wasn't applauding. I'm trying to think of the right word to describe the kind of look he was sending our way. *My* way. Hot? Burning? Scorching? Pick one.

Once Zack stopped hopping and I'd persuaded him to behave himself, he and I moved slowly through the whole dance several times. The Desperado Wrap is not an easy dance to do. All of our country-dancer wannabes imitated our movements with varying degrees of skill. And then we put it to music.

Believe me, even when he's behaving properly, Zack is one smooth partner. He *really* knew how to do the

Desperado Wrap. Every intimate movement. Every nerve-tingling sexual nuance.

Before the dance was over, butterflies were galloping around my private parts and I was entertaining thoughts about vows of celibacy not being worth the paper they're written on, and giving mental admonitions to my weak knees to pull themselves together.

In short, I was a wreck. That dance would have turned me on if I was doing it with Freddy Whosit from the nightmare movies. Doing it with Zack was like foreplay. I was ready to give up celibacy. Really ready.

"You out of shape, Charlie?" Zack asked as we headed back to the bar through an admiring crowd of patrons. His arm was around my shoulders. It felt heavy. Warm. "Not pumpin' any iron lately?" he went on. "You seem to be breathin' heavy."

I gave him a look that was intended to broil him to an apologetic cinder but it somehow came out feeling languorous.

Smiling, he dipped his face down close, his lips brushing my hair as he murmured, "We'll dance again later, okay?"

I tried to tell myself I had no idea what this statement really meant. But I knew. And I didn't object. I kept hearing Savanna's voice telling me, "Just nail him, Charlie. Get it over with." Savanna was pretty savvy about sexual stuff. I wondered if I should take her advice. Sometime in the future, maybe.

I know, I know. I was pathetic. Have I ever pretended otherwise?

During the break, Zack and I and the Cervantes

brothers went up to my loft so we could fill Angel and Miguel in on what we'd learned from Roxy. Savanna wanted to spend the time on the office telephone with Jacqueline, which was just as well. Unfortunately, at the moment, Savanna had a conflict of interest. She was our friend, but she was now married to Bristow, who constituted "authority." We would, of course, give Bristow an edited version at a later date.

Zack plucked Benny out of his cage and took him over to my creaky old rocker. Benny was in rabbit heaven. He adores Zack. Or at least he adores his big hands. I guess they make him feel secure.

I remembered Savanna on her wedding day saying women loved big hands, too. I found myself looking at Zack's big hands and remembering that when I was still in high school a girlfriend and I did a study on how many boys in our classes had big hands. We'd heard there was a correlation between their hands and a certain other part of their anatomy. Being good little girls, we made no attempt to find out if that was true. It was quite a few years before I discovered it was a myth.

I realized Zack was squinting sexily at me as if he knew exactly what I was thinking. "Shouldn't Ben have a lady rabbit to keep him company by now?" he asked.

I sat down on my secondhand sofa. "He doesn't need one, if that's what you mean. I had him neutered."

The ensuing silence was fraught with indignation. All three men looked at me as if I'd said something obscene. "He'd be ODing on testosterone, acting too territorial," I explained. "Harder to train in all ways. Too aggressive. He might even bite people."

Zack held Ben up to his face so he could look him in the eye. "You have my sympathy, bud. Not much I can do but offer some advice. Never trust a woman again."

Miguel made a sound that might have been agreement.

"Let's get started, okay?" I suggested. "We don't have too much time."

Miguel came and sat next to me. Angel stood with his back to a wall, as he usually preferred to do, arms folded more for comfort than as a negative sign.

"That woman believes I killed my father?" Miguel exclaimed when I was partway through Roxy's story.

"That seemed to be the general idea," I said. "However, she also thought your mother might have committed suicide in spite of what the deputies said. And she thinks it's possible that Sal Migliatore killed your father."

"Sal's my choice, too," Angel said. "Seems he and our father quarreled a lot. Sal was the one rented the locker. He was the one paying the rent on it. He put . . . the body in there. If he hadn't died it would still . . . our father's body would still be in there."

I wished I could tell him Sal had been pretty well ruled out as the murderer by the lab, even though he'd been involved in the cover-up, so to speak. But if Bristow was given cause to doubt what he called my discretion, he'd never pass me information again.

"I guess we may never know exactly what Sal did and didn't do," I said.

"Maybe *she* killed him," Miguel said.

"Roxy?" Zack queried. "She was crazy about him,

she said, and she wasn't the only one to say so. That reminds me—one time on *Prescott*—"

I interrupted hastily. "Women have been known to kill the men they love," I said.

Zack's eyebrows climbed. I guessed he couldn't imagine any woman who loved him doing anything violent to him. Unless it was lovemaking, of course. I could imagine that making love to Zack could get pretty violent. I could imagine . . . It was getting pretty warm in my loft, I thought. Maybe I should open a window.

"Our father told Roxy he was going to leave her," Miguel said. "That would make her mad, don't you think?"

"She expected Vic to come back," I pointed out. "It had happened before and he always came back. All she had to do was wait and her life would go back to being the same as usual. According to all the gossip, it was nowhere near being the first time. Why should she suddenly get violent about it this time? Anyway, why would Sal Migliatore help Roxy, given that he didn't like her?" I hesitated. "What about Roxy's brother, Hank?" I suggested. "Have you met him?"

Angel and Miguel exchanged a glance and nodded without comment.

"He's a sleazy sort of guy," I said. "He was around at the time. Living with Vic and Roxy."

"Sleazy is too kind a word," Miguel said.

"But what's his motive?" Zack asked rhetorically. "You think he'd kill his sister's lover because the dude left her? What's it to him? He stayed on with his sister after, same as before. Seems like Vic wasn't supportin' him. He has a job. Something to do with plumbin', didn't Roxy say?"

Miguel shook his head. "I don't think any of this is going to help *our* situation."

"We had to go into the police station and take a lie detector test," Angel said out of the blue.

"A polygraph test!" Zack exclaimed, startling Benny. Zack rubbed the spot behind Ben's ears that seemed to be one of his erogenous zones and the little rabbit mellowed out immediately.

"We didn't *have* to take the test," Miguel corrected. "What Timpkin says is that so far we are just being *interviewed*, not interrogated. Only because we are related to the *decedent*, he says. He loves that word, decedent, throws it around like a cow chip. Keeps assuring us we're having a friendly discussion. The lie detector test—polygraph test—was for the purpose of clarifying things, he says. No charges being filed, he says."

His mouth was a grim line. "I've had friendlier discussions with a two thousand pound Brahma bull named Tornado."

"Detective Sergeant Timpkin was born hostile," I said.

"That was the scariest, most intimidating thing I ever went through," Angel said. "They start you off with this thick bunch of forms where you have to answer questions about everything you ever did or didn't do. Then when they get you hooked up, they ask only a few of those questions, some of them several times, until you are convinced you must have shown some kind of criminal response somewhere along the line, even though you *know* you didn't do anything."

Zack pulled his lower lip between left thumb and forefinger to show he was thinking. "Timpkin has to be hostile," he offered. "A police officer can't believe anythin' without proof. Has to question everythin'. That's the dude's job."

Our TV police expert. He was probably right, though, I conceded.

"Polygraph isn't as important as it's made out to be," Zack continued. "It's based on the idea that when you tell a lie, you get stressed out and that shows up in the test. But some people get stressed out just doin' the test, and some people don't get stressed even if they're lyin' through their teeth. But sometimes just the act of takin' the test makes people confess."

"So, what was the result of the polygraph test?" I asked.

"They said some of the answers were inconclusive," Angel said.

Miguel's mouth curled. "Timpkin was trying to scare us into saying we killed our father. That test showed nothing and the clown knew it. I could tell the way the guy—the guy doing the testing—was acting, there was nothing there for anyone to go to the gas chamber or get a lethal injection for." He paused, eyebrows raised. "Murderer gets a choice in California. Did you know that? Democracy in action."

I noted he still hadn't said outright that he hadn't killed his father. I remembered Bristow telling me one time that a guilty criminal had a hard time actually saying the words "I didn't do it." He or she might say,

"I'm innocent," or "You can't prove a thing," instead. Which basically was what Miguel had just said.

I could imagine Miguel covering up stress well enough to fool a machine, but I couldn't visualize Angel lying at all. Withholding information, yes. He was never a big talker, but he'd always seemed painfully honest. And honorable.

After Angel, and Miguel, left the loft, I put Benny back in his cage. He immediately scuttled into his cardboard box. The day before, I'd given him an old worn-soft T-shirt to wrestle with and he'd dragged it into the box. Now he scooted it around with his forepaws and front teeth, making it comfortable, I supposed. I carried the cage into the bathroom and turned on the nightlight as usual, so I could go in the night without falling over the bunny cage. I made sure Ben had food and water; then Zack and I headed for the door, turning out lamps as we went. My loft looked large and shadowy in the dim light coming up from the parking lot. I was glad to return to the bright lights below.

When the open dancing started, we all went about our various duties which for me meant doing an occasional dance with a patron and once in a while helping out serving beer or wine.

Miguel stayed around. Now and then I caught him watching me with that same tight-lipped, verging on cynical smile. I couldn't imagine him ever breaking out a breathtaking, to-die-for smile such as Angel let loose every once in a while. Miguel was much too controlled to let loose of anything. But he did have some attractive qualities and that tight smile was one of them, even though there was something behind it that spoke of aloneness, as distinct from loneliness. Loneliness had too weak a sound for a tough hombre like Miguel.

I remembered him saying he was a loner, and going on to say Angel had told him I was one, too. The difference was that sometimes I did get lonely.

I managed to sneak out while Miguel was looking in another direction, and went to work in the office on the Web page. I checked the mail before shutting down, but there was no anonymous message and I decided with some relief that the earlier one really had just been someone's stupid idea of a practical joke.

I went back into the main corral around closing time to help ease people out the door. Miguel had left, I was glad to see. The man disturbed me in some atavistic way. Almost like hair rising on the back of your neck, you know? Or at least feeling that it was. I couldn't decide if I liked him or was afraid of him.

Zack and I were the last to leave the main corral. I walked out with him to the streetside door so I could lock up behind him. He hesitated after opening the heavy door, one hand on the door handle. "You wanna come pick up a pizza at Feriga's and take it to my house?" he asked.

I thought briefly of fixing him something in my loft, but I was feeling vulnerable, and if Zack was on my turf it might be difficult to dislodge him, whereas if I was at his house I could leave anytime I wanted to.

Okay, I admit to faulty reasoning again. I knew damn well, after my reaction to the Desperado Wrap, that I'd been fooling myself about having either my emotions or hormones under control where Zack was concerned.

Yeah, I know. You guessed.

But I really didn't relish going back up to my shadowy loft alone. I looked beyond Zack to the deserted parking lot. It was foggy around the edges. I wondered if anyone was hanging around, watching. I thought that for some unknown reason I didn't want to be alone right now.

"Hang on a minute," I told Zack, and went to fetch my leather jacket from the office closet where I usually kept it. I was afraid if I ever took it up to my loft I might absentmindedly leave it draped on a chair and risk Ben chewing it. He was partial to leather.

"Okay," I said, as I locked up behind us. "If we can get the fresh vegetable pizza, and we drive separately."

Zack gave me his bad-boy grin. "We'll get one pizza for you and one for me," he said.

After hanging up our cowboy hats in Zack's foyer, we set our pizzas on the island counter in the kitchen. "You want me to hang your jacket?" Zack asked.

Something in the way he asked made me decide to say no. "I haven't warmed up yet."

He cocked his head to one side and treated me to his slanted eyebrows and crooked smile. "That jacket is part of the fantasy that weird lady wanted to know about," he said. "My recurring fantasy."

"I'm not interested in your fantasies," I reminded him.

"You should be. This one has your name on it." His smile became more knowing. "It's like this, Charlie. You look damn dangerous in that jacket. I see you in that jacket, feel the butter-softness of it. I have this ongoin' fantasy where I go back to bein' Sheriff Lazarro and you're a suspect in some crime or other and I go about gettin' you to assume the position. Up against the wall. So I can check you for concealed weapons."

I took the jacket off and handed it to him. He grinned and took it out to the hall. One thing about Zack: when he was refused, he gave in gracefully. Which was remarkable when you consider how seldom he was refused.

Mine was a great pizza, garden fresh and flavored with pesto. Zack's was dripping with cheese and filled with pastrami and onions and thick meat sauce and anchovies. He kept trying to get me to taste it. I kept trying to get him to taste mine. Pizza isn't much for romantic symbolism, but hey, you work with what you've got.

We ate at the island counter, sitting side by side on high stools, our arms brushing once in a while. We talked about Benny and his new tricks with the cardboard box and T-shirt and about Savanna and how happy she and Bristow appeared to be. We agreed that occasionally marriage seemed to be okay for some people, though it definitely wasn't for either of us.

Then we wandered into Zack's living room, carrying our glasses and what was left in the bottle of burgundy, and settled down on the white larger-than-life, down-filled sofa to watch the news on TV.

I could feel all kinds of vibrations coming from Zack. He kept looking at my face instead of the TV. He had a way of looking at a woman as though he was recording every feature on some internal mechanism, assembling a picture he could look at in private moments. It was flattering and at the same time mesmerizing.

I knew that all I had to do was to turn my face slightly and he would lean forward and kiss me.

And eventually, I did turn to look at him.

That's when I saw it.

It was standing in the corner of the room, right where the light from the television screen would make it visible in its entirety—a life-size cardboard cutout of Sheriff Lazarro, as played by Zack Hunter.

Zack looked startled when I jumped up, but he laughed when I walked over to look at his alter ego. "What d'ya think of my friend, Charlie?" he asked.

"Where on earth did you get this?" I asked.

"Rudy DeSilva got it for me. Some catalog company is sellin' them at thirty-five dollars a pop. Sellin' out fast, Rudy says. You can get a ton of different people—the Duke even."

The legendary Duke, John Wayne, of course, was one of Zack's heroes. Rudy had been one of the directors of *Prescott's Landing*. I'd met him for lunch once, with Zack, in a Monterey restaurant. Rudy had also been one of the directors of Zack's comeback series a few months before—a new *Prescott's Landing* series that had stretched any intelligent person's sense of disbelief to its logical snapping point. Rudy was obviously a man of uncommon discernment.

I walked back and forth in front of the figure. It was wearing Zack's signature black Western clothing, plus chaps—*shaps* as Miguel would have it. He was standing in a gunslinger's crouch, gun drawn and apparently just fired, judging by the cloud of white smoke that covered his right shoulder.

As I walked, the eyes in the shadow of the sexily tilted cowboy hat seemed to follow me, just as Zack's were following me.

I bubbled over with laughter. "Only Zack Hunter would have a cutout of Zack Hunter standing in his living room."

"He reminds me of the good old days," Zack said, sounding wistful.

Getting up, he came over to stand beside me. "I *liked* bein' Sheriff Lazarro," he said. "Now it doesn't look as if there will be any more episodes. Westerns aren't popular any more, they say."

He sighed. "In Hollywood, everyone talks about *they*. '*They* say it's out, over, kaput.' '*They* want to do it this way or that way.' No names. I think maybe nobody real is ever involved. It's just an imaginary *they*."

His eyes were as shadowed as those of the cardboard facsimile. It was really weird standing between them. I suddenly lost most of my amusement at the situation and felt a wave of sympathy for this man who was, after all, my friend and partner. After years of enjoying maximum popularity, it would have to feel pretty rotten to be told the parade was passing you by.

"I'm sorry, Zack," I murmured, touching him lightly on the arm.

That was a mistake. Like most male animals, Zack had an unerring instinct for when a female of the species weakened, and never failed to take advantage of it. The words were hardly out of my mouth before I was enfolded in two iron-hard arms, getting kissed as only Zack Hunter knew how to kiss, which was to say gently, warmly, sensually, skillfully, and irresistibly.

I let myself sink into him for all of fifteen minutes, returning his kisses with openmouthed fervor, relishing every tender moment. I loved that Zack's hands didn't roam. I hate being grabbed and pummeled while my mouth is busy. Good kissing should be concentrated on for its own sake.

"I need more wine," I murmured when we surfaced to breathe. "I have to think about this."

He laughed softly, confidently, and steered me back to the sofa, my knees having developed a peculiar wobble.

"We could finish the wine off in bed while you're thinkin' and I'm lovin'," he suggested, one arm holding me in close to his shoulder.

"We might spill it on the sheets," I said. Don't ask me why I said such a stupid thing. Some last-ditch defense mechanism my brain had devised to protect me, I think. "It's safer on the sofa," I added.

He laughed again. I could hardly blame him. "Well, let's for sure play it safe, Charlie." He put my glass in my hand. "No hurry, darlin'. There's plenty of time. I've waited a long time for this."

He reached for his own glass.

"Speaking of playing it safe, Zack. I have to tell you, with your record I'm not sure I should ever go to bed with you."

"My record?" He seemed genuinely puzzled.

"Women, Zack. You change women as often as you

change your cowboy shirt. Not only do I not want to be one in a long line of conquests, to be replaced when the next dolly twitches her I hips at you, but I'm not sure *you're* safe."

The frown increased, then cleared. "Oh, you mean all that stuff about safe sex? I use protection. Always. I told you that before."

"I don't know if that's enough," I said, meaning I still didn't want to be one in a long line of conquests.

Zack jumped up and strode off down the hall and into his bedroom. How did I know it was his bedroom? I'd gone through it once on the way to his swimming pool, which was in a courtyard out back. What did you think?

He reappeared with a piece of paper in his hand and presented it to me with a flourish. Red printing. The name of a medical lab at the top. "What am I supposed to do with this?" I asked.

He grinned.

HIV, it said on the left. Negative, it said on the right.

"Look at the date," he said.

It was dated two weeks ago. "I get checked every couple months, Charlie," he said. "Doc said it was a good idea for anyone who was sexually active to get checked regularly. Gave me a whole bunch of literature to read, too."

"And you read it, I suppose."

He nodded solemnly. "Sex is good, Charlie. I enjoy sex more than most anythin', but sex isn't worth dyin' for. So see, I was okay two weeks ago. Haven't been with anyone since."

"Not even Missy?" I asked. I hadn't heard him mention Missy, his flight attendant number-one girlfriend, in some time. Come to think of it, it had been a while since I had heard of or seen any of his collection of dollies—who were mostly young, shapely females, tall and willowy. They came in several ethnic varieties—Zack was an equal opportunity lover.

He frowned again. "Just can't seem to whip up as much interest as I used to, Charlie. You know—Missy's a lot younger than me."

"That never bothered you before. Almost everyone in your doll brigade is a lot younger than you."

He laughed. "You and Savanna still call my friends my doll brigade?" He was silent for a minute; then he looked at me solemnly. "I've just noticed lately that very young chicks—sorry, *women*—don't have much conversation."

My oh my! The man was growing up, maybe?

"I never thought conversation was your goal," I said.

"Guess I got used to havin' stimulatin' discussions with you, darlin'," he said, then looked at me sideways. "Stimulatin' bein' the important word there." He raised an eyebrow. "So what do you say, Charlie?" His grin was back and turning sly. "That is, if *you* check out okay."

Still bemused, I gave him an answer instead of a retort. "I was checked when I had that cone biopsy in January. Clinic policy."

"I'll accept your word you haven't had sex since," he said with a knowing grin.

"I haven't had sex in more than two years," I said.

Wrong thing to say.

He looked distinctly pleased. "It'll be like startin' over, Charlie," he said.

"Not according to Savanna," I said, remembering her insistence on her wedding day that I couldn't go back to being a virgin. I wasn't going to share that with Zack.

"May I have a little more wine?" I asked.

Delaying tactics.

Zack poured.

"You really think there'll be no more *Prescott's Landing?*" I asked, gamely making small talk.

He nodded, looking solemn again for a moment. But then he smiled. "I did pitch an idea that Rudy liked the sound of, so things may not be as bad as they look, Charlie. He's goin' to have the writers take a look at it, see if they can come up with a script for him to take to a producer he's worked with a few times."

"What kind of idea?" I asked idly, feeling pretty sure it would be as dumb as the Sheriff Lazarro episodes.

"You remember *Cheers?*" he asked.

I nodded. I'd enjoyed *Cheers*, at least the earliest shows. Series shouldn't be allowed to go on too long, I thought; sooner or later they always started going downhill.

"This would be a sort of *Cheers* with chaps," Zack said.

I frowned at him and took a fair-size gulp of burgundy. I think I had a prescient moment there. I could feel a chill running through my veins. It had nothing to do with the burgundy, which was, of course, at proper temperature. Zack had the same kind of cabinet at home that he kept at CHAPS. He was very particular about the care of wine.

"*Cheers* with chaps," I echoed.

He chuckled. "Give you half a dozen guesses where I got the idea, Charlie. Four partners in a country-western tavern. The tavern would be the focus of every episode. Rudy thought we could maybe make it a mystery show. Add another dimension. Lead characters runnin' into dead bodies, just like you and me. A different story every week, but the same locale, same continuin' characters for viewers to get hooked on. We could include some line-dancin' and funny situations and some eccentric characters and . . . what's wrong, darlin'?"

My horror was evidently showing on my face. Setting the wineglass carefully down on the coffee table in front of us, I stood up. I was experiencing the full fight-or-flight syndrome. I was either going to deck him or leave.

"Haven't you ever learned the difference between television and reality?" I demanded. "Have you any idea what would happen to your sense of reality if a show like that was produced? Not to mention the exploitation involved."

He stood up, looking uncertain and puzzled.

"Good night," I said, heading for the door. It wouldn't matter how much I attempted to explain what I meant, he would never understand.

"Charlie," he said, and he sounded so bewildered, I was half tempted to stop, to try really hard to explain, hoping to convince him of the impossibility of his idea so we could go on with what had been about to happen.

But fortunately my brain had begun operating again. It took over from my traitorous body and sent commands to all parts to keep going. I grabbed my hat and leather jacket from the foyer closet, closed Zack's door gently behind me and got into my Wrangler and drove back to CHAPS. I didn't even look around the parking lot to see if anyone was there. By the time I climbed the stairs to my loft, I'd persuaded myself I was glad something had happened to save me from certain disaster.

Almost glad.

CHAPTER 9

So hey, what's the best way to wash a guy right out of your hair? Nope, the answer has nothing to do with any kind of shampoo. The answer is—get another guy. Right.

The next morning, I arbitrarily decided that Benny needed a checkup. Sure he was as perky as ever, but I convinced myself his eyes looked a little less shiny than usual.

I had a harder time convincing Dr. Brian Andersen, the veterinarian. "This is one very healthy bunny," he said after checking Ben from whiskers to tail. "What kind of hay are you feeding him?"

"Alfalfa."

"Better to give him Timothy hay. Alfalfa will give him too much calcium."

Well there, it was a good thing I'd brought Benny in after all!

Brian put Benny back into his pet carrier with gentle hands, secured the door and looked at me with inquiring blue eyes. Nice blue eyes. Clear and healthy-looking. And interested.

"I'd like to ask you some more questions about Vic Smith and his family," I said.

His face closed down immediately and he busied himself wiping down the stainless-steel examining table. "Thought there was something on your mind," he said, his voice clipped, almost hostile. "What's your interest in Vic? You never did say why you were at the wake."

"I'm just—it's not for myself. I'm helping a friend."

"A worthy motive." Definitely hostile. Washing his hands at the sink stand against the wall, he glanced up at the wall clock. "I have to make my rounds. Sorry."

"Maybe I could accompany you?" I suggested.

The pinkness around his ears said plainer than speech that he didn't appreciate the suggestion, but, to my surprise, after taking a couple of minutes to dry his hands very thoroughly, he nodded. "My vet tech will keep an eye on Benny," he said.

I had an idea it was not normal for him to be rude, and he couldn't quite bring himself to go too far with it, but it was still fairly obvious that he'd turned off the charm. And the vibrations.

Leaving the pet carrier in the veterinary technician's care, we set off across a wide strip of grass to a concrete building behind the clinic where pets were boarded. "School's out," Brian commented. "Lot of people off on vacation, so we're pretty well filled up."

The indoor kennels consisted of a long row of enclosed pens with runs behind them for dogs, a special room Brian said held cages for the odd gerbil, guinea pig, or rat, another room where he allowed cats to roam free.

I was impressed by Brian's kind but professional manner as he checked each animal. At about the fifth stop, I realized he wasn't going to talk until I did, so I asked him why he minded me asking about Vic now when he hadn't seemed to mind at the wake.

He was crouched down looking into the right ear of a cocker spaniel and took a moment to answer. "At the wake your questions seemed natural, considering the wake was about Vic. But it seems to me you came in here purposely to ask about him again, which makes your questions much more suspect. What are you up to, Charlie?"

Honesty is occasionally the best policy. "I'm trying to find out enough about Vic's death to clear Angel and Miguel Cervantes," I said, and waited for him to ask who they were.

"Vic's sons," he said.

"You've met them?"

He shook his head. "Roxy told me about them when they showed up last fall right about the time Vic took off." His clear forehead knotted above his nose. "The Cervantes brothers know you are going around asking questions about their father?" he asked.

"They asked me to help. Asked *us* to help. Me and Zack. They *are* suspects and I want to get them off the hook."

"At whose expense?" he asked.

His ears were still pink. I looked at him thoughtfully. He wasn't talking about money. "Whose expense do you think will be involved?" I asked, then threw out a guess. "Roxy's?"

"She's a friend. She told me Miguel was mad enough to kill when he came to her house in October."

"That doesn't mean he did kill."

He shrugged.

"Was Vic also your friend?" I asked.

"Yes." He hesitated.

"Did you like him?" I persisted.

A half-smile lifted the corner of his mouth. "When someone's been murdered, it's best you tell everyone you liked him."

"But you didn't?"

"Most of the time I thought he was a nice guy, but I didn't like the way he treated Roxy. All those younger women, getting younger all the time. Did she tell you about Bambi?"

I nodded.

"And she still kept right on loving him," he said, looking wistful.

Hmmm.

He rubbed the cocker's head, then moved on to the next pen. "Shetland sheepdog," he said, when he caught my inquiring glance. "Commonly known as a sheltie." The tricolored dog lifted his right paw to shake hands with me in a very dignified manner. I obliged.

"Vic was okay otherwise," Brian said. He was checking out the sheltie's teeth, making a clucking sound. He seemed very uncomfortable, I thought. Or maybe he just didn't like the look of the sheltie's teeth—they seemed a bit grungy around the gums to me.

"What do you think of Roxy's brother?" I asked.

He didn't mind talking about this one. "Let me count the ways," he said, straightening up. "Repulsive? Nasty? Disgusting? You getting a message here?" He made a note on a chart on the wall and we moved on to the next pen.

"Loud and clear. And I happen to agree. He grossed me out the minute I met him. What do you know about him?"

"Roxy told me her father threw Hank out of the family home in Texas a year ago. He cut off Hank's allowance because Hank didn't take kindly to work and tended to squander money."

"He was getting an allowance? Why? He's hardly a kid."

Brian was checking over one of a pair of fuzzy tan mixed-breed puppies who were wiggling with delight to have company. I crouched down beside him and petted the other pup. Benny would have a fit if he smelled dog on me, but I didn't often get a chance to play with puppies. "The name Spangler seems familiar to me," I added.

Brian laughed. "You must have been contemplating your toilet bowl. The Spangler Corporation has been making potties for several generations. According to Roxy, the family owns a huge factory on the west side of Houston."

"Was Roxy cut off by her father, too?" I asked.

He considered for a moment. "I've never asked her. She didn't say so." He hesitated again. "I don't think anyone likes Hank except Roxy. I'm not sure why she's so fond of him, but maybe they were happy together as kids. Sal sure didn't like him."

I was suddenly alert. "Sal? You mean Sal Miglia-tore? Vic's boss? How did he know Hank?"

Brian's mouth tightened as if he was sorry that last comment had escaped him. "I'm not sure I should be talking to you, Charlie. You're not officially connected with all this. I don't see why I should satisfy your idle curiosity."

"Idle!" I could work up some hostility myself if he kept talking like this. "I've explained my connection, Brian. I'm hardly asking you for state secrets."

He shook his head. I didn't think he'd have any more to say and regretted my sarcasm.

"Hank worked for Sal for a while when he first came to live with Vic and Roxy," he said after a moment, surprising me again. "Sal couldn't stand him, got rid of him pretty damn quick. I understand Sal didn't get along with Vic, either."

"So Roxy told me. It seemed weird to me that they'd work together for all those years if they didn't like each other."

"People *are* weird," Brian said tersely. "That's why I work with animals."

"How did you know Sal?" I asked.

I waited, but he gave a last back rub to the pups and moved us on to the next pen without adding anything further.

"I wouldn't say I *knew* him," he said finally.

"What would you say then? Was he a customer? Did he have a cat? A dog?"

He shrugged. "Most of what I knew of Sal came from what Rox—well, Roxy and Vic had to say."

He wasn't making eye contact, I noticed. Which made me very inquisitive. I mentioned earlier that I've always been a student of body language. Since I've been involved in detecting, I've learned to watch for it when I'm questioning someone. You'd be surprised how much it gives away.

"Sal was the contractor for this whole complex," Brian added offhandedly, gesturing expansively around him. "He didn't show up on the job often, though."

Roxy had said she thought Sal might be gay, might have made a pass at Vic. Was Brian gay, too?

The vibrations had not returned. But they had definitely been there on previous occasions. I supposed he could be bisexual.

As though he'd read my mind, Brian suddenly turned away from the very large German shepherd he'd been checking over and looked at me with a fair amount of intensity. Nope, there wasn't a glimmer of sexual interest there anymore. "Are you through, Charlie? I probably have patients waiting for me in the clinic."

Part of the reason I'd come here was to see if anything would transpire between Brian and me, so I could get over this ridiculous infatuation I had for Zack. But I'd evidently managed to alienate the man. Way to go, Charlie.

I hadn't really liked the idea of using one man to help me get over another anyway, I told myself.

"I have to get back to CHAPS and help Zack supervise the refinishing of the dance floors anyway," I said, gathering remnants of dignity around me like a comforting blanket.

"Uh-huh."

He escorted me to the outer hall. When I left him and went to pick up Benny, his smile was polite but nowhere near as friendly as on former occasions. Not a successful interview, I conceded to myself. Maybe I'd try again at a later date.

I hit right on lunchtime traffic. Gridlock, for a while, then five miles an hour in some stretches. But what the heck, it was a nice day and I'd left the ragtop off the Wrangler. I tossed my cowboy hat into the back-seat. The sun felt good on my bare head. I fancied I could smell the red, white, and pink oleanders in the median over the exhaust. I had a country-western sta-tion playing on the radio.

Ben dozed in his carrier, but I spent the time use-fully, going over my conversation with Brian, trying to figure out why I had the distinct feeling he'd been holding out on me.

All the same, it seemed forever before I exited the freeway and drew up at the traffic light outside the entrance to Memorial Park, a couple of blocks from CHAPS.

That street is one way, so the arched entrance was pretty close. I glanced over at it, thinking that I hadn't been in it for some time and I should visit soon. Way back in the nineteenth century the town of Bellamy Park originated there with some kind of military encampment. The park was well kept but not too mani-cured, and featured all kinds of shrubs and flowers and trees, plus a jogging trail, tennis courts, playing fields.

I looked back at the light, which was still red. Just as I began to think it might not be functioning, some-thing hit the hood of the Jeep with considerable force and bounced off into the street.

My first thought was that the object was a baseball. Cussing kids and school holidays, restraining myself from dashing out and tracking down the miscreant, I leaned over the door to see what the object was. About then, another object came flying through the air and smacked me on the forehead.

Everything did not go black, but I did see a few stars and stripes and flashes of zigzagging light.

Almost immediately, cars behind me started honking and I woozily realized the light had changed to green. Somehow I got the Wrangler going and kept myself reasonably alert until I made it into CHAPS's parking lot.

My head was throbbing. I put a hand to the place, but there wasn't any blood. I leaned back against the seat and closed my eyes. I was going to have a hell of a bruise, I thought. The Wrangler, too. I should go find out who was playing in the park and give them a talking-to.

I just kept sitting there. I couldn't seem to make the movements necessary to get out of the Jeep. And I was beginning to feel vaguely nauseated. I suppose I was in shock. Somewhere in the back of my confused mind I was glad to be home safe. Somewhere else in there I wondered when I'd started thinking of that loft above CHAPS as home.

Time seemed to pass.

"What the hell happened, Charlie?" a male voice asked.

I turned my head, wincing as pain shot like a lightning bolt through my head. Miguel Cervantes had materialized alongside me. Speaking slowly and carefully, I explained what had happened. "I was parked at the light by the park," I added. "I guess it was kids playing baseball. Someone knocked a couple over the hedge. Got a home run or two for sure."

Miguel opened my door and reached around me to unfasten my seat belt. I smelled the clean odor of soap. "What are you doing here?" I asked.

"I came to see you," he said. "I've been waiting in the entryway there. Too much racket inside. Zack said you'd be along shortly. Took me a minute to figure out that was you sitting in the Jeep. Wondered why you didn't get out."

"Zack? Zack's here? Why is Zack here at this time of the day? Did I pass out? What time is it?"

"Bunch of guys here, Charlie. Doing something to the dance floors."

Oh, God. The refinishing job.

I finally figured out how to move my feet and body so I could get out of the Wrangler. Miguel helped. I hate to admit it, but sometimes it feels very very good to have a strong male around to lean on. On the way out, I brushed against something hard on the seat and picked it up. A rock. A fairly large rock. "I guess it wasn't a baseball," I said.

"Most likely still kids who did it," Miguel suggested.

"Benny," I said, resisting as he started easing me toward CHAPS. "Benny's in the car."

"Your rabbit? I'll come back for him."

I shook my head, and moaned as pain lanced behind my left eye, but I wasn't about to take another step.

"I'll get you to the entry, then come back for him."

That seemed like a good plan and I let him guide

me onward. I leaned against the doorjamb until he returned with Benny's carrier and opened the heavy door.

The noise of the electric sanding machines was horrendous. I put both hands to my head, forgetting the rock was still in my hand. It made contact with my forehead and I cussed and leaned against the wall, groaning. "I don't think I can make it," I said when I could speak.

I didn't know if Miguel heard me or not. When I managed to open my eyes, he had disappeared. Then I saw him in the foggy distance, setting Ben's carrier down at the foot of the stairs. A heartbeat and he disappeared again. He came back eons later with Zack.

Zack asked no questions, so I guessed Miguel had explained the problem. I realized at the same moment that if I could figure that out, my brain must be functioning again.

Next thing I knew I was in Zack's arms being carried up the stairs to my loft.

"Hey," Miguel exclaimed. "We were going to carry her up between us."

"I can handle it," Zack said.

"Frankly, Scarlett, I don't give a damn," I muttered, and I thought Zack laughed, but wasn't sure.

"Well, I do," he said, and kissed me gently on the cheek, on the undamaged side of my head.

I could still hear the sanding machines in my loft, but the sound was at least muffled and I could feel myself beginning to unjangle. Zack laid me down on my bed, made up an ice pack from the cubes in my freezer and a dishtowel, and told me to hold it over the lump.

I looked at him blankly. "You have a humongous lump," he said, then placed the ice pack himself and put my hand over it.

"I suppose you learned how to do that on *Prescott's Landing*," I muttered.

The ice pack felt heavy and painful, but after a minute or so, the cold penetrated and it wasn't so bad.

Zack told Miguel something that made Miguel disappear again. "He's gone to get a better ice pack from the downstairs freezer," Zack told me as he brushed my hair off my forehead in the gentlest way imaginable. Then he yanked off my boots, which caused a few weak tears to form in my eyes.

Miguel returned with a soft gel pack he'd wrapped in a cotton dishtowel and draped it over my forehead. I could have kissed him. It felt wonderful. He looked down at me in his intense way.

"I'll be okay," I assured him. "I'm starting to think straight."

"That's a change," Zack's voice said from the direction of the bathroom. From the sounds, he was getting Ben established in his cage. He came out and tore a piece of newspaper off the pile I had in my magazine rack, then took it in to give Ben to play with.

I thought of the time I'd had to have a surgical procedure early this year and Zack had taken me to Dr. Hanssen's clinic, waited for me, brought me home and taken care of me.

Now here he was taking care of me, and my rabbit, again.

I felt a wave of love for him at that moment. Love. Not lust. I groaned aloud. I did not need to be feeling love for Zack Hunter.

"What did you come to see me about?" I asked Miguel.

His stern face appeared above me again. "It can wait," he said. "I'll come see you tomorrow, maybe."

And that's about all I remembered for a while except for Zack telling me he wanted to call my doctor and what was his name again. I told him not to bother, the only doctor I had here was Dr. Hanssen, and he was a gynecologist.

I dozed. Somewhere in there Zack said he had *his* doctor on the line and he wanted to know if I'd lost consciousness when I was hit.

I thought back. Laboriously. "No," I decided. "But I did see flashes of light, like the kind you get with a migraine. Um—scintillating scotoma."

"Whoa!" Zack exclaimed. "That kind of vocabulary, your brain is awake and workin'." He passed the message on, then told me the doctor had said the temples were the weakest part of the skull and I was lucky not to have a concussion. If I got nauseated or blacked out, had a change in personality or poor vision, I was to call him. I'd probably have a headache for a while, which was to be expected, but if it increased steadily, that was another red flag. As long as I hadn't passed out and there wasn't any bleeding, however, I was probably going to be okay and I could go ahead and sleep.

"Probably okay?" I asked, but I didn't hear any answer.

* * *

When I came back to my surroundings later in the afternoon, I had the mother of all headaches. Zack was still there. Zack had called Savanna and she'd brought over some of her killer chicken soup that was guaranteed to cure all ills.

I inhaled a bowlful and took a couple of Tylenol, which the doc had suggested and Zack had picked up at the drugstore. After a half hour or so, I began to feel as if I might live.

The floors were done, Zack said when I remembered them. I immediately felt guilty for not being there to help supervise. I needn't have worried. Three things at CHAPS Zack was fussy about. The temperature of the wine, the quality of the beer, and the state of the dance floors. He reminded me that we'd closed CHAPS for this evening so we could be sure the protective finish on the floors would be thoroughly dry before it was danced on. I felt relieved. I didn't have to do anything. I sure didn't feel up to doing anything.

After changing into a chaste nightgown in my bathroom, I climbed back into bed and told Zack what little I had found out from Brian. "He wasn't too happy to have me questioning him," I admitted.

"Should have taken me along," Zack said. As if Brian would have opened up to him!

Eventually, I remembered the part about Roxy's family and the potty factory. Zack immediately went into the bathroom to look at my toilet. "It's a Spangler," he said when he came out. "I didn't like that dude," he added.

"Roxy's brother, you mean? I know, I didn't, either—"

"Not him. I sure didn't take to Hank, but I was talkin' about the other dude, Brian whoever."

"The vet? What's not to like?"

He shrugged.

"Why don't men ever try to work out why they feel a certain way?" I asked. "Women are always figuring out the whys of things. Guys just say what their reaction is and leave it at that."

He shrugged again. "What difference would it make?"

"Theirs not to reason why, theirs but to do and die?" I suggested. "A guy wrote that. Alfred, Lord Tennyson. 'The Charge of the Light Brigade.' 'Into the jaws of death, into the mouth of hell rode the six hundred.' "

"Maybe you're still confused," Zack said.

I wasn't confused at all. Getting hit by a rock had apparently stimulated a part of my brain that hadn't produced anything in years. Blunt-object acupressure. My father had loved "The Charge of The Light Brigade," and had often read it aloud to me when I was a child. He'd loved it for its cadence, by the way, not for the stupidity of the officers who ordered the charge.

"Brian's okay," I said, just to be ornery. "I'm thinking of dating him."

Zack sat down on the edge of my bed and gave me the benefit of his crooked smile and slanted eyebrows. "He's not romantic enough for you, Charlie. Name me one movie hero was ever named Brian."

"I'm not looking for a movie hero," I said with as much firmness as I could manage. "I'm not looking for anyone, but if anyone did come along, he'd need to be a nice guy who would respect my mind and think of me as something more than a warm body."

"A warm and sexy body," Zack said. "Leanin' toward skinny, but still sexy. Somethin' to do with the way you move. Especially when you dance."

I ignored him, and closed my eyes. "I'm going to sleep now," I said. "Thank you for taking care of me, but I'll be just fine on my own now."

"Sure, Charlie," he said. Amusement was clear in his voice.

"Lock up on your way out," I said.

"Sure will," he said.

I fell asleep. Literally. One minute I was conscious; the next I'd stepped into a black hole. Wherever I landed was warm and dark and very comfortable.

When I woke up again it was morning. My headache had receded to a dull pain in the area of the lump. Zack was asleep on my sofa, his legs hanging over the arm.

I went into the bathroom and checked on Benny. He was working on his salt lick—all bright-eyed and bushy-tailed. He had plenty of food and water and clean litter.

I looked in the mirror.

"Aaaaargh," I said, loud enough to make Ben scuttle around in his cage.

I had a huge swelling on the left side of my forehead. Alarming streaks of black, purple, and green swirled through each other, like a marble cake. There was enough color leaking out around my left eye to suggest I was going to have a black eye before too long. My head began throbbing to the beating of my heart. "I see any kids anywhere near that park, I'm going to kill them," I told Ben as I fished a couple more Tylenol out of the bottle Zack had brought in.

Ben rolled his eyes sideways. Rabbits do that.

After putting in a new roll of toilet paper, I gave him the cardboard center from the used roll and he picked it up in his sharp teeth and started beating on the cage wire with it. It would keep him happy for a while; then he'd shred it.

When I came out of the bathroom, Zack was standing up, stretching. He had a great-looking body and he was obviously in good shape. I'm not terribly heavy. In fact I'm distinctly fat free—you might even say bony—but I'm five ten, and he'd picked me up as easy as could be and toted me upstairs.

"What?" he asked with a lazy smile.

The best defense is offense. "I thought I told you I'd be okay on my own," I said.

"That's quite a shiner you've got comin', Charlie," he said, cupping my face in his hands and leaning in to examine my eye closely.

I did not need this face this close to mine when I was feeling vulnerable again. He hadn't shaved yet, of course. Is there anything sexier than a dark-haired man's face with its lower half shadowed?

"Go home and get some proper rest," I said, backing off.

He grinned at me. "Seems like you're back to normal, Charlie," he said. To my surprise, he pulled on his boots and gathered up his cowboy hat and headed out.

By midmorning I was feeling, though not looking, a little better, though the thought of any strenuous activity was nauseating. I decided the most I was up to was doing some work on the Web site. Taking Ben along in his cage for company, I headed down to the office and booted up the computer.

Then checked the E-mail.

There was another letter from anon311.

I didn't make any connection with Shakespeare this time. My first instinct was to hit the delete key and zap the letter into cyberspace without reading it. But then I changed my mind. It was probably best to know what the practical joker, or whatever he was, had to say.

The message was short. Simple. Self-explanatory. It chilled me to the bone and made my throat and stomach close up so tight, I had trouble breathing or even thinking.

It said: "It could have been a bullet."

CHAPTER 10

The first anonymous E-mail had said, "Don't you think you'd better quit while you've a head?"

And the rock had hit me on the head.

I called Zack. His phone rang five times, but just as I was trying to decide if I should leave a message on his answering machine when it cut in, he answered.

I told him about the E-mail and about the previous one. And what Macintosh had said about anonymous remailers.

"Call Bristow," he said.

"I guess I should, yes. I'm just afraid he'll think I'm being paranoid."

"It doesn't matter what he thinks, Charlie. Someone's threatenin' you. Listen, hang on a second."

There was a silence. Maybe he'd changed his mind about one of his dollies, since I'd left him frustrated. Maybe he'd gone back to doing whatever he'd been doing with the dolly when I called. I couldn't hear any breathing.

"Sorry, I had to get a robe on," he said. "It's chilly in here. Air-conditionin'."

Great. Now I had an image of a naked Zack stuck in my head.

"I'll be over there as soon as I can get dressed and mobile," he said. "Don't open the door to anyone until I get there, okay?"

A fine security guard I was, sniveling to Zack whenever anything happened.

While I was waiting, I thought about what a good friend he was to me. As impatient as I could get with him from time to time—let's face it: he could be a dense dork without hardly trying—I had to admit he was always there for me in a pinch.

But this wasn't something he could make go away. Sighing, I picked up the phone and called the Bellamy Park Police Department.

Bristow wasn't in, but the brisk-voiced person I talked to promised to let him know I needed to talk to him ASAP.

Zack arrived before Bristow called back. I met him at the door carrying Ben's cage. "Something just occurred to me," I said as I let him in. "Didn't you say you'd scheduled your poker game for this afternoon?"

"No problem, Charlie," he said. "I called the guys and canceled. I also reckoned I'd come in tonight so you could be sure to have the night off. I want you to take as much time off as you need to get feelin' good again. Angel and Savanna will be here."

I was touched that he'd cancel a poker game for me and offer me some recovery time as well.

There was a sudden silence between us, and Zack's eyebrows slanted up in a questioning way. Seemed a good time to find him something to do. I handed Benny's cage to him and he carried it up to the loft for me, put it on the floor, opened up the top and started petting the rabbit.

Deciding I was hungry, I set out the toaster and a crusty loaf of stone ground wheat bread, then put together some tuna, chopped green onion, diced tomato and olives with some low-fat mayonnaise, heated up a pan of Savanna's chicken soup and brewed a pot of kona-blend coffee.

"I put a call into Bristow," I said as I plunked bread into the toaster. "I'm hoping he'll call back soon."

The words were barely out of my mouth when somebody rang the doorbell at CHAPS's entryway and the extension in my loft blasted the airwaves. It sounds a lot like a Klaxon. It made Benny jump. Me, too. "I need to find a way to tone that thing down," I muttered as I headed out and down.

Bristow was standing with his back to the door, hands in jeans pockets, surveying the parking lot. He turned with a smile when I opened the door, then did a double take.

"That's why I called you," I said. "I got hit by a rock yesterday. Outside Bellamy Park."

I didn't want to stand in CHAPS's entryway while I explained. "Have you had lunch?" I asked.

He shook his head.

"I'd have thought now you're married you'd be eating right."

"I never eat a formal lunch, Charlie—takes too much time out of the day. I'll grab a bagel when I get downtown."

He was still gazing at the lump on my head. "What did you get hit by—a meteor?"

"I'll show you," I said, and he finally came in and let me close the door.

After he worked gamely at expressing no surprise over Zack's presence and the two of them did their usual 'you Tarzan, me Tarzan' handshake, I pulled up another chair to the table, gestured him into it and put a plate, soup bowl, knife, and spoon in front of him. He dug right in. I've noticed people who swear they don't need food will always eat it if you make it easy for them.

"Did I hear you right?" he asked around a mouthful of toast and tuna. "You said you'd called me?"

"You didn't get the message?" I frowned at him. "Why are you here then?"

"I wanted to share some astounding news before you hear it on television or read it in the newspaper. But I'd prefer to hear about this rock you stopped first."

"Charlie was real woozy when she got home," Zack said. "Miguel hauled her out of her Jeep and then I carried her up here."

"This happened yesterday and you've been here ever since?' " Bristow asked with a smirk.

"Mostly," Zack said with a smirk of his own.

"Uh-huh!" Bristow darted a sly glance at me as if to check why I wasn't commenting, then, fortunately for him, changed the subject.

"So why did you call me?" he asked.

"I thought at first the rock thing was an accident,"

I said. "I figured maybe kids playing in the park. But now I don't think it was an accident after all."

He settled back with an expectant expression on his lean face.

"Here's what happened," I said. "I was driving back to CHAPS and I got stopped at the light right outside Memorial Park. It's a one-way street and I was next to the park entrance. Something bounced off the Wrangler's hood. I thought it was a baseball. I leaned around the windshield to look at the dent and then something hit me on the forehead. Not hard enough to knock me out, though I was disoriented for a while. Again, I thought it was probably kids playing baseball in the park, but when I was getting out of the Wrangler, I saw this rock on the seat."

I got up and brought the rock from the kitchen counter where I'd left it.

"Fingerprints, Charlie," Zack said in a chiding voice.

"Can't get fingerprints off a rock unless it's a polished stone, Zack," Bristow said. "You need a smooth, dry surface in order for the excretions from the pores of your fingers to leave a print."

I was afraid Sheriff Lazarro was going to argue, so I started telling Bristow about the first anonymous E-mail I'd received and what Macintosh had told me about remailers.

"Interesting," Bristow said. "You are the first person in my experience to get a threatening E-mail."

"A trendsetter, that's me."

"You said you'd decided the rock bit wasn't an accident?" Bristow queried. "What led you to that conclusion?"

I went over to my sleeping area and brought back the second E-mail, which I had printed out and brought upstairs with me.

"Hmmm," Bristow said after he'd read it carefully. "Too bad it's not like the old days—crooked letter 'M' to give the identity of the typewriter away."

He sighed. "I'd have to agree with you, Charlie. Someone's giving you a warning." He gave me a hard look. "Maybe I should give you a warning, too. Whose feathers have you been ruffling?"

"We talked to Roxy," I said.

"And Gloria Blatt," Zack added.

"Herb's wife," I explained to Bristow's cocked eyebrow. "Herb's Budget Storage."

"Dill Eisenhardt, the dude who found Vic's body," Zack contributed.

"He wouldn't talk to us," I said.

Bristow looked at Zack. "You said Miguel Cervantes was here before Charlie came home?"

"He came lookin' for Charlie a few minutes before she drove in. He said he saw her come into the parkin' lot and waited by the door, then saw she wasn't gettin' out of the Jeep. Went over to investigate."

"You weren't with him while he waited?"

Zack shook his head.

"So we only have his word that he was hanging around here? I'm not enamored of taking one person's word for anything. I want witnesses for everything." He mulled for a couple of minutes. "How *many* minutes between Miguel asking about Charlie and Charlie arriving?"

It was Zack's turn to frown. "I don't know. I had

the floor-sandin' crew here. Miguel showed up. I told him Charlie was expected anytime. She was supposed to meet me in the main corral at one o'clock, but she hadn't shown up. I told him that and he took off. Next thing I knew, he was back, sayin' Charlie'd had an accident. Could have been ten minutes, could have been half an hour."

Bristow looked at me questioningly. "Where were you?"

"I went to see Brian Andersen. The vet. I took Benny in for . . ." I really don't like lying to the police unless it's absolutely necessary. "I had a couple of questions I wanted to ask him," I amended.

"You never did say how come I didn't get an invite," Zack complained.

"I was hoping Brian would ask me for a date."

Zack narrowed his eyes. "Yeah, you mentioned you were thinkin' of datin' him. Did he ask you out?"

I shook my head. "I've been wondering if he might be gay."

Bristow raised his eyebrows. "A guy doesn't ask you out, you decide he's gay?" He set down his soup spoon and pushed the empty bowl out of the way. "Maybe we should leave Charlie's love life out of the discussion until I get caught up here?" he suggested.

"Let's do that," I agreed, then plunged in before Zack could get me in any deeper. "I talked to Brian about Roxy and Vic," I confessed.

Bristow gave me a jaundiced look.

"Well, here's a case that's been widely reported in the media and I know some of the relatives of the deceased. There's some law I can't discuss the case with a friend?"

Bristow laughed shortly. "Remind me. Dr. Brian Andersen who might possibly be gay fits in where?"

"He takes care of Roxy's cat. He was a friend of Vic's."

I wasn't sure if I wanted to tell him what I'd learned from Brian or not.

Zack gave me some thinking time. "So what can you do to protect Charlie?" he asked.

Bristow shook his head. "Not a whole lot, I'm afraid. If whoever threw that rock had thrown it from a vehicle and Charlie had noted the license plate of that vehicle, I might have been able to do her some good, but . . ."

"I think it came from inside the entrance to the park," I said. "I never did see who threw it."

"What about that threatenin' letter?" Zack asked. "Isn't it against the law to threaten someone?"

Bristow nodded, then sighed. "Unfortunately, as far I've ever heard, there's no mechanism set up to deal with someone making a threat by E-mail—the law has not caught up with technology. There's also a problem in that E-mail can be easily altered."

He thought for a minute before going on. "While the rock-throwing could be deemed a battery or an ADW—an assault with a deadly weapon—without any other clues we have nowhere to go. If anything further happens . . ."

"There was one other thing," I said. "But I'm not sure it was a real thing. Still, it sort of scared me at the time."

I explained about the figure I'd seen moving between the bank and CHAPS, and how the guy had ended up going into the convenience store at the intersection. "I decided probably it was someone picking up some milk or cigarettes," I added.

"And probably it was," Bristow agreed. "All the same, it's another element to consider. When was this?"

"Tuesday, June seventeenth, late, after CHAPS closed."

"Which was after you'd talked with whom?"

"Roxy, Gloria, a little bit to Brian at the wake. A little bit to Macintosh after the first E-mail. He's trying to track the sender down."

Bristow nodded slowly.

"If this was *Prescott's Landin'*, we'd have a couple deputies assigned to keepin' a watch over Charlie," Zack said.

"*Prescott's Landing* has all that advertising revenue," Bristow said dryly. "We have to depend on taxpayers." He glanced sideways at me, the corner of his mouth quirking mischievously. "Maybe Zack should move in here with you, Charlie. Just until we get this whole business resolved."

"Over my dead body," I said, then shuddered a little. The lump on my forehead throbbed in sympathy.

"What I suggest," Bristow said, looking earnest, "is that you should keep a log of any future incidents. Any future threats you receive. Anytime you see anyone hanging around CHAPS or acting in a suspicious manner. Also, should any of these situations repeat, call the station and let me know. If I'm not there and it's urgent, call my private beeper, the one I keep in case Savanna or Jacqueline needs me."

He gave me the number and I wrote it down on a handy paper napkin. "Furthermore," he added, pushing back his chair, "I would urge you to behave cautiously. Which means you should not go riding around in that hot wheels toy of yours without its hard top on."

"You said you had news," I reminded him as he stood up. I wasn't about to make any promises.

"I'm getting to it," he said. "I just have to use your conveniences first."

We could hear him talking to Ben in the bathroom. He always addressed him with dignity, calling him "Ben, my man."

After a minute, Zack stood up and said he had to get something out of his pickup.

When Bristow came out, he was carrying Ben. He sat down with him in the rocker and began stroking him with a gentle finger. Benny closed his eyes and vibrated.

Zack came back in carrying his cell phone. "You afraid you might miss a call from one of your dollies?" I asked.

"I told you, Charlie, the brigade has been disbanded," he said with a meaningful grin. "I brought the phone up for you. I want you usin' it for now until I can get you one for yourself. Take it with you everywhere you go, just in case there's another incident and you need to call for help when you're away from here. Anyone calls for me, tell them to call me at home."

He was looking unusually solemn. He cared about me and my welfare. He really did. It was a good thing

Bristow was there or I might have given him a grateful hug and God knows what that might have led to.

"Thank you," I said.

The famous green eyes smiled warmly into mine.

Bristow cleared his throat. "My news," he said, "is this." He waited until he had our complete attention, then came out with his bombshell. "Detective Sergeant Reggie Timpkin is out of action and in the hospital. He was shot yesterday."

I stared at him, my own problem suddenly dwarfed. "Is he okay?" I managed.

"He's alive. And complaining mightily last I heard. Driving the hospital staff out of their gourds. His wound may require surgery."

"Where did he get shot?"

"Right here in Bellamy Park." He relented before I had a chance to get indignant. "In the posterior."

"What happened?" Zack asked.

"While off duty, he came across an individual who'd parked illegally on San Pablo Avenue downtown. Told him he'd have to move his pickup. Individual didn't take kindly to the suggestion. Swears Reggie never said he was a police officer. Insists Reggie came on all feisty. There was an altercation. Outcome being that the individual reached into the cab of his truck and pulled out a hunting rifle."

He paused, shaking his head. "According to the individual, Reggie grabbed the gun, there was a struggle and the gun went off. According to Reggie, he was unarmed, so he prudently took off looking for cover and the individual shot him in the rear before he could reach any. I am inclined to believe Reggie. Difficult for a bullet to go through Reggie from back to front if they were struggling over the rifle. Luckily for Reggie, the bullet went clean through without hitting any major organ, but Reggie's out of service for quite a while."

"That's awful," I exclaimed, though I could certainly see how someone could get instantly mad at Reggie; he was easy to get mad at. "I bet he did identify himself all the same," I said. "He's meticulous about proper procedure. Is he going to be okay?"

"May have to have a replacement hip. Docs aren't sure yet."

Zack and I were both silent for a while, mulling over this startling news. Then Bristow handed Ben over to Zack, pulled out his notebook and looked at me expectantly.

"What?" I asked.

"Timpkin will consult on this case, but he is basically *hors de combat*," he said.

"So you said." Light dawned. "You're in charge of the case now?"

"As of two hours ago. Seems likely to me you were thinking you'd gotten away with passing on very little information, but you were wrong. So how about you rake around in that splendidly busy mind of yours, Ms. Plato, and tell me everything that is in there to do with this case, leaving no stone or memory chip unturned?"

He was all cop suddenly. Nothing friendly in his gaze or voice. I recognize a moment of truth when it looks me in the eye.

CHAPTER 11

I started with the wake. I noticed that Bristow was especially alert when Zack and I talked about Hank Spangler. His pen stopped moving across the lines of his notebook and he didn't ask another question for several minutes, just sat there with his chin on his fist looking like Rodin's Thinker. Then he wagged the pen at me so I'd carry on.

"Have you met Hank Spangler?" I asked.

"I have indeed." His expression told me that getting acquainted with Hank Spangler had been no more of a pleasure for him than it had been for me.

"Mr. Sleaze," I said.

"His daddy makes potties," Zack said.

Bristow nodded. "So I understand."

"According to Brian Andersen, Hank's daddy cut off his allowance," I said. "Roxy told him Hank wasn't overly fond of work, but addicted to spending money. I guess the family was pretty wealthy."

Bristow's eyebrows asked for more.

I told him about Hank coming to California and living with Vic and Roxy for the last year and about him working for Sal Migliatore, which he seemed to know. I added that the two men hadn't hit it off, which he hadn't known.

"Brian didn't know if Roxy got cut off, too," I said.

"I had a talk with Hank Spangler," Bristow said.

"At the station?" I asked.

A glimmer of amusement showed in his amber eyes. "At the station."

"He's a suspect?"

He just looked at me.

"What did he say?"

Zack laughed.

After a second, so did Bristow. "You are incorrigibly inquisitive, Ms. Plato."

"I'll take that as a compliment," I said, and met his gaze, eye to eye.

He shook his elegant bald head in a helpless way that indicated surrender. I like that in a man. "Okay. Privileged information coming up," he said. "A couple days before Angel and Miguel's mother, Malena Cervantes, was killed, she telephoned Roxy's father, Warren Spangler."

"The potty king," Zack said.

Evidently the idea of someone actually making toilets tickled our man in black. Had he thought they grew on trees?

"She told him she'd found out her husband was having an affair with his daughter?" I suggested.

"Hank told you that?"

I shook my head. "I'm guessing. Excuse me. Deducing."

"Correctly. It seems Warren Spangler told Malena he would put a stop to the affair. Hank was in Warren's office being dressed down at the time. Overheard the whole arrangement."

"Well, Warren would hardly put a stop to it by killing the wife," I said. "Malena's murder had the effect of sending Vic and Roxy off together."

"It would seem rather a self-defeating action on Warren's part, yes."

Zack was ruminating next to me. I could almost hear the wheels turning in his brain. I took Benny from him and put him down on the floor for some exercise, but he squatted on his haunches and started washing his face with his front paws instead. His ears were on alert status. Evidently he was interested in the conversation. Sometimes I thought he could understand more than we gave him credit for.

"So, did Hank think Vicenzo/Vic killed Malena?" Zack asked.

"He said he's always believed he did. He also said Vicenzo called Warren from California to tell him he'd just heard Malena had been killed and to swear that he was innocent. Roxy also swore to her father that Vicenzo was innocent. According to Hank, Warren believed them and gave them money to tide them over until Vicenzo found work. There was also a suggestion that bribes had been paid to the then sheriff."

"Sheriff Grigsby," I said, which got me another look. "Angel thought Long John Silver Sterling, the guy who wanted to get Vicenzo into baseball, might have done the bribing."

"So he said. Maybe Long John bribed somebody, too. He's dead so we can't ask him. Warren *isn't* dead, and I'm trying to get the current sheriff to look into his part in this affair. The sheriff seems somewhat reluctant. According to him, Warren is an outstanding citizen, the murder was a long time ago, clues are now covered in mud, and so on and so forth."

He glanced from me to Zack. "Go on with your story." This time he let us get through all of it without interruption.

"Brian said he didn't know if Roxy got cut off without a penny, too," I offered again when he didn't comment.

"As far as I could determine, Roxy was her father's most precious possession, so disinheritance seems unlikely."

"Her father's possession?" I echoed.

"I'm quoting Hank."

"Ick," I said.

Bristow stood up, but didn't start toward the door right away. Instead, he passed a hand over his smooth head and looked troubled. "A couple of Sheriff Grigsby's deputies had one other suspect in mind," he said finally.

"Miguel," Zack said.

"Why would you think that?" I demanded.

"One of the *Prescott's Landin'* episodes was like that. Mother killed, father suspected, but all the time it was the elder son who did it. Seems his mom wouldn't let him stay out past nine o'clock and he got more and more resentful until he just exploded and killed her."

I was about to make some comment about weak motivation, but Bristow nodded solemnly. "People have been killed for less," he said.

"You suspect Miguel yourself?" I asked.

He gave me his closed-off, don't-even-try-to-read-my-mind expression. "My thinking processes are still engaged, Charlie. I'm not naming suspects in either murder at this stage. I'm not ruling out the possibility of Miguel being involved, however. Mother, father, maybe both. I'm always inclined to go along with Occam's Razor, a scientific rule of investigation given to us by English philosopher William of Occam, which states that of all the theories that fit the known facts, the preferable one is the simplest."

"Miguel was fifteen years old when his mother was murdered," I protested.

"Fifteen-year-olds have been known to handle a gun," Bristow pointed out.

"Charlie's sweet on Miguel," Zack said. "She doesn't want to believe he's guilty of anythin'."

"I am not sweet on *anyone.*"

There was enough emphasis in my voice that Ben quit bathing and scuttled under the sofa. He had this ongoing project under there—pulling out all the stuffing with his front teeth. I cleaned out a pile of it every week. Someday that sofa was going to discover it had been eviscerated and would collapse like a balloon that had run out of air.

I yanked Benny out, nuzzled him for a while, then took him into the bathroom and put him into his cage.

Bristow was at the door when I came out. He grinned at me. "I see why someone would want to frighten you off, Charlie. You're a pretty good investigator. If I was a sheriff I'd deputize you."

He frowned. "However—I have not deputized you, or *you*," he added to Zack. "I think it would be a wise

idea for you to cease and desist from involving yourselves in this investigation, as of this moment. Is that
clear?"

We agreed that it was. We didn't agree to obey.
Bristow didn't seem to notice that, which indicated to
me that he wasn't all that serious about warning us
off.

"Be sure to pass on any other information you happen to come across," he said as he opened the door.

"You just told me to stay out of it," I reminded him.

"So I did," he said. Just before closing the door
behind him, he popped his head around it, flashed a
smile, and said, "Take care of that lump, Charlie. Looks
like you're getting a black eye, too. People used to use
raw steak for that. You not being a red meat fancier,
I guess you wouldn't want to do that."

"So, I guess the Hunter/Plato detectin' duo is out
of business," Zack said after the sound of Bristow's
footsteps had faded down the staircase.

"No way," I said briskly. "Bristow wouldn't have
said what he did about passing on information if he
hadn't expected us to come up with some. That warning
to back off was just a formality."

Zack looked doubtful, so I kept talking. "We stop
now, whoever sent that anonymous E-mail is going to
think he scared me."

"That might not be such a bad thing," he said.

"It would be very bad for my pride," I said. "On
the other hand, if I keep on investigating, I might be
able to get whoever sent that E-mail stopped. anon311
has to be connected with the crime. May even be the

murderer. I can't just sit by and let him get away with murder."

"The police—"

"The police do a terrific job. Bristow will do a terrific job. But we can talk to people without jeopardizing the outcome of the case. We don't have to worry about the fruit of the poison tree. We're just a pair of nosy people trying to ferret out the truth."

"You look great when you get all wound up, Charlie," he said. "Your eyes get really blue. Never knew anyone had blue eyes as vivid as yours. Of course, the lump and the black eye tend to spoil the effect."

"Cut it out," I said. "This is important. We have to help Angel and Miguel."

"What if Miguel did it?"

That gave me pause. "Then we'll find that out and he'll go to prison."

I felt exhausted suddenly, and my head had started throbbing again. "I don't think I'm up to doing anything today," I said. "And I'm definitely taking you up on your offer of the night off, although I feel guilty about deserting you all on a Saturday. But we could get back on the job tomorrow."

"Doin' what?" he said.

He was coming up with a lot of good questions lately. I sat down on the sofa and thought about it for a while and a name popped up I hadn't even considered before. "Otis Reeder."

Zack looked blank.

"He was the guy who identified the body of Vic Smith/Vicenzo Cervantes. He worked with Vic. Maybe *he* knows something."

It took me a while to find a phone listing for Otis Reeder. Turned out he lived in Half-Moon Bay, on the western edge of the San Francisco peninsula. Coast-side, the locals call it. He'd be at home the next day building a new garage, he said. His wife had bought a secondhand Pontiac Grand Prix and it needed a roof over its head. Her last car had sat out in the driveway and developed a bad case of rust. One of the penalties of living near the ocean.

He was promisingly talkative, I thought.

His address was in the same area as the Arts and Crafts Cooperative, which was close enough to the ocean you could hear the surf while you wandered around the gardens.

I'd stopped in to the Arts and Crafts co-op several times after driving through the hills to Half Moon Bay. They had a nice little restaurant with outside seating in the rose garden and they served their meals on Blue Willow china.

In my former life as wife to Rob Whittaker, plastic surgeon and swordsman extraordinaire, I had collected Blue Willow. But I'd left it all behind in Seattle when I left Rob. One of the decisions I'd made at that time, besides the one about remaining celibate the rest of my life, was that I was never going to get attached to possessions again. Possessions possess you—not the other way around. I'd stuck to my marriage longer than I should because I loved our beautiful Tudor house on the shores of Puget Sound, and everything in it. When I finally realized I was miserable and those "things" weren't going to restore me to anything even remotely connected to happiness, I headed south with only my clothes and my Jeep Wrangler.

Coming across Blue Willow china still gave me a kick, though. It reminded me of my parents. They'd both loved blue and white—my dad because they were the Greek national colors—and had used that combination to decorate their Greek restaurant in Sacramento.

I read some more in my woman-in-jeopardy novel after Zack left. I was hoping the main character might get a threatening letter and come up with some creative way of dealing with it, but all she had was some guy stalking her and odd sounds that turned out to be her cat. I put the book down and went to sleep, woke up hearing music coming from CHAPS, and was comforted.

Otis Reeder was a commercial flower grower. We found the man himself between the house and a couple of huge greenhouses so full of color they looked like impressionist paintings. Otis was putting up drywall inside the new garage. "We're going to heat it," he said, "so it made sense to insulate it."

Otis was African-American, a large man in all ways—maybe six feet, five inches tall and three hundred pounds, all of it fairly evenly spread around. He had a very cheery smile and friendly-looking dark eyes. He wore one of those caps that adjust at the back—a white one that said "Reeder Nursery" on it. He'd bought the nursery when he retired from construction, he told us.

"What's the other fella look like?" he asked me when the preliminaries were over. He hadn't recognized Zack at all.

I'd used makeup judiciously, put on my sunglasses and tilted my cowboy hat forward. I had thought the lump and the black eye were impossible to see. Evidently I'd thought wrong.

"I walked into a door," I said.

He looked at Zack suspiciously. "I'm tempted sometimes," Zack said, "but so far I've managed not to do it."

Otis grinned. "Didn't mean to sound unsympathetic. It looks painful. Doors make mean enemies."

"It feels painful. When did you retire?" I asked to get us on topic.

"When Sal Migliatore died," he said. "Sal was a pretty good boss. I didn't want to go to work for anyone else. Figured I'd get into something different. My wife worked for years for a florist in Los Altos, learned to do all kinds of exotic arrangements. She already knew all the ins and outs of bonsai. She got to know a lot of people. She's really the boss. She tells me what to do and I do it. Right away."

I smiled at him, then wished I hadn't. Smiling squinches up the area around the eyes. "Sounds like the natural order of things to me," I said, then I took a deep breath. "Mr. Reeder—"

"Otis," he said.

"Okay, Otis, it is. I'm a friend of Angel Cervantes."

He frowned, but he turned out to be puzzled rather than annoyed. His brow cleared almost immediately. "Never knew Vic's real name until the papers came out with it. But he mentioned Angel and another boy often. Miguel. Vic told me he'd lost them in a custody fight."

Vic had often stretched the truth. Under the circumstances you could hardly expect him not to.

"He really missed those boys," Otis added.

"I understand you worked with Vic."

He nodded, then turned aside to take hold of a sheet of drywall and hoist it onto the sturdy plastic sawhorses that stood in the middle of the garage. Zack made a slight move forward as though to help him, but he swung the wallboard into place as easily as if it was made of cardboard.

"Kind of a temperamental fella," he said, picking up a pencil and eyeing a sheet of paper that had notes scribbled on it.

"In what way?" Zack asked.

Sheriff Lazarro reporting in.

"Thought of himself as an artist. Did nice work, but my idea of an artist is someone paints a picture, makes a sculpture, that kind of thing. Someone who can make an arrangement of flowers that makes you wish you *could* paint. My wife Dodie makes art out of flowers every day. Nowadays you've got people who make fancy sand castles and animals and stuff out of wet sand—they call themselves artists! Then there's people who make pictures out of dryer lint, or tie a bunch of different kinds of wires together and call it art. As for Vic—I don't count someone who makes kitchen cabinets an artist, no matter how good-looking they are."

I didn't agree with him, having seen some nifty uses of wire and dryer lint, as well as the cabinets in Macintosh's kitchen, but I've learned you don't argue with someone you're trying to get information out of. It tends to make them shut down.

"I liked Vic all the same," Otis went on. "He was a fun fella. Hardworking, too. I admire anyone works hard. Whether it's digging ditches or running the country. He had two jobs, Vic—making cabinets and doing the wood finishing in Sal's houses, and bartending at Grumpy's—that's a bar in Dennison."

He shot a glance at me under wiry black eyebrows. "Vic was a good-looking fella. Liked the ladies more than he should, though. He was standing here right now in my place talking to a fine-looking lady like you, he'd have a date by now. Never could figure out why his wife put up with his behavior. My wife now, she'd have my guts for fiddle strings."

"We understand Vic and Sal Migliatore weren't too friendly toward each other," Zack said.

"You understand right." He shook his head, then bent over the sheet of drywall with a retractable tape and began measuring for cutouts. He'd reached the window in the wall he was working on.

"Sure surprised me that Sal would kill Vic, though. Sal had a temper, but I never would have thought he was the murderous type. And then to put the body in a storage locker! What a dumb thing to do. 'Course he *was* mortal sick!"

It wasn't up to me to disabuse him of the notion that Sal was the murderer. He'd find out whenever the truth came out.

"Why did Vic keep working for Sal if he didn't like him?" I asked.

He scored the lines he'd drawn with a box knife, then

reached for a long skinny saw with a yellow handle. "I don't know that he didn't like Sal," he said when he was through cutting. "He didn't seem to mind him too much. Sal was the one had a grudge of some kind against Vic, though who knows what it was."

He straightened and looked at me. "How come the son hired you, you don't mind my asking? I don't mean, why you—I mean, why does he want all this looked into? Cut and dried, I would have thought."

"Well, there are some other circumstances," I said vaguely. He seemed satisfied.

He lifted the drywall and put it in place against the wall. It fitted around the window and the electric outlet perfectly. "I didn't socialize with Vic," he said. "All I know of him was working with him. My wife wouldn't have stood for me going to Grumpy's Tavern."

Mrs. Reeder certainly seemed to have him under her thumb. Not that I'm criticizing. That situation was reversed for so long it may take men a few centuries to take over the world again.

"When did you last see Vic Smith?" Zack asked.

Another good question. Zack was getting pretty good at this stuff, considering he didn't have a script. Though come to think of it, he might be *quoting* from a script. It was still a good question.

"Funny you should ask that," Otis said, then paused while he drove screws into the drywall with an electric screwdriver. He was very fast and the screws looked equidistant.

"Last time I saw Vic, he was getting into a car with that little fella," he said.

"What little fella?" Zack and I asked in unison.

Otis put down his screwdriver and grinned good-naturedly. "Guess I came up with something interesting, huh?"

"Talk!" I exclaimed.

He nodded, took off his cap and scratched his head. He had a good head of hair, thick and gray and tightly curled. Putting the cap back on, he said, "I've debated telling someone about this, wasn't sure if it was significant or not, but now that you've asked—" He looked at Zack. "Nobody asked me that question before. I didn't want to tell the little fella I'd seen him. He struck me as having a mean streak."

"Do we have two little fellas here, or what?" I asked.

He shook his head. "Only one. Same little fella came on TV the day Vic's body was found. Same little fella asked me to identify the remains. Reason I didn't want to tell him I'd seen him that day—there was something about that time struck me as wrong somehow. Made me nervous. Anyway, that was the same little fella got shot downtown Bellamy Park yesterday morning. Saw it in the newspaper this morning."

"Let's be clear on this. You're talking about Detective Sergeant Timpkin?"

"As ever was."

I exchanged a glance with Zack. I guess we were both stunned. It was a couple of minutes before I could even think of anything to say.

"You're saying you saw Vic Smith getting into a car driven by Sergeant Timpkin? On the day he disappeared."

"That's about the size of it."

"Willingly?"

"Seemed like."

"Did it look as if he was bein' arrested?" Zack asked.

Otis shrugged. "He wasn't handcuffed, nothing like that."

My brain was in turmoil, trying to figure out exactly what this might mean. At the same time, my stomach was tightening, because I knew I had to tell Bristow about this, and he was going to know Zack and I had carried on asking questions after being told not to.

"Where was this?" I asked.

"One of Sal's houses. A spec house. It was going to be opened up for public viewing in the next day or two. Out in Mountain View. Vic was putting fasteners on the kitchen cabinets that day. I was up on one of the roofs, finishing up the trim on the outside. Difficult stuff, scalloped. Car drove up, little fella got out and rang the doorbell. Had no idea who he was at that time. Vic came to the door and they talked; then Vic got into the little fella's car."

"You hear what they said?" I asked.

"Nope. Too far away. Wouldn't have listened in anyway. Not the nosy type."

He was smiling. I wasn't sure that wasn't a dig at me.

"And you never saw Vic again?" Zack asked.

"That's right. I left soon after. Vic must have come back after a while, because his pickup was gone when I got there the next day. Sal told me a couple days later Vic had done a runner with some little teenage gal named Bambi of all things. I never did see Vic again until that same little fella asked me to go with him to identify Vic. Because I'd worked with him. So I did."

He shuddered a little, then turned away to separate another sheet of drywall from the stack and hoist it onto the sawhorses. He picked up his pencil. "Don't ever want to see anything like that again. Turned my stomach for a week that did. Even had nightmares. Told Dodie she's to have me cremated when I go. Had it put in my living will. Don't want to think of looking like that."

He made his measurements and drew his lines and straightened up again. "Can't truthfully say I identified Vic," he said. "I identified his watch and his medal. He wore them always. Told me once they were his most prized possessions. I also told the little fella about Vic's bum shoulder and he made a note of that."

"The medal and the watch," Zack said. "Were they easy to see? Would the detective have seen them when Vic went with him in the car?"

Otis crinkled his forehead. "Well, I should think . . . No, I don't really know. It was a pretty chilly day. I was wearing a windbreaker. The house didn't have any heaters going yet, so Vic was wearing jeans and a sweatshirt, long sleeves, crew neck. So the detective wouldn't necessarily have seen them. Might have seen the chain to the medal."

"Do you know what day it was?" I asked.

He shook his head. "Real chilly day is all I recall. We finished the house up in November sometime. So it was before that."

I racked my brain for any more questions that might

be in there and came up with only one. "Did you ever meet Bambi?"

"Not so I remember. Young women came by wherever Vic was working, so I might have seen her, but never did get introduced that I recall."

"You ever hear what Bambi's full name was?" Zack asked.

I gazed at him with admiration and he looked smug, but after Otis thought hard for a while, he said, "No, don't believe I did."

"Would you and your friends like some coffee, honey?" a female voice asked.

We all turned.

"My wife, Dodie," Otis said, love evident in his voice.

She was petite and slender. Maybe five feet tall. Size four at the most. Gray curly hair like her husband's. Probably close to the same age. Very attractive in leggings and a pink smock. *She tells me what to do and I do it,* Otis had said. Well, she did have a determined-looking chin.

"You're Zack Hunter," she said to Zack. "I heard you lived on the peninsula. Girlfriend of mine saw you in Lenny's Market over in Bellamy Park one day. Said you were buying Lavosh in the bakery—some kind of cracker bread. Almost had a heart attack, she said. Can I get your autograph for her—she would just die!"

"Happy to oblige, ma'am," Zack said.

Otis looked at me inquiringly. "Zack plays Sheriff Lazarro on *Prescott's Landing*," I told him. "TV," I added when he still looked blank.

"Never watch TV," he said. "Get all the news I can stand in the newspaper. Dodie now, she's addicted."

Dodie had dashed out and was now returning with a notepad and ballpoint in hand. "Could you make that a couple?" she asked eagerly.

Otis rolled his eyes.

"Thank you for your time," I told him. "I'm going to have to report our conversation. Detective Sergeant Bristow's in charge now. You'll probably be hearing from him. He's a nice guy—you'll like him."

"Glad to hear it."

"Thank you for the offer of coffee," I said to Dodie. She smiled and nodded, but her attention was mostly on Zack. Which you'll remember I was used to.

CHAPTER 12

It was Tuesday evening before I could get hold of Bristow. I guessed now that he had double duty he was staying pretty busy. Savanna confirmed that when she arrived at CHAPS. "I saw more of that man when I was single," she grumbled. "This town has had more murders since our wedding than in its entire history."

That was something of an exaggeration, but I wasn't going to argue with Savanna when she was already in a negative mood. Bristow was at the station now, she thought, so I went into the office and called in.

I'd thought he would explode when I told him Zack and I had talked to Otis Reeder, but he took the news fairly well. "I might have known you'd take my warning as a challenge," he said mildly. "How's the lump?"

"Gone down some, but it still hurts," I said, hoping to arouse enough sympathy, he'd forget to chew me out.

His voice sounded severely clipped after I told him what Otis had said about Reggie picking Vic up. "I'll talk to Detective Sergeant Timpkin," he said.

"What's the latest word on his health?" I asked. I hadn't had a chance to look at a newspaper all day.

"He's doing as well as can be expected," he said flatly. "I understand he's already cordially hated by his nurses, but they tell me he is coming along quite well and surgery may not be necessary after all."

"Well, that's good, I guess," I said. "I don't suppose having an artificial hip would have improved his personality."

"You say Otis Reeder did not remember the date when Vic went for a drive with Timpkin?" he asked.

"Just that it was before they finished the house, and they finished the house in November. He said it was a real chilly day." I hesitated. "Otis also said Vic must have come back to the house afterward because his truck was gone next time he looked."

Silence.

"I guess someone else could have come for the truck, though, huh? Sal Migliatore, maybe? Did Timpkin know Sal Migliatore?"

"Everyone knew Sal Migliatore," Bristow said heavily.

"Do you remember me telling you that Vic almost threw Reggie Timpkin out of Grumpy's because he got in a fight with a guy who accused him of cheating at pool?"

I could hear Bristow breathing into the receiver at the other end of the line. "Remind me who it was told you that?" he asked.

I had to think a minute. I needed to start taking notes. "Roxy," I said.

He didn't comment.

"That reminds me," I said. "I promised Roxy I'd

ask you how come she can't get Vic's body back. She's anxious to get him properly buried."

"Is she?" He paused, then said formally, "In pursuit of an investigation, a medical examiner may keep a body for as long as he needs to. The length of time he needs to keep it varies widely. He has the last word on that."

"I'll pass that on if I see her again," I said, then went back to the previous topic. "I guess there was bad blood between Timpkin and Vic, after Vic threw him out of Grumpy's, huh?"

Bristow snorted. "It means Vic told Roxy there was an incident with Timpkin at the bar. That's all it means. I'll talk to Ms. Roxy, too, Charlie. You don't need to take on that chore."

His voice was heavy with sarcasm, which I chose not to mention. I didn't want him getting mad at me and making me shut up shop.

"Well, I just thought you ought to know," I said.

"You thought right."

He paused and I figured he was about to hang up on me, but then he asked one more question. "This guy Reeder. Did he mention Bambi?"

"Only to say he didn't think he'd ever seen her, but apparently women hung around Vic all the time. Must have had some kind of animal magnetism, that man. Mr. Reeder said he couldn't recall ever hearing Bambi's full name."

Bristow let out a sigh that was almost a growl. He was obviously feeling frustrated by this case.

"Any idea yet who did it?" I asked.

His response was immediate. "Good-bye, Charlie."

That sounded rather final. I guessed he hadn't a clue.

CHAPS was fairly lively for a Tuesday night. At someone's request I taught the redneck stomp. It took me a while to get everyone in straight rows with space to pass each other, then organize them into double rows back to back, not to mention getting all the box half-turns worked out. I was glad when break time came and I could climb up on a stool at the main corral bar and accept a Pellegrino water from Angel.

"How's it going?" Angel asked. He looked worried. He wasn't asking about the dancing.

"I don't know. Bristow's on the job, I guess. Zack and I are considering what to do next."

I had told Angel that Bristow had warned Zack and me off the case, adding I didn't really think he meant it. I'd also caught him up on what we'd found out so far, and told him that Miguel was under suspicion.

Evidently Angel didn't want to ask any more questions at the moment. His attention had moved away from me to something over my right shoulder. I swiveled around on my stool and saw his former love, Gina Giacomini, talking to a man in full cowboy rig, including a gray Stetson that was far too high-crowned for such a slightly built guy. Gina herself was in jeans and a fringed shirt from Buttons & Bows, but she still looked punk with her multicolored spiky hair and black lipstick.

"You want me to invite Gina over for a drink?" I asked, swiveling back.

Angel's face closed down to a bronze mask.

About then, one of the waitresses came over to get an order, so I waited until she left, then said, "I never did understand why you two broke up."

"She liked that other guy," he said, referring to someone Gina had accompanied to CHAPS a couple of times shortly after New Year's.

I let my exasperation show. "She only got interested in him because you broke up with her," I reminded him. "She wanted to make you jealous. You said you had something you had to do, that you'd made a vow. So okay, now we know the vow had to do with finding your father—you didn't want romance getting in the way. But Gina doesn't know any of that. Why don't you explain it all to her and start over, Angel? You had something really nice going there."

"Not until this police investigation is over, Charlie," he said flatly.

"Why not? Friends aren't just for good times. Friends want to be with you when things aren't so good, and that's when you need friends."

He shook his head. "I'm not laying this problem on any woman," he said. "When we get it settled, when we find out who killed my father, then we'll see."

"Maybe Gina won't be available then."

"Then it wasn't meant to be."

"You're getting all mystical on me again."

He gave me the now-you-see-it-now-you-don't smile that every once in a while flashed on and lit up his whole face. He was just as suddenly solemn. "That is my family legacy," he said. "When I was just a little kid, my mother taught me about fate and how everything happens according to a plan."

I don't agree with that theory myself—I think we all have total free will to lead or mess up our lives any way we want to. But it was too much of a novelty to hear Angel talking about feelings for me to argue with him.

Another waitress showed up, and I waited again. Then Savanna came over with an order. I figured I could pursue this part of the conversation in front of her. "Did your mom teach you to see auras?" I asked.

Savanna's interest perked up. "I talked to your husband," I told her.

"More than I've done all day," she said. "Did he say what time he'd be home?"

"Nope."

She sighed; then we both looked at Angel.

He shook his head. "Nobody taught me. I saw auras as long as I can remember. When I was a little kid I used to call them the pretty lights. I thought everyone could see them. One time I said something about them to my mother and she told me she could see them, too, and so had my grandmother, her mother, but most people couldn't. She told me some people think you are crazy if you talk about such things, so mostly I don't."

"Can you see my aura?" I asked.

The smile appeared again, for a second or two longer this time. "Talking to a woman about her aura is almost as dangerous as trying to guess her age," he said. "I've learned not to do it."

"Come on, Angel. I'm curious."

"Everybody knows that, Charlie."

I looked at him and he raised his hands in mock surrender. "It's a little dim today, Charlie, because you're hurting. Usually it goes between yellow and orange. Sometimes gets close to red, when you're irritated, like when you look at Zack." He grinned. "Maybe a little passion in there, too."

"What does yellow and orange mean?" I asked, ignoring the passion crack.

"You're a thinking woman, and friendly, approachable."

"What about me?" Savanna asked.

Angel looked at her and smiled. Looking at Savanna makes most people smile. "Blue—for calm, and charisma."

"Did you read Gina's aura?" I asked.

"Yes." His expression effectively closed off all further communication on that subject.

Savanna sighed again, over Angel this time.

"I suppose if we do find out who killed your father, you'll come up with another excuse to avoid getting involved with Gina," I suggested.

He managed a half-smile that barely showed under his Pancho Villa mustache. "Could be, Charlie, but I hardly think you're one to talk. Haven't seen a whole lot going on in your love life."

"Isn't that the truth," Savanna said, then hoisted her loaded tray and moved away.

"There's nobody around worth having a love life with," I said.

"Miguel likes you."

"He has a weird way of showing it."

"You like him?"

I thought about it while I drank some mineral water, then shook my head. "I think I'm a bit afraid of him."

He didn't rush to defend his brother as I'd thought he might. "He's a tough guy," he said.

"Does he see auras, too?"

"No."

"Roxy said he scared her to death when the two of you went to see her last October."

"He was okay till she said she was the woman our father and mother fought over. He always blamed *that* woman for our mother's death. His theory was always that our mother yelled at our father again about that woman and our father killed her in a fit of anger. So, it's only natural he should get mad at Roxy."

"She said he tore through the house like a madman. She thinks it's possible he killed your father."

"That's crazy. We went together looking for our father after we found out where he lived and worked. Our father was missing before Miguel came to Bellamy Park."

"You're sure of that? There's no way Miguel could have got to your father *before* joining up with you?"

Sudden anguish showed on his face. "What?" I asked.

His mouth worked. "A thought. It doesn't mean anything."

"It means something to you."

He shook his head. "It's only that the detective contacted Miguel when he discovered where our father was living. Miguel was on his way out of town for a rodeo, so it was a couple days before he could let me know."

"And you think maybe in that couple of days he

could have driven up here and killed him, then got in touch with you and pretended to be looking for him?"

"No!"

The word came out loud enough to make a few people nearby look over at us.

Angel pulled out a bottle of mineral water and took a healthy swig. The streak of red over his cheekbones faded, but the agony in his eyes didn't go away.

"How did Miguel get along with your mother?" I asked.

He drank more water, set the bottle down. "I was just a kid, remember."

"You said once that your mother thought she should have called him El Diablo. Seems to me that would indicate they didn't get along too well."

"They met head to head like a couple of rams sometimes, sure. Miguel always did have a temper. Our mother, too. Very fiery woman. He inherited the temper; I got the auras. But she loved us both. And our father. And Miguel and I loved her. She put up with a lot."

"So what did she and Miguel fight about?"

"I told you that before, too. The usual kid stuff. Miguel staying out till all hours, drinking, smoking—he quit before he was twenty, but in his teens he smoked a couple packs a day. And he always liked girls a lot. Our mother used to pace the floor waiting for him to come in, grumbling to herself in Spanish; then they'd go at it for an hour. Neighbors used to complain."

If the neighbors complained, then someone would remember that Malena and Miguel had fought. If that was the case, Bristow would possibly have been informed of it by the sheriff he'd talked to. Fifteen years old, though.

But Bristow had pointed out that fifteen-year-olds were capable of handling a gun.

"You recall me telling you both that Roxy thinks Miguel might have killed your mother? Miguel was very angry when I told you that, remember?"

His face flushed up again. "Of course he didn't kill our mother. She was our *mother!*"

Once again the agony—accompanied by doubt—was showing. The agony was understandable. He'd lost his mother and his father long ago. He'd lost John and Yvonne Sterling who had taken him in. Miguel was all the family he had left.

"Here's Miguel now," Angel said, suddenly looking relieved.

I wasn't sure if he'd been worrying about where Miguel might be or if he was just glad to get the spotlight taken off himself.

"Hey," Miguel said, sliding onto the stool next to me. He had a bruised cheek, a wide Band-Aid on his chin.

Angel slid a bottle of beer in front of him.

"Your eye's getting to look real colorful," Miguel said to me.

He was right. Last time I'd looked, it had gone an interesting combination of green and yellow.

"You're looking a bit the worse for wear yourself," I said. "People are going to think we got in a knock-down-drag-out bout."

"Could only enhance my reputation," he said, then

hesitated. "I drove down to Salinas yesterday. Benefit rodeo."

I wondered if he remembered he wasn't supposed to leave town. But I wasn't going to start anything. I wondered how good he was at throwing rocks. He had the muscle for it. "You participated?" I asked.

"Yeah."

That was all he was going to say? "What happened to your chin?"

"Bull whipped his head back. One of his horns caught me on the chin. Didn't throw me, though. Couple of stitches was all."

"You win the event?" Angel asked.

"Sure."

Could there have been any doubt?

"I haven't had a chance to thank you for helping me the other day," I said. "You never did tell me why you came to see me."

He looked down at his beer and spun the bottle awkwardly between the palms of his hands. Probably he was one of those guys who was embarrassed by gratitude. "You ever find out who threw the rock?" he asked, ignoring my implied question.

I shook my head. I could do that now without feeling as if a knife was stabbing me in the eyeball—though it did produce a weird, almost electronic, humming sound. Maybe there was a hole in my brain.

"You feel up to dancing with me tonight, Charlie?" Miguel went on, giving me one of his intense glances. "I need some action. I get right antsy hanging around Bellamy Park."

"Are you a good dancer?" I asked.

"Nothing to it. The two-step calls for the same skills as riding a bull—rhythm, timing, a sense of balance."

I laughed, and he produced his tight smile.

"I guess you miss the rodeo when you're up here," I said.

"I surely do. Not just the adrenaline rush—which is humongous—but I miss being active, being outside. That's where I want to be when my time comes—outside, with my boots on."

"I miss being outside, too," Angel said. "Every once in a while I think about riding my horse, early mornings at the ranch—dew on the grass, shining in the sun. The sounds the cattle make, my horse breathing. From the back of a horse, a man can see a long way."

That was quite a speech for Angel. Almost poetry.

"Sure," Miguel said. "Working daybreak to midnight. Spend half your time on a tractor. Boring."

"I broke and trained my own horses," Angel protested. "Nothing boring about that. Had some good little dogs, too. Border collies. Loved those dogs more than any woman I ever met."

He was looking over my shoulder again. Three guesses who he was looking at.

"I'd rather win a hundred and fifty thousand a year risking my neck than sit around watching dew on the grass," Miguel said, turning to see where his brother's interest lay, nodding slightly when he'd figured it out.

A tinge of red appeared on Angel's cheekbones. I was afraid he was in for more teasing, but Miguel just went right on talking about bull-riding. "Taking what can't be controlled and controlling it—that's the way to live. Rodeo is a great lifestyle, Charlie. Freedom.

Money. Pushing to the limit. Traveling. You don't make any money standing still. Houston Livestock Show and Rodeo, Dodge City, Reno, Phoenix, Calgary, Cheyenne, Fort Worth, Denver, San Antone, Las Vegas for the NFR. National Finals Rodeo. Only way I know is to go after life like it's got to be roped before it gets away. Though I might take to ranching in a year or two, especially if I get a few more broken bones and a few more horns poking at me. I'm getting too old for bull-riding. Maybe I'll find me a woman and settle down. You have a hankering to be a rancher's wife, Charlie?"

"I don't hanker to be anyone's wife," I said.

"Good steady job," he said. "Long John's wife, Yvonne, was a little bit of a thing, but tough as leather. Worked harder than Long John, harder than any of the hands. Takes a special kind of gal to love a cowboy, rodeo *or* ranch style."

"I doubt I'm up to the job," I said, then asked as casually as possible, "Was your mother tough, too?"

"She could outride the two of us when we were kids," he said. "Give me a whupping soon as look at me. Yeah, you could call her tough."

"Sounds as if you didn't get along too well."

I could feel Angel looking at me. But he didn't give away that he'd already told me that.

Miguel took a long swig of his beer. "My mother chewed my rear out from the day I was born. My fault. I was always testing the rules. She had a lot of rules. Thought I hated her and her rules until the day we found her dead and I knew all at once that I'd loved her, admired her guts. Never had the chance to tell her. That's why I made the vow about killing my father, I guess."

There was a cold and distant look in his eyes now.

About then, Sundancer started up the music again and Miguel cocked an eyebrow at me. At the same time, I saw Zack coming toward us from the stage area. I didn't know if he was planning on asking me to dance, but I decided of the two men, he was the most dangerous to my peace of mind. I hadn't yet come close to forgiving my lapse the previous week.

Miguel turned out to be a smooth dancer. His two-step was fairly straightforward without too many fancy variations and I was able to follow him easily. I liked that. Some of our cowboy-wannabes do a two-step like the woman is a contortionist. The morning after dancing with someone like that, I show up at the chiropractic clinic.

"You getting anywhere with your detecting?" he asked in what he evidently intended to be a casual voice.

"Not really. I gave Angel a rundown earlier. He'll probably tell you all about it."

"Probably." We danced sedately around the floor a couple of times. "Angel says you're hung up on Zack," Miguel said.

"For someone who rarely talks about himself, Angel has a way of talking too much about me."

"It's true then." That cynical grin was beginning to irritate me. "What is it, television glamour? All hat and no cattle, you ask me."

I remembered Miguel watching when Zack and I danced the Desperado Wrap. Zack wasn't watching me dance with Miguel. Zack was dancing with a plump little redhead in a leather miniskirt and boob-enhancing sports bra top. Some people's idea of country-western apparel is a little unusual. Maybe we ought to institute a dress code.

"I wasn't asking," I said shortly.

"Reason I came to see you Friday, I was going to ask you out," he said after a minute's silence.

"I can't go out," I said. "I work nights."

"I was going to ask if you'd like to drive down to Salinas with me Saturday, see the rodeo."

"Sorry I blew the opportunity," I said. And I really was. I hadn't watched rodeo in a long time. Never had much of a chance to see it. It would have been fun to see someone I knew perform. Not that I knew Miguel all that well, but still . . .

Was this why he'd taken to staring at me so intensely? He had something in mind where I was concerned? Men did get attracted to me from time to time. I'd never figured out why; I certainly wasn't the curvaceous, sexy type like Savanna. But it did happen. Maybe my pheremones were calling to his pheremones.

He was looking at me, reading my mind. As we were close to the same height, both wearing cowboy boots, our eyes were on the same level. "We could try some other kind of date, some other time," he suggested.

Although a while back I'd almost decided I was ready for some extracurricular activity with *somebody*, I didn't think it would be very wise to get interested in Miguel until I was at least sure he hadn't murdered anyone. Besides, if there was any sexual chemistry, it wasn't operating where I was concerned. This man still made me very nervous.

"I'll think about it," I said.

"Hung up on Zack," Miguel said knowingly.

"I am not hung up on any man."

"Whatever you say, Charlie." He grinned. "I've heard tell there are two rules for arguing with a woman. Trouble is, neither of them work."

CHAPTER 13

The lump didn't feel too bad the next morning, nor was it quite so colorful, so I decided to hit the gym for a workout. I deliberately avoided the street that goes past Memorial Park.

I don't remember if I've said anything lately about the gym I use. It's in Condor, the town next to Bellamy Park. Disabuse yourself of the idea that this gym looks like whatever you are used to at your local Y, or at a hotel fitness center. Think back quite a few years to when a bench-press and leg-lift machine were separate items. Place them next to a leg-press with a built-in squeal, a rowing machine, and a treadmill that won't go over three miles an hour unless you gallop on it. There's a barre on the mirrored wall. A stair-stepper that often has an out-of-commission sign on it. No TV. No music, unless you bring your own portable tape player. Which I do.

But it's clean and it's usually empty in the morning and it suits me, even if the air-conditioning always smells sort of stale, like airplane air. At least there *was* air-conditioning. The morning had started off with a pretty high temperature. It was going to be a hot day.

I was through with the weight-resistance machines and leaping like a roadrunner on the treadmill when Detective Sergeant Bristow walked in unexpectedly. I slowed down immediately, switched off the treadmill and pulled my headset off, cutting Ricky Van Shelton off in the middle of "I Am a Simple Man."

Bristow worked out at Dandy Carr's in downtown Bellamy Park, but he had come to this gym a couple of times before—both times when he was working on a case. I really think he liked to talk to me because it clarified his own thinking. Usually, I came up with some ideas of my own, and he seemed to respect my intelligence. I like men who respect my intelligence. A lot.

"Did you grill Timpkin about him picking up Vic?" I asked right away.

He smiled tiredly and sat down on the bench press. "Good morning to you, too, Charlie. You're looking a little less colorful this morning." He sighed. "Haven't been able to talk with Reggie. He had to have surgery after all." He glanced at his wristwatch. "Even as we speak. Hip replacement. I'll give him a couple days to recover before I set up the klieg lights for the third degree."

He sighed. "Reggie will probably be transferred to admin. after this. Guess we'll be rooting around for another detective."

I had an idea Reggie wasn't one of Bristow's favorite law-enforcement officers any more than he was one of mine, but he was much too much of a gentleman to say so.

"I'm going to agitate for a female," Bristow said, which brought him a smile of commendation from me.

"A female officer can often defuse a situation a male officer would be inclined to stir up," he said.

You see why I like this man?

I sat down in the leg press seat. The area around my eye was throbbing a bit after all my exertions, so I was just as glad to take a break. Evidently Bristow hadn't come here to work out anyway; he was in his usual "uniform" of jeans and polo shirt and he had all his police stuff on his belt.

"I had a talk with Otis Reeder," he went on when I was comfortably settled. "Seems like a nice guy. He did, of course, confirm what you told me. Then he told me something else—one of the things *nobody* had told me before ..." He paused to give me a meaningful look. "Seems our two Cervantes brothers went to see Sal Migliatore at one point in this ongoing saga. This was around the time that their father disappeared from Bellamy Park. Seems Angel and Miguel talked to Sal's secretary and she told them where Sal lived. She began worrying recently that maybe she shouldn't have told them, so she talked to Otis about it."

Curiosity is my middle name. "Where *did* Sal live?" I asked.

He pulled his notebook out of his jeans pocket and flipped a couple of pages. "Magnolia Avenue, number twenty-three."

I recognized the name of the street and mentally filed the address. I put my next words together carefully. "I take it you are saying Angel and Miguel didn't tell you they'd talked to Sal?"

"They did not. I was given the impression they had relied for all information on the private investigator they'd hired. Whom I've interviewed, by the way. He has a good reputation, doesn't step over the line. He's been helpful to me on several occasions. He did *not* know the brothers had come to the area themselves. He did *not* know they had visited Roxy, or that they'd talked to Sal."

"Roxy didn't tell you they'd gone to see Sal?" I asked.

"I asked her why she'd omitted that part. She said she told 'the boys' who Vic worked for and where his office was, but she didn't know they'd visited. I'm inclined to believe her, though she may be shielding them, of course. They *are* Vic's sons. Roxy has been cooperative from the start. She's as anxious as I am to find out who killed her man. She reiterated that Sal apparently disliked her, so it stood to reason he hadn't informed her that the boys had come to see him."

My turn to talk. Sometimes loyalty gets pulled in two directions. Bristow was eyeing me sternly. And there was nothing significant in what Angel and Miguel had told me about Sal Migliatore.

I sighed. "They said Sal was obviously ill, on oxygen. They got the impression Sal didn't like Vic very much. But all he told them was that he didn't know where Vic had gone. Praised Vic's work. Said he'd always understood Vic and Roxy were very much in love and very happy together. He thought maybe Vic had some kind of seizure or had an accident and had amnesia."

I didn't think it was necessary to add that Angel had said Sal's aura was black.

"That's it?"

"As far as I know."

"Why do you suppose they didn't include that in their statement?"

"Maybe you didn't ask the right question."

He laughed shortly. "Yeah, the old excuse. Nobody asked me. Same one Otis Reeder used."

"Well, in Mr. Reeder's case, he was dealing with Timpkin. Timpkin would put anybody's back up."

"True." It was his turn to sigh.

"You think it's significant that Angel and Miguel went to see Sal?"

He gave me a jaundiced look. "Come on, Charlie. Sal's the guy who wrapped the tarp around the body and rented the storage locker. Angel and Miguel kill their father, stash him away somewhere. They go talk to some of the people who work for Sal, find out Sal never liked Vic. They go to see Sal, and he helps them dispose of the body."

"Why would he do that?"

He grinned. "You've detected the weakness in my argument, Ms. Plato. Maybe he really *hated* Vic. Maybe Vic did him a bum deal sometime. So he was happy to help dispose of him. I don't know, Charlie. I'm throwing out wild theories hoping one of them will trigger some proof."

"I can't imagine either Angel or Miguel being dumb enough to put a body in a storage locker."

He nodded. "I have difficulty with that, too."

"If they were in cahoots with Sal, they'd surely have

either moved the body or kept the rent paid up after he died," I pointed out.

He was looking around the ceiling. "They don't supply any music here?"

"You want to listen to Ricky Van Shelton?" I asked, indicating my portable tape player.

"Mozart would be better," he said. "Beethoven, maybe. Or Bach." He looked at me solemnly. "Your supposed ancestral relative, the philosopher Plato, believed music created a sense of order and harmony necessary for intelligent thought, careful analysis, and faithful discussion. We could use some of that about now. Much as I admire Mr. Van Shelton, I doubt he could do all of that for us."

He stood up. "I hesitate to call in the Cervantes brothers for clarification until I have more to go on. I'll talk to some more of Migliatore's acquaintances, see if anyone has anything to offer."

He rubbed the back of his neck, looking suddenly weary. "Trouble is, I have a heavy caseload now that Timpkin is out of circulation."

My ears perked up. "I guess you have more urgent things to do."

"Everything is urgent," he said, then headed for the door, pausing before leaving to say, "It would be just as well if you did not discuss this conversation with either of the Cervantes brothers."

"My lips are zipped," I said.

After the door closed behind him, I absentmindedly started pushing on the leg-press pedals while I thought over what he had said. It had sure sounded to me as if he was looking for a little help as far as Sal Migliatore was concerned.

And he hadn't said I shouldn't tell Zack.

No, whatever I ended up doing—if indeed, I could think of something to do—this time I wasn't going to take Zack along. This time I was going to go it alone.

Because of my wish to avoid the street that went past Memorial Park, I took yet another route home to CHAPS. One that coincidentally took me past Magnolia Avenue. Naturally, having heard Bristow speak of this street, I turned in. It was a dead-end street, I noted, middling upscale, quiet, tree-shadowed like most of the streets in Bellamy Park.

There was a magnificent magnolia tree in front of number 23—as it was the only one, I guessed that's where the street got its name. A sprinkler system was producing minirainbows over the front lawn. On the other side of the driveway, a Barbie all-terrain vehicle in pink-and-blue plastic and a small inflatable wading pool indicated there was a toddler in residence.

For no particular reason I parked across the street, a couple of lots back, where I could keep an eye on the house without being too obvious about it. I had no idea what I thought I could gain by this maneuver. The house no longer belonged to Sal Migliatore. Sal Migliatore was dead.

It was a very attractive house. Large, too—it just about filled the entire lot. It had a soaring peak to the roof and was built of stained rather than painted wood. Almost churchlike. The front was all windows, becoming triangular at the top. A couple of wings stuck out on each side.

A very pretty black woman and a little girl of about two, both wearing white shirts, yellow shorts, and sneakers, came out of the house while I sat there. They walked off down the street, hand in hand, talking animatedly.

Mothers and daughters always looked great together. I'd had maternal instincts once, but they had gone into anaphylactic shock every time my ex-husband's two kids had come to spend summers with us. The stress had been too much for them and they had died. The maternal instincts, not the kids.

I realized that I needed to go potty. I've always had a problem with that. In life's most poignant or beautiful or tense moments—I need to go potty. It's a curse. In the movies I've seen, TV or big screen, no sleuth worth his fee needed to potty in the middle of a stakeout. Maybe it was because I was an amateur. Getting a license probably strengthened a sleuth's personal plumbing.

It occurred to me that lately I was making references to television or movies almost as often as Zack did. Maybe it was some kind of virus and I'd caught it from him.

The Wrangler was heating up. Following Bristow's directive, I had put the hardtop on. The windows were down but there wasn't any breeze. The heat was adding to my discomfort. I crossed my legs.

As though that had been a signal, the front door of the house next door to the former Migliatore residence opened and a petite elderly white woman appeared, wearing denim shorts with a matching sleeveless shirt and Nikes. Her snow-white hair curled around her pleasant face. She was tugging on a leash that was attached to a collar on the reluctant neck of a large cocker spaniel with really long "feathers" on his legs.

The rest of the dog finally emerged onto the porch. Then sat. Aggressively. The woman squatted to pet his head and talk to him. Then she stood up and moved on in a brisk, competent sort of way. The dog followed, but his stub of a tail was clamped firmly between his legs and his head drooped in a disconsolate way.

I thought of a dog I'd met during the last investigation I'd been involved in. Also a cocker spaniel, though female and a darker golden color. Champers. Short for Champagne. Owned by Thane Stockton, whose wife had been a murder victim. My second thought was that Mr. Stockton's house contained eight bathrooms.

The Old Stockton Place, as it was known locally, featured wrought-iron gates that included a checkpoint at the head of a long long driveway edged by palm trees. The house itself could have passed in *Architectural Digest* for a French château.

Thane Stockton, accompanied by Champers, was waiting for me at the foot of the stone steps that led up to his baronial front door. Evidently it was the servants' day off. Thane didn't have live-in servants; he liked his privacy. He was also agoraphobic, which was the Greek name for fear of the marketplace. In other words, he rarely ventured outside the grounds, and then only under protest and with company.

I noticed as I parked the Wrangler that since my

last visit the iron bars had been removed from all the windows. I thought that was a good sign.

Although he was a shy man—midforties, my height but slightly stooped, with blue eyes and a lot of sandy hair—Thane was obviously delighted to see me. So was Champers, who folded herself nose to tail like a cashew nut and wiggled all over to show her feelings. Both man and dog had good reason to like me, I might add modestly. To know about that reason you'd have to be familiar with my last adventure, and as I don't want to bore the people who do, I won't go into all that here. Suffice it to say, Thane and Champers liked me and I liked them.

I explained my facial bruises when I caught Thane looking at them—using the same old "walked-into-a-door" excuse, wondering briefly if anybody ever did get a bruise that way, and if they did would anyone believe them?

I also apologized for any residual odor I might have brought along with me. I'm not much of a sweat-producing person, but I had worked out and then sat in a hot car for some time.

"Are you forgetting Rory has been living with me off and on?" Thane asked.

I was hardly likely to forget. I was the one who sort of nudged a homeless man named Rory—full name Roderick Effington the Third—and Thane into getting together. Rory was known for his aroma, which even Thane's eight bathrooms hadn't quite eliminated. The living arrangement had worked fairly well through what was left of the winter, but once spring showed up, Rory had decided he was homesick and had gone back to his packing-case bungalow under the bridge that crossed Flood Creek, which was actually dry. Have you noticed how often names of places live on long after they've lost their significance?

I asked permission to use one of Thane's palatial bathrooms, and after I'd achieved the relief that surpasses all others, I gave myself what my mother used to call a "Spitz bath" in the large pedestal sink, carefully wiping down the brass fixtures with a paper towel when I was done.

The part of the mansion that Thane lived in—he had most of the rooms closed off and dust-covered—was blessedly cool. When I came out and followed my garlic-smelling nose to the enormous country kitchen, I found that Thane had set out bowls of gazpacho and thick slabs of focaccia, one of my favorite breads.

The cold soup was delicious, and there was an olivata spread to put on the hot bread—a thick paste of pureed ripe olives, garlic, and olive oil.

We sat at the table that overlooked the gardens, which featured rhododendrons and camellias as big as trees. The flowers crowding the formal beds rivaled Dodie Reeder's greenhouses for color. The lawns were as manicured—and as incredibly green as Pebble Beach golf course down Monterey way.

Champers took up a position on an oval rug with a soft pile that had been placed halfway between the kitchen and the dining area. She lay there flat on her stomach, her head stretched out, chin on the floor, dark eyes following our every move. I'd eaten here before when Rory was still in residence and knew that this dog was so well trained, she would not budge from that spot until Thane gave her permission.

After we were through eating, I broached the possibility of my borrowing Champers the next morning. Thane's pale blue eyes gleamed with curiosity. "I'm sort of working on a murder investigation," I explained. "I need Champers for cover."

He smiled. "I'm glad to hear you are still in business, Charlie. You ought to get a license."

"I've thought of that myself, but I'm not sure I've put in enough hours in security work. I'll have to figure it out someday."

I had worked as a night watchperson for a concrete company while I was putting myself through the University of Washington, and then I was listed on CHAPS's books as security guard as well as accountant and line-dance instructor. My pay for serving and protecting CHAPS was my rent-free loft. I wasn't sure that would qualify as professional employment as a security guard.

Besides, I enjoyed my life at CHAPS. For now, anyway.

"So what do you think about me borrowing Champers?" I asked. "I'd only need her for a couple of hours or so, maybe less. She won't be in any danger, I promise you."

"After all you've done for me, Charlie, you can borrow or take anything I own," Thane said gallantly.

We exchanged a smile of pure friendship; then Thane produced a couple of slices of the sinfully decadent chocolate cake he seemed to have on hand whenever I turned up.

Those who know me know that I'm a health food nut. But even purists have to give way to weakness once in a while or be thought fanatics. If I'm going to fall off the wagon, the cause is going to be chocolate every time—nothing else is worth the guilt trip.

Such a dessert, of course, must be eaten in companionable silence, with only an occasional faint murmur of enjoyment.

"This stuff should probably be against the law," I said as I licked the last traces from my fork.

Thane picked up my plate and headed for the sink. "Since when have you obeyed every letter of the law, Charlie?"

I was still mulling that question as I drove away down the long avenue of palm trees. But by the time I reached the highway, I had managed to rationalize my interference one more time. Detective Sergeant Bristow could hardly borrow Thane's dog in order to strike up a conversation with a woman who just happened to be the neighbor of the man who had hidden Vicenzo Cervantes's body in that storage locker. This wasn't interference; it was a service to the community.

CHAPTER 14

After I picked Champers up the next morning, I drove straight to Magnolia Avenue. The cocker spaniel sniffed the Wrangler's passenger seat—where Ben's cage usually sat—all the way. I hoped she wouldn't decide to mark it as her territory.

It was another hot day. Instead of my usual Western gear, I'd put on shorts, a loose T-shirt with the slogan "Attitude is Everything," sneakers, and a ball cap. My idea of a disguise. The bruise on my forehead had paled enough so I could cover it with makeup, and I'd turned up some larger-lensed sunglasses to hide my still-discolored eye.

I parked just around the corner of Magnolia Avenue, and prepared to keep vigil. It was close to eleven, just about the time the woman and her dog had gone for a walk the previous day. I could only hope she was a creature of habit.

She wasn't.

It was a few minutes after noon by the time the door of the house next to Sal's opened and woman and dog emerged.

By that time I was feeling sweaty and irritated—

as though the woman ought to have followed my schedule—and Champers was totally somnolent. She resisted all my attempts to drag her out of the car until the other cocker was within smelling distance. Then she shot upright and leaped out so fast she almost knocked me over, and started yanking me on the leash in the opposite direction to the one I wanted to go.

The male cocker immediately gave chase, leaping and posturing like an antelope in a *National Geographic* TV special, dragging his owner behind him.

This was ridiculous. I dug in my Reebok heels, hauling Champers to an abrupt halt. The male cocker skidded into her and swung around her a couple of times, hopelessly entangling the leashes.

"Cocker spaniels have minds of their own, don't they?" the woman said, panting, as I tried to sort out whose leash belonged to whom. "I saw you trying to get her out of the car. My Poopsie is exactly the same way. Cockers are nice dogs most of the time, but if they don't want to do something, my, don't they let you know who's boss? Sometimes when I take Poopsie walking, I have to carry him a couple of blocks until he's used to being out of doors. He much prefers being in the house. But he also likes to eat, so he has to have his exercise, don't you, Poopsie?"

Since I've taken up nosing into other people's business, I've come to love talkative people. Interviewing this woman was going to be as easy as getting wet in a cloudburst.

Poopsie wasn't paying any attention to his owner. He had quite obviously fallen madly in love with

Champers at first sniff and was making a huge fuss over her hindquarters.

Men are all alike—one-track minds.

"This is Champers," I said.

"Well, that's an unusual name for a dog," the woman commented. As though Poopsie wasn't.

"It's short for Champagne," I explained, then held out my hand. "My name's Charlie Plato."

"Well, that's unusual, too!" She gave me some fingers to press. There are still a lot of women who don't know how to shake hands. What's so difficult about it?

"I'm Willie Peregrine," she said, then let out a peal of very musical laughter. "I know. I'm a fine one to talk about unusual names. Willie's short for Wilhelmina. And I got stuck with Peregrine from my late husband, Vern, God rest his poor digestive system."

She seemed in no hurry to move on. I guessed she was lonely, glad of the chance to talk to someone, anyone. My lucky day.

"I like your T-shirt," she said.

"Most women do."

"You live around here?" she asked.

She'd even provided an opening. It was time to revert to spy mode. "I've lived in Bellamy Park a couple of years," I said. "I have an apartment on the east side, but I'm starting to get interested in a house. I came to take a look at this neighborhood today, but it appears all the houses are beyond my price range."

"Nothing less than six or seven hundred thousand dollars on this street," she said. "Couple of them worth over a million. Wasn't like that when Vern and I moved in, let me tell you, or we'd never have left Oakland.

Our mortgage was paid for before Vern died or I wouldn't be able to afford to stay here."

"Which house is yours?" I asked craftily.

"Come and take a look," she said.

Poopsie refused to lead the way—he wanted Champers right in front of him so he could follow nose to tail. It was my guess he had not been neutered. It was a damn good thing Champers wasn't in heat.

"There it is," Willie said.

I made admiring sounds, though in truth I couldn't imagine such a small house being worth six or seven hundred thousand dollars. As soon as I could do so naturally, I indicated the house next door. "That's a very attractive design, too," I said. "I do like lots of windows."

"Do you? Seems an awful lot of bother to me. Cleaning them, I mean. Mrs. Fairbairn thinks so, too—she's the young African-American woman recently moved into that house. Sandra Fairbairn. Nice husband, white, not that it makes any difference to me. He works long hours—some kind of executive in Silicon Valley. All that computer talk is beyond me. *She's* nice though quite shy, which makes a big change from the previous owner. And their little girl is darling."

"The previous owner?" I echoed, trying not to pounce.

"Sal Migliatore," she said, rolling out the name as though she'd practiced it several times. "He was a building contractor, built several of the houses on this street, including my little one. Can you imagine my house being worth that much money? It's ridiculous. It's barely a thousand square feet!"

"Location is everything," I said, quoting Roxy.

"That's what the real estate people keep telling me. They are forever harassing me to sell out and move. They see a nice fat commission, I suppose, but what's the point? Vern and I lived here all our married life, raised three kids here. I know where everything is."

She indicated a bench under a walnut tree and I escaped gratefully into the shade. Anyone who has orange hair and Scottish skin doesn't dare hang out too long in the sunshine.

Poopsie was still sniffing around Champers, who was being remarkably patient in a dignified, disinterested sort of way.

"Mr. Migliatore was a good builder," I said, looking at the house next door.

"Not bad I suppose."

There was definitely a tart note in her voice. "I'm getting the feeling you didn't like your former neighbor."

"Oh, he was likable enough, but . . ."

I waited.

"He was a terrible flirt."

I blinked. This didn't jibe with what Roxy had said. She'd gone so far as to call him a mysogynist.

"Oh, I know what you're thinking," Willie said archly. "Why would a man flirt with an old lady like me?"

"I wasn't thinking that at all," I said truthfully.

She put a hand to her beautiful hair in unconscious primping. "It made me very uncomfortable. Not that he wasn't an attractive man, but, you know, Vern was always around and . . ." Her voice trailed away, but not before I heard the note of regret in it.

So she'd probably fancied Sal. *An attractive man.* How had Roxy described him? Tall, gray hair, gray eyes, an old man.

Well, the perspective at forty was not the same as the perspective at eighty. Possibly it was Willie who had done the flirting. And maybe been rebuffed?

"He'd come over for a coffee sometimes," she went on. "But Vern didn't like it, so I eventually had to tell him to stop."

She had a funny sort of smile on her pleasant, ordinary face. If it hadn't seemed so ridiculous, I would have thought it was salacious.

Sometimes it's best to remain silent. But awfully difficult to do. Maybe that's why "You have the right to remain silent" is included in the Miranda warning. Reverse psychology. Soon as you think of keeping your lip zipped, you want to talk.

"He got a new girl anyway," Willie said, then tilted her head to one side. "I guess I'll never know now who the mystery girl was."

I don't know how I did it, but I kept my voice low and casual when it wanted to squeak and shriek. "Mystery girl?" I repeated.

"Vern called her the nooner." She giggled.

Champers had tucked her butt under her and was glaring at Poopsie. I didn't blame her. How could you get serious about a guy named Poopsie?

I waited.

"Sal never married, you know. We thought at first he might be a homosexual—I can never get used to saying gay. But the way he acted around women, well! I asked him once why he hadn't married and he said his mother had married four times, each time disastrously and that had cured him of ever wanting to. I could understand that—marriage isn't all it's cracked up to be. And I always thought it was up to Sal whoever he wanted to entertain. But Vern said he wondered why the girl always had such a secretive air about her. No fool like an old fool he used to say, but there was a wistful note in his voice. He would have liked a mystery girl calling on him, I suppose. Though I don't know what he'd have done with her." She laughed merrily.

I was beginning to get a fairly clear picture of Vern.

"Did she visit often?" I asked.

"Two or three times a week, always around eleven-thirty in the morning. She'd stay a good two hours, then scuttle into her car and drive away. Went on for months."

I tried to send a subliminal message: *Say something about the car, the make, the color, the license plate, something!*

Nothing.

I managed a laugh that sounded false even to my ears. I guess I'm not that good an actor. "A mystery girl. How intriguing. Was she dark and sinister or fair and menacing?"

She had to think about it.

"She always wore a hat. A big straw hat with a brim and a black ribbon around it. A sun hat. I wore a hat something like it myself when I had breast cancer and had to have chemotherapy."

Her smile was reminiscent, and sad. "My hair fell out in handfuls. But it came back curly—isn't that amazing? Must have been the radiation."

She looked at the mass of orange frizz hanging out from my ball cap and I could almost read her mind wondering if radiation had caused that mess, too.

"You called her a girl—she was really young?"

She sighed. "Well, dear, it all depends if I had on my distance glasses or my reading glasses. I can't abide bifocals. They make me dizzy as a frog in a flash flood. Anyway, most people look very young to me. She was very slim. No boobs worth mentioning. But I couldn't ever see much of her face. She'd drive up, park in the driveway and whisk on into the house, whisk back with her head down when she came out."

"What kind of car?" I asked. Not a very subtle question, I know, but sometimes you go with whatever comes in your head.

She thought about it. "It was an old car, I guess," she said. "I wouldn't call it an old beater, though— that implies something neglected. This was well cared for—more in the way of a classic car, like they have at rallies."

My heart skipped a beat. We were closing in on an identification. "I love those old cars," I said. "I saw a parade of them a couple of weeks ago, going through downtown Palo Alto. Did it have fins?"

"Fins?" She shook her head. "I don't think so." She made a clucking noise with her tongue. "I never can remember what those old cars are." She laughed. "Can't remember the new ones, either. Too many of them. And they all have such fancy names. And the colors nowadays. Isn't it amazing the range of colors there are? Mr. Fairbairn next door, I asked him the color of his new car and he said it was called raspberry!"

I tried a different tack. "That was funny, your husband calling the young woman's visit a nooner. Was he an old guy—this Sal whatever it was?"

"Migliatore. I suppose *you* could call him old. He was in good shape, though, remarkably good shape. Until he came down with cancer. He sure didn't ever have a beer belly like Vern's. I'd have pegged him around fifty-something, which in my considered opinion is a fine age period for a man, but Vern and I were behind him going into a movie once, just before we found out he was ill, and he bought a senior ticket— which in our local theater means you are sixty-five. That girl wasn't any senior citizen, though, that's for sure."

She laughed her merry laugh again. "You'll understand when you're older, Charlie. A very strange thing happens as you advance in years. Older people get younger and so do younger people. Fifty-year-olds look like Generation X to me. You, now, have surely just this minute graduated from high school." She sighed. "I remember when I thought eighty was prehistoric, yet here I am."

Her mouth twisted whimsically. "My doctor is sixty-four and he seems like a kid to me! So it gets difficult to define age. It's all relative anyway. Sal was young compared to me, but obviously not too old for his lady visitor."

"You really think there was some hanky-panky?" I asked casually.

"Well now, Charlie, I didn't go peek in his bedroom window, but she was in there long enough—that's for sure. Of course, if Sal was anything like my Vern, it wouldn't take more than five, six minutes tops. Wham bam and snoring before he ever got to the thank-you."

Another peal of laughter.

"Why do old guys so often go after much younger women?" I asked.

"Makes 'em feel like *they* are young, dear," she said promptly.

Again I thought of Roxy, who had talked about old men and the fountain of youth.

"I never did have a chance to see the mystery woman from the front, but she looked like a teenager from behind," Willie said, after squinting into the middle distance for a while.

"A teenager!" Could the "mystery girl" have been the ever-mysterious Bambi?

Willie read my exclamation as shock. "I know. It's hard to believe a youngster could find a senior citizen attractive, but strange couplings happen all the time. I'm forever amazed at why people marry the people they marry. No rhyme or reason to it. 'Course people probably wondered why I married Vern. Wondered myself more than once."

Going-on-sixty Vic had had an affair with seventeen-year-old Bambi. Why not Sal Migliatore? Maybe Sal had found out Vic was about to run off with Bambi? Nobody seemed to know where Bambi had come from or gone to. Could it be that Sal had disposed of her, too? Somewhere else? Another storage locker?

I needed to get hold of Bristow and tell him about Sal and his mystery woman, who might just be young enough to be Bambi, and who, as far as I knew, hadn't been run to earth yet.

"I'd better get going," I said, standing up.

Willie's face fell.

"I'll come back and visit when I have more time," I promised.

"You'll bring Champers? Maybe we could take a walk together; there's a real nice trail starts a couple of blocks over." She waved in a vaguely westerly direction.

"Sure," I said. Champers was already straining at the leash in the direction of the street, Poopsie happily sniffing again. If I did come back, and I usually did try to keep promises, I'd have to come up with some excuse for leaving "my" dog at home.

I held out my hand, but Willie ignored it, electing to give me a hug instead. "Champers isn't really my dog," I blurted out. Nice people always bring out the truthful side of my nature. "I'm just walking her for a friend."

"How sweet of you!" Willie gave me another hug, then held firmly on to Poopsie's leash as Champers dragged me off the property.

As soon as I'd delivered the cocker spaniel back to Thane Stockton, I headed straight for CHAPS and called Bellamy Park Police Department's nonemergency number. Bristow wasn't at the police station, I was told. There was no answer at the apartment he and Savanna had moved into. I left a message on their answering machine, then tried to remember Bristow's beeper number while I hunted for the napkin I'd written it down on. Which of course I couldn't find.

I called the station back and asked for Sheila, who

had been on duty when I first met Bristow. I'd run into her a couple of times since then when some reason or other took me to the station. Maybe she'd remember me.

She didn't.

"I really need to get hold of Detective Sergeant Bristow," I told her anyway. "I have some important information for him and he's not answering his beeper."

"Well . . ." The pause did not sound promising. "You want to leave a message?"

"I've been in the station a couple of times with Zack Hunter," I said, desperate enough to drop Zack's name.

"Well, sure, I remember now," she said. "You're the skinny redhead."

Not my description of choice, but hey, if it got me Bristow's location, I'd accept anything. "I don't know what's going on," Sheila said. "Far as I know it isn't any kind of secret. He's at Bellamy Park Hospital—the emergency room. He called in an hour or so ago."

"He had to take someone in?" I couldn't bother him in that case. My news would have to wait.

"Way I heard it, he went in for himself. Said there'd been a minor accident and to call his wife and have her meet him at the hospital."

"An accident!' "

"He *said* everything was fine. Nothing to worry about."

I was in the process of hanging up. "Okay, thank you," I said.

Two minutes later, I headed down the stairs, still in my shorts and T-shirt "disguise."

Zack was about to pull open the outer door as I

barreled into it and shoved it open. "Excuse me, ma'am," he said politely, then belatedly recognized who was beyond the sunglasses and ballcap. "Charlie? Where you goin' in such a rush?"

I told him what Sheila had said. "Supposedly Savanna's there with him. I'm going to make sure he's okay, and see if they need any help with Jacqueline or whatever."

"I'll come with you," he said at once.

"The partners' meeting," I reminded him. The four of us usually met in the office on weekdays at three in the afternoon to get CHAPS ready for the evening's invading hordes. "We were going to talk about this thing of renting CHAPS out on Monday evenings and maybe for club lunch meetings."

"Yeah, I was comin' to tell you I couldn't make it. Macintosh wanted to schedule the poker game for this afternoon."

"Well, sure, poker has to come first."

He nodded, impervious to sarcasm. "I'll call Macintosh from the truck and tell him I can't make it. I can call Angel, too. We might as well cancel out the meetin' in case we can't get back in time. Especially as Savanna's not available, either. I'll just tell Angel to come on in ahead of openin' time, okay?"

"I forgot to bring your cell phone," I said, starting to unlock the door.

"I have a new one. I want you to keep that one."

I started to protest; then I thought, Heck, I do a lot of work for CHAPS.

If that sounds ungrateful it's because I didn't want to admit to myself that I was coming to think of Zack more and more as someone beyond a friend, someone who was unfailingly kind to me. Someone I might almost come to care for. Deeply. As in love, rather than lust.

Given Zack's history with women, that would be even dumber than sleeping with him. Maybe what I needed to do was to sleep with him so then he'd dump me and stop my stupid feelings for him in their tracks.

How d'you like that reasoning? Women can be way dumb where men are concerned. You may have heard me say that before.

The hospital was not too busy. We were able to find a parking place quite easily. We were hurtling toward the emergency department when we rounded a corner and literally bumped into Taylor Bristow and Savanna.

Savanna's eyes were red-rimmed.

"What are you two doing here?" Bristow exclaimed.

I didn't want to risk Bristow asking me who had told us he was at the hospital. It's not a good idea to get sources in trouble. They think twice about being sources in the future. "We were in the neighborhood," I said, thinking fast, though not too believably. "We thought we'd stop by and see how Timpkin was doing."

Bristow's eyebrows rose to where his hairline might have been once upon a time. But he didn't question the statement, except to point out that the wards were in the opposite direction.

"This place always confuses me," I said.

He glanced at the bands of bright color on the walls that indicated directions to all facilities, but again refrained from comment.

"More to the point," I said, "what are *you* doing here? I hope nothing's wrong with Jacqueline?"

"Jacqueline's fine," Bristow said. "She's spending the day with her grandmother."

Tears welled up in Savanna's large dark eyes. She doesn't often cry, but when she does, she does it beautifully. "It's not Jacqueline—it's Taylor," she said, her voice breaking.

He put his arm around her. "I'm going to be fine, honey. This sort of thing happens all the time." He looked at me. "Tell her I'm going to be fine," he said.

"What sort of thing?" I asked.

A frazzled woman carrying a baby and dragging a screaming toddler by the hand stopped to comfort the two-year-old, who didn't want to be comforted. Within seconds, the baby joined in. She had terrific lungs. I guess the smaller the person the louder they have to be, to avoid getting stepped on.

"The coffee shop," Bristow suggested, and we followed along.

"It was just a kid," he said, after we were all seated with steaming mugs of unnaturally black coffee in front of us. "I arrested him yesterday. No problem. Bellamy Park High. Dealing on school property. Fifteen years old. We've had a major increase in drug traffic at the local schools and we're shorthanded, so I've been driving by whenever I had a free moment. I took the boy in and booked him. Next thing I know he's right back on the street again. This time at the grade school. Laughing at me."

He sighed. "So just to show how dumb I can be, I got mad and put him up against the wall and patted him down kind of roughly, not carefully, and he had a needle in his jacket pocket. Damn thing poked me in the hand."

Zack sucked in his breath, but I was still waiting for the rest of the story. So far it didn't sound too serious. Obviously Bristow hadn't been hurt in any vital way—he was his usual vigorous-appearing self.

"The kid bein' tested for HIV? " Zack asked.

I got it then.

Savanna sobbed.

Bristow tightened his arm around her. "Savanna hasn't gotten used to being a cop's wife," he said. "I keep telling her I'm more likely to get shot in a routine traffic stop than to contract AIDS. Needle-stick injuries happen all the time. Chances of me coming up with HIV is anything from one in three hundred to three in a thousand, depending on whose statistics you read. Last figures I heard, close to a million health care workers get stuck one way or another every year. Very few AIDS cases result. Medical student here says almost everyone she knows has been stuck by a needle."

"The boy checked out positive for HIV," Savanna blurted out. "We just got the results."

"It doesn't mean I'm going to be dead next week," Bristow said.

"Don't say that!" she wailed.

Bristow raised his gaze to the ceiling. "I can see it's going to be really fun at home for a spell. It's too bad they closed down the AIDS vigil. I could have bought a tent and moved in for the duration."

The AIDS vigil was an encampment of tents that

was pitched in front of San Francisco's civic center to call attention to the disease. A lot of people tried in a lot of ways to get rid of it, but it managed to hang on for ten years until a big storm blew it out of existence.

Savanna sobbed some more.

"I'm kidding," Bristow assured her.

Cops usually have a twisted sense of humor. Helps them face the stuff they have to face on a daily basis, I guess.

So far, I'd been too shocked and worried to say anything. I must have looked it, too.

"I wasn't stuck deeply," Bristow said to me, in the same reassuring tone he'd used on Savanna. "The needle didn't poke me in a vein or an artery. And it isn't as if the kid has full-blown AIDS."

"What happens now?" Zack asked.

"They've already started me on AZT, among other medications," Bristow said. "They say it's safest to treat the situation aggressively within two hours, just in case. But I'm going to be perfectly okay," he added to Savanna.

He took a sip of his coffee, winced and set the cup down. "Re your inquiry," he said, and I looked at him blankly.

"You said a few minutes ago that you were here to ask about Detective Sergeant Timpkin," he said.

I tried not to blush.

"Reggie's doing fine physically," he said. "Not so good mentally. He doesn't like being confined."

He hesitated. "By the way, I talked to Reggie last night and established that he took Vic into the station for questioning on the day Otis Reeder saw the two of them driving away."

"Questioning about what?" Zack asked.

"Seems Timpkin heard about the private investigator poking around Bellamy Park asking about and flashing computer-aged photos of someone who looked a lot like Vic Smith. He hauled Vic in to find out why he was being looked for. He was still pretty mad about Vic wanting to throw him out of Grumpy's the day he got in a fight. He'd hoped to learn something he could teach him a lesson on, he admitted, but Vic convinced him there was no reason any PI would be looking for him."

He paused in a way that indicated there was more coming. "Vic also got him to admit he shouldn't have gotten in the fight in his bar. Seems he and Reggie basically kissed and made up, so to speak. After Vic was identified, Reggie had reported to the chief that he was probably one of the last people to see Vic alive. He was not able to determine who the PI was, or his location. I informed him Angel and Miguel had hired a PI and told him who he was and that I'd talked to him."

He stopped to think again. "This morning, I canvassed the neighborhood where Vic and Otis had been working. Several neighbors recalled seeing Otis on the roof of the house, and seeing the police car come and pick Vic up. They were all agog, one of them told me, but the man on the roof told them he had no idea why his colleague had been hauled off. An hour later, the police car brought Vic back and dropped him off. The man who'd been on the roof had already left. Someone

came by in an old Mustang. Then a van drove up—
one that belonged to the building contractor. Sal Migliatore. Nobody noticed when any of these people left.
It must have been after dark, a couple of people
thought. End of story."

"Too bad," I said. "I'd love to have pinned it on
Timpkin."

"Your vigilante nature is running amok," he said,
but he was smiling when he said it.

"So are you going to try to trace the Mustang?" I
asked, and then thought—Hey, wait a minute: a Mustang would surely qualify as a classic car.

I was about to pass on what Willie had told me, but
then Savanna suddenly blurted out, "The doctor said
it'll be six months before we can be sure Taylor didn't
get infected. They told us we should get some mental
health counseling and modify sex practices until we
know for sure."

"Forget modify," Bristow said. "No way I'll risk
any sex until we get the word."

"You *do* think you're in danger," Savanna said, looking as though she was going to burst into tears any
second.

"I'm just not willing to take chances where you're
concerned," Bristow said.

She looked at him steadily for a couple of minutes,
her eyes lustrous. "You can't mean that you're actually
going to stop . . ." She broke off.

"There's nothing to worry about. Mostly, we can
live our lives the way we were doing before this, but
we have to take proper precautions."

"That doesn't mean we have to give up sex altogether," Savanna protested.

I felt superfluous. Zack raised an eyebrow at me, evidently feeling the same. I decided it wasn't a good idea to bother Bristow with possible evidence about Bambi right now.

Standing up, Zack and I both expressed sympathy and encouragement and exchanged hugs all around.

We didn't talk at all on the walk back to Zack's pickup. "Bummer," Zack said heavily after we'd climbed in and fastened our seat belts.

I nodded. "He'll be fine," I said with a confidence I was far from feeling.

"Sure he will." Zack's voice was no more convincing than mine.

"They both will," I said, with even less conviction.

CHAPTER 15

Traffic was relatively light on the way back to CHAPS. After a while, I told Zack what I'd learned from Willie Peregrine. We discussed the possibility of the mystery woman being Bambi, and that she might have driven a Mustang, but couldn't really reach any conclusion without further evidence.

"You going to call Macintosh and set up the poker game after all?" I asked as we drove into CHAPS's parking lot.

He shook his head. "I don't feel up to it now." He looked very somber and I felt another wave of affection for him.

"Bristow and Savanna are going to be okay," I reiterated.

"I know." He sighed, and relapsed into silence again, but as we walked toward CHAPS, he made an obvious attempt to lift himself out of the doldrums. "How 'bout I inventory the bar," he suggested. "Angel was plannin' to do that today."

"Sounds good to me."

I went directly into the office. I felt restless. The information Willie had given me kept clamoring in my brain, which was trying desperately to make sense of it.

Ben was safely in his cage upstairs, probably napping in his box. I really needed to get more work done on CHAPS's Web site, I decided. I'd signed on some time ago for AOL's "bring your own access" program, the access being my Independent Service Provider. I could get unlimited time for only $9.95 a month, and a free Web site. I'd already registered it at http://members.aol.com/chapsclub. Feel free to visit anytime.

A few minutes later I was bringing in E-mail—mostly fan letters for Zack. We needed to set up a separate account for him where his fans could swoon over him to their hearts' content without filling up CHAPS's mailbox.

Buried in the middle of Zack's fan letters was another E-mail from anon311@moonstorm.com.

My stomach tied itself into a couple of knots and I stared at the monitor screen for a good two minutes, then finally clicked the letter open.

"If you don't stop, it could be a bullet for sure next time."

When the paralysis finally released me, I went to the door and yelled for Zack.

He read the message two or three times, just as I had. "You gonna call Bristow again?" he asked.

"I think Bristow has enough on his mind right now. Besides, he's already told us there's nothing he can do."

"Gotta do something, Charlie," Zack said, putting his hand on my shoulder.

My hormones responded to the warmth of his big hand with a full-size whomp! Oh, great—just what I needed, proof positive that thinking I was cured of my infatuation for Zack had been premature. I hadn't experienced a whomp in quite a while, and had almost convinced myself that apart from that one episode of backsliding, dancing the Desperado Wrap with Zack, I was whomp-free forever.

Shrugging his hand off in what I hoped seemed a casual way, I picked up the phone. "I'm calling Macintosh."

As usual, Macintosh insisted he had nothing better to do than to bring aid and comfort to a friend. He arrived twenty minutes later, said, "Let's sit in then," and took over my computer.

A worried look came into his brown eyes as he read the E-mail. "What does it mean?" he asked.

"Charlie had a letter in between the first one and this one," Zack said. "Someone threw a rock at her from the entrance to Memorial Park, while she was parked in her Jeep at the stoplight. The next day there was another anonymous letter sayin' it could have been a bullet. And now this one."

"The rock missed?" Macintosh asked.

"The first one hit the Wrangler, the second one hit me on the head," I told him. I touched my forehead. "I'm using makeup to cover up the bruises."

"She had one hell of a lump," Zack said.

Macintosh peered up at my face. *"It could have been a bullet,"* he repeated. *"It could be a bullet for sure next time."*

"Exactly," I said, and he pursed his lips and said he'd better get to work.

"I wasn't able to track down your anonymous E-mailer before," he told me after some tense minutes of tapping on the keyboard and squinting at the screen. "Remailers have a tendency to come and go. They mostly don't make any money, you see. I did ask around. Those who administer anonymous remailers will not tolerate criminal activity. I could find no one who uses moonstorm as a domain. Just now, I took another look at a couple of Web sites that list remailers. I'm not finding any clues this time, either. It's possible your correspondent set this bogus domain up for his own nefarious purposes. I'll give it another try at home, lassie, but I cannot promise a thing."

He looked at me sympathetically. "Are you afraid?"

"Well, that's my first reaction each time," I admitted. "But then I get angry. This guy is messing with my head." I grimaced at the unintended pun. "I want to find out who he is."

"You've been continuing your investigation, I take it."

"We haven't run into anyone who's a computer whiz," Zack said.

"As far as we know," I added.

Macintosh tugged at his beard. "I'm not able to offer much help."

There was a brief silence.

"Sorry about the poker game," Zack said. "We're shorthanded today."

"Nothing wrong, I trust?" Macintosh asked.

"Everyone's just busy," I said hurriedly before Zack could say too much.

Zack gave me his amused-eyebrows expression.

Macintosh looked from one to the other of us, evidently catching on to the sudden air of secrecy.

"Is your investigation not going too well, then?" he asked.

"We found out a lot of stuff, but none of it seems too useful," I admitted. A thought occurred to me. "Did you ever hear any talk about Vic Smith and a girl named Bambi?"

Macintosh smiled. "What a fine name. I see her with big doe eyes and soft skin and lots of doe-brown hair."

"We don't know the color of her hair," I said. "Apparently when Vic took off, she was the reason. Roxy says she was around seventeen."

He shook his head. "What a foolish man he was." He sighed. "I'm sorry. I've no knowledge of any girl that young in Vic's life. Or of anyone of that name. It is not a name I would forget."

He stood up. "I'll make contact with some people again and see if I can turn up anything new on your remailer."

Halfway to the door, he paused and turned around. "I've a mind to tell you both something. Though I'm not fond of gossip, you understand. I've long since been deathly afraid of gossip myself, so I'm averse to speaking out of turn."

His Scots accent was even more noticeable than usual.

Zack and I glanced at each other.

And waited.

"I'd always known that Vic dallied with the ladies from time to time." He paused again. "I heard gossip at the wake that Roxy herself had an affair."

I felt my eyes widen. "With who? Whom?"

"Och, I've blanked out his name. Yon veterinarian. The one who was at the wake."

"Brian Andersen?" There was a noticeable squeak in my voice.

"Aye, that's the man."

"Charlie's sweet on him," Zack said. "You may have broken her heart."

Macintosh gave him a startled look, then turned his mild gaze on me. "Is that a fact? How very interesting. Not that he's the only man Charlie's sweet on, I'm sure."

Yet another alert friend who'd noticed my stupid fixation on our man in black.

"I'm not sweet on Brian," I said firmly. "I liked him when I met him, but . . ."

I was remembering the wistful look on the vet's face when he talked about Roxy loving Vic in spite of his womanizing. "How reliable was your source?" I asked Macintosh.

"David told me. He saw them coming out of a motel together, said by the look of them he didn't think they'd been discussing Sumatra's health. This was a few months ago. I don't recall exactly when."

"Sumatra?" Zack queried.

"Roxy's cat," Macintosh and I said together.

"I don't suppose it has anything to do with Vic's death," Macintosh said. "But it's been a weight on my mind. Not enough for me to go to the police, but enough to make me uneasy."

"I'll look into it," I said.

"Not without me this time," Zack said.

I agreed we'd go together the following morning. I had no desire to check for vibes with Brian Andersen anymore. Which made me even more pathetic than usual. The fact that Brian and Roxy had been intimate had turned me off Brian instantly, but Zack had been with any number of women since I'd become a partner in CHAPS, and I still couldn't get over this stupid infatuation.

Of course, with Zack, there was no murder to worry about. My mind popped up an image of Brian Andersen's open, friendly face and clean-cut Scandinavian looks. It was impossible to believe he could have been involved in Vic's murder.

Yeah, sure, like all murderers have slicked-down black hair and little beady eyes.

I was surprised to see Savanna helping Angel set up the bar when I reported downstairs for duty that evening. I took her aside on some lame excuse, not sure she wanted Angel to know what was going on with Bristow.

"You didn't have to come in tonight," I scolded her. "Bristow needs you more than we do. I doubt we'll be busy tonight; it's too nice an evening after such a hot day. People will be wanting to cool off, not gallop around a dance floor."

"Taylor went shopping," she said, surprising me.

"He's not going to let a little thing like the specter of AIDS slow him down."

There was a bitterness in her tone that was highly unusual for our normally serene partner. The only other time I'd heard that note in her voice was when she'd told me about her ex-husband Teddy Seabrook picking his lovers out of the line-up of patients at the massage-therapy clinic she'd owned before buying into CHAPS. At the time she hadn't even known Teddy was gay, never mind cheating on her. Finding Teddy in bed with a truck driver she'd been treating for a job-related back injury had put her off her whole profession and she'd sold the clinic, on the other side of Adobe Plaza, to Leah Stoneham, who was a physical therapist. And unmarried. Which state, I kept reminding myself, was the very best state to be in.

"I don't blame you for being worried, honey," I told her.

"That's not all of it," she said. "You heard what he said. No sex. He means it, too. No kissing even, he says. He's out shopping for a bed for himself. He's going to clean out the spare room—the one I was hoping to make a nursery out of sometime—and he's moving in there until he's sure he's clean, as he puts it."

"He didn't seem to think it was such a big deal," I said.

"He insists it's not. But he's still being fanatical about protecting me and Jacqueline. It's either separate bedrooms or he moves back to his old condo—it hasn't sold yet."

There were tears in her eyes again. "I love that

man with everything I have, Charlie. I'm afraid for him and I'm afraid for us."

I put my arms around her and hugged her, and felt her tremble. "You'll both come through this stronger than before," I said. Normally, I hate platitudes, but sometimes there aren't any other words to offer.

"Sure," she said, unconvinced.

CHAPTER 16

Brian Andersen was not the kind of guy to be over-whelmed by meeting Zack Hunter. I remembered he'd previously made some kind of negative crack about *Prescott's Landing*. He wasn't too overwhelmed to see me either when Zack and I showed up at his clinic the next morning. He was polite, obviously wondering why he'd been blessed with our presence, but there was no sign of the friendliness he'd exhibited to me before this whole business of Vic's murder had come up.

It's a difficult situation—asking someone if he had a love affair with a woman whose husband has been murdered. Especially when the murderer has not yet been discovered. I had rehearsed my discreet opening gambit all the way there. Not aloud, unfortunately.

"We've heard you and Roxy Smith are intimately involved," Zack said the moment we got past the initial suspicious greetings. I gave him a look, but he was in full Sheriff Lazarro mode and paid no attention.

"I don't see where my social life is any of your business," Brian said, bristling and clenching his fists.

"We're here to make it our business," our man in black said, squaring his not inconsiderable shoulders.

The atmosphere in the vet's office was suddenly more like a rodeo than an animal clinic, with Brian as a headstrong calf and Zack getting ready to rope him and bring him down.

"Oh, for heaven's sake," I butted in. "We're not trying to start any fights. We're trying to decide if we need to go to the police with this, Brian. I'm sure you can understand it's important evidence, considering Roxy's husband was murdered by person or persons unknown."

"Is that supposed to be an accusation?" he asked, not at all mollified by my soothing tone.

I shook my head. "It's a request for cooperation. Some friends of ours are suspects in this case and we know they're innocent. We're trying to help them prove it."

"There's a presumption of innocence in this country—they shouldn't have to prove it."

"You know as well as I do, it doesn't always work that way," I said.

"We can always talk to Roxy," Zack said.

Brian flashed him a look of pure hatred, but I saw a change of expression in his eyes. He was wavering. Sometimes Zack's bull-in-the-chute method worked surprisingly well.

"I didn't touch her while Vic was still living with her," Brian said. He sat down abruptly on his office chair, as if his blood sugar had suddenly dropped, which it probably had. "Sumatra was having a bladder problem. That's fairly common in toms that have been neutered. Roxy brought him in. She told me about Vic running off with some teenager named Bambi. You asked me about her before."

I nodded.

"She told me Vic suffered from occasional impotence and he was going through just such a period when Bambi showed up at Grumpy's and gave him a shot in the arm, so to speak. She said she'd thought he'd be back in a month or two, but now it was four months and he hadn't been in touch. She was worried. And lonely. Vic's sex drive was pretty low, she told me. Then added that hers wasn't. It was pretty obvious she was coming on to me, and well, I was attracted to her, always had been. It just . . . happened."

"Are you still . . ." Zack hesitated.

I was afraid he was going to ask Brian if he was still boinking Roxy—it was just the sort of tactless thing he would do. "Are you still together?" I asked.

Brian sighed. "Off and on, yes. It's no big love affair, just a couple of people with needs to satisfy." He looked directly at me. "You surely don't suspect Roxy, do you? She told me the police were pretty well convinced Sal Migliatore, the building contractor, killed him."

"We suspect everyone," Zack said heavily. Evidently he was still following one of *Prescott's Landing*'s scripts. They seemed to have been cut into his brain with a hammer and chisel.

"We haven't ruled her out, or in," I said. I wasn't sure you could rule anyone in, but I didn't think either of the men was paying attention to word usage at the moment. "I guess we really just wanted to know if you and Roxy got involved before or after Vic disappeared."

"So now you know."

I was disappointed. I'd hoped to be able to hand Bristow another suspect to take his mind off not only Angel and Miguel, but his own troubles as well.

"I'm very fond of Roxy," Brian said.

Which sounded to me as if the affair was running out of steam. "Very fond" does not a relationship make.

Men have this way of making statements that sound very romantic and loving but on examination mean nothing. "I'm madly in love with you" can later be called a joke. "I love you dearly." Qualified. "You can count on my love. I'm very fond of you."

What women are looking for are those three little straightforward words: "I love you." Why is that so hard for a guy to say?

Not that I'm interested for myself, you understand; it just makes me wonder.

"When did you last see Vic Smith alive?" Zack asked. This line had worked okay with Otis Reeder. He'd come up with the tidbit about Detective Sergeant Timpkin, which had been interesting for a while, even if it hadn't worked out.

"About a week before he vanished," Brian said. "I dropped in at Grumpy's for a drink with a . . . friend."

So Roxy wasn't his only interest. Maybe I'd imagined vibes. No, I knew vibes when I was bombarded by them.

"Do you go to Grumpy's often?" I asked.

He nodded. "I used to go fairly regularly. Not so much after Vic disappeared. It's a pubby kind of place—the same people go all the time. Most people don't get drunk; they go for the sociability. There are dart matches, a couple of good pool tables, a big-screen TV, that sort of thing."

I nodded, visualizing it. "So you were there a week before Vic disappeared," I prompted.

"Vic and I got talking," he went on. He thought for a minute, looking more relaxed now, more like the friendly man I remembered. "He was complaining about Hank Spangler. Roxy's brother. Said he was costing him money and he wished he could persuade Roxy to kick him out."

"He wanted to get rid of Hank?" Zack asked, suddenly on the alert again.

"Hated the guy, according to what he said."

I ruminated for a while. "You said you'd never met Bambi?" I muttered.

"I never did," he said, sounding indignant, as if I'd accused him.

"I'm just trying to sort things out in my brain," I said. "You don't happen to know how Sal and Roxy got along, do you?"

"Roxy never mentioned Sal to me. Except to tell me he had died. Which was around the time we started—going together."

I remembered thinking at one time that a lot of people connected with this case were dead. Malena, Vicenzo, Long John Silver Sterling and his wife Yvonne, Sal Migliatore. There was something significant in that, I felt, but I had no idea what it might be.

My bruised eye gave a twinge and I thought to ask Brian one more question. "Did you tell anyone I was here asking questions the other day?"

He didn't have sharp cheekbones like Angel's, but

the area where they would have been came up with a pink stripe. "What do you mean?" he asked.

"Someone saw me parked outside Memorial Park when I was on my way home. Whoever it was threw a rock at me and hit me on the forehead." I took off my sunglasses so he could see where the bruise had spread to my eye.

"What makes you think that was connected with you being here?" he asked.

"Whoever threw the rock sent me an E-mail to *tell* me it was connected."

The flush deepened. "My name was mentioned?"

I didn't answer.

"I guess we need to talk to Detective Sergeant Bristow," I said to Zack, who nodded and stood up on cue.

"I called Roxy," Brian admitted. "I thought she ought to know you were here. But she didn't answer the phone."

I waited, sensing there was more.

"I left a message on her answering machine," he went on finally. "I said you'd been here asking questions about her and had just left."

He hesitated. I waited again.

"It's possible, I guess, that Hank heard the message." He let another beat pass, his usually smooth forehead creasing into corrugated lines. After a deep sigh, he said, "Hank is very much into computers, Charlie. Roxy told me he's addicted to the Internet, always surfing the Web. He's always wanting her to hang out with him in chat rooms, most of which she says are pretty boring. He spends hours in one that's devoted to vintage cars."

My eyes must have widened.

"What?" he asked.

"What kind of vintage cars?" I asked.

He shrugged. "We didn't get into specifics that I recall." He frowned. "But now that I think about it, Hank owned an old car that he kept in superb condition. An old Mustang. Roxy borrowed it once when . . ."

He broke off and my mind filled in the blank with salacious details.

"She said Vic used to get mad at Hank because the phone line was always busy when he wanted to call in or out," he went on hastily.

Hank.

An image of curly blond hair around a sunburned bald spot popped up in my mind, accompanied by gooseberry eyes, a sweaty pink face, and a pudgy body. A finger poked slyly into my palm.

Hank.

I liked Hank as the murderer. It's always good when the sleazy guy turns out to be the bad guy. Makes everybody want to stand up and cheer.

I had no desire to give Hank Spangler the third degree, all the same, but I thought maybe it wouldn't hurt if Zack and I talked to Roxy again, with a view to winkling out whatever she knew about Hank's involvement in Vic's murder. For all I knew, there were all kinds of collusion going on here. Bambi might be someone Hank had introduced Vic to for purposes of his own. Could be he'd loaned *her* his old Mustang— the classic car Willie associated with Sal's mystery girl.

* * *

Zack called Roxy as soon as we got back to my loft. I was quite sure she'd be more inclined to accept an invitation from him than from me. Following a script we'd agreed on, he told her some interesting facts had turned up in the case and he wanted to discuss them with her. He suggested she meet him at CHAPS.

We saw her Lincoln Town Car drive into CHAPS's parking lot as we were stacking our lunch dishes in my dishwasher. Benny was hip hopping around the loft when she rang the doorbell and he did one of his leaps into the air, came down and skedaddled under the sofa.

Zack was laughing as he went down to bring Roxy up.

She looked very slender and businesslike in a navy-blue pinstriped pantsuit that had a masculine cut. Pantsuits were apparently her signature clothing. I'd never wanted to be too coordinated myself—a sign of my disorganized personality probably—but the style had come back in recent months and it suited her admirably. Her hair was parted at one side and combed very severely.

I thought that if you weren't close enough to her to see her face, you could mistake her for a very young man.

"Have you ever hung around CHAPS at night?" I blurted out as I dried my hands on a dishtowel.

She looked startled. "Why would I do that?"

"I thought I saw someone who looked like you from up here one night," I said lamely. "The person was standing at the corner of the bank, then went around and across the street to the convenience store."

"Well, it wasn't me," she said firmly. And the denial had the ring of truth. Not everyone who strolled through a mystery scene belonged in the mystery. Whoever that young man was, he'd probably been going about a normal errand when I happened to see him.

Zack and I had discussed what questions to ask Roxy and had agreed he'd do most of the quizzing as she was much more likely to be open with him.

Having made a mess of the opening remarks, I retired to one of my straight and very uncomfortable dining chairs and waited while he metamorphosed into Sheriff Lazarro.

"That's a great suit," he commented after Roxy seated herself in my rocker.

That comment wasn't in the script, but it was probably beyond Zack to greet a woman without saying something complimentary.

She smiled an acknowledgment. "What's this all about?" she asked with a vague gesture of her right hand. "What new information do you have?"

"We heard your brother Hank likes messin' around on a computer," Zack said, leaning forward on the sofa. "We also heard he drives a Mustang."

"So? That car is Hank's baby. He spends hours polishing and . . ." Roxy's eyes narrowed. "What about it?"

Apparently Zack didn't remember what I'd told him about Sal's mystery girl arriving in an old car. "What about the computer?" he asked cleverly to cover up his lapse.

Roxy shrugged. "Hank's a computer nerd, sure. California's full of computer nerds. The whole world is. Hank was on the Internet when he was still in Texas, way before most people ever heard about it."

A note of pride had crept into her voice. "He designed the Web site for my father's business and for the company he works for now. He even did one for my real estate company. I'm a technophobe—you won't get me anywhere near a computer."

"Charlie received a couple of threatenin' E-mails from someone," Zack said. "Seems to have been someone who knew somethin' about computers, set up his own . . ."

"Domain," I supplied when he went blank and looked at me, the actor waiting for his prompt.

"That same person threw a rock at me," I added, watching Roxy's face.

The expression in Roxy's pale green eyes changed from one that portrayed innocence to something that was much more guarded. At the same time, her lips clamped tightly.

I was willing to bet she knew something about that rock.

Getting up, she walked over to the window and stood looking out. She might not be the "young man" I'd imagined was hanging around CHAPS, but she had a youthful way of walking—a generally youthful appearance. She was obviously comfortable in her body. I remembered Brian saying she was a jogger.

So what was I thinking? No matter how youthful she looked, she wouldn't have been the mystery girl who visited Sal Migliatore every day at noon. She'd barely known Sal. And Sal hadn't liked her.

She'd said.

I swallowed—hard—and mentally kicked myself. Because I liked Roxy, and maybe because she was such an attractive woman, I'd allowed myself to believe everything she said. As though beauty on the outside meant the inside was flawless.

I stood up. "Would you excuse me for a minute?" I said, and exited the loft before either of my guests could answer. It took me less than a minute to find Willie Peregrine in the office telephone directory. She answered on the first ring. Definitely a lonely woman.

"What did the mystery girl wear?" she asked when I posed my question. "What does it matter what she wore?"

"I'll explain later," I said. "I'll come over and we'll have a long talk about it. Right now, it's just a story I'm interested in."

"I'd like you to visit, Charlie," she said wistfully, and I vowed to myself I would keep my promise. "Are you a newspaper reporter or something?" she asked.

"Something like that," I said.

"I thought you seemed awfully interested in that story," she said. There was a brief silence. "Well, she wore a lot of different things. She was always very smart. In the beginning she'd be in nice dresses, or jackets and skirts. She liked pleated skirts. And the hat, of course. Vern said she wore the hat so no one would know who she was—she did keep her face down going in and out of the house."

She paused. "After Vern died, I noticed she was wearing pants more often." She gave an embarrassed kind of giggle. "Well, now that sounds as if she wore pants because Vern died. I never was good at keeping my sentences straight, Vern always said. Mrs. Non Sequitur, he called me."

"Did the mystery girl ever wear pantsuits?" I asked.

"Oh, I guess I didn't say. Yes, she often wore matching jackets and pants the last few months. Not jeans—tailored pants and jackets. Some of them looked like silk. Very nice. I tried a suit like that on in Macy's once—made me look real squatty." She sighed.

"Did the mystery girl drive a Mustang?" I asked.

"I don't *know* what kind of car it was, Charlie," she said.

I made another promise to come over and explain everything later, then hung up. I put in a call to the police station, but Bristow wasn't in. I asked Sheila to try to track him down and have him call me and she said archly that she would if I promised to bring Zack in to the station sometime soon. I told her I'd have Bristow bring him in in handcuffs and turn him over to her and she sucked in her breath and said that would be even better. I hoped she was joking. I hoped she knew *I* was.

I went slowly back up the stairs, my brain seething with questions.

Roxy had said Sal didn't like her. She'd also said he didn't like women. Period. Yet Willie had chattered about "the way he behaved with women"—and that he'd flirted with her. And his mystery girl had visited regularly.

Roxy had said she'd never used a computer. I'd

gotten so hung up on what Brian said about Hank having an old car and a computer, I'd passed over him saying Roxy had told him the chat rooms were boring. How could she know that without having used a computer?

If someone lied once, weren't they more likely to lie several times? Especially for self-protection.

Could Roxy have lied about Sal not liking her?

Sal was dead. There was no way to find out how he'd felt about women. Or about Roxy.

Roxy had said that Vic had run off with a girl named Bambi. To me, to the police, to Brian.

Could she have lied about that, too? Vic was dead; there was no way to ask him.

Sal had told Otis that Bambi had hung around Vic at work. But Otis, who worked with Vic, knew nothing about her.

Sal had wrapped Vic's body. Sal had *known* Vic had been murdered even if he hadn't murdered him himself. So he'd lied about Vic going off with a girl named Bambi.

Sal was dead.

According to Roxy, Bambi had hung around Grumpy's. She'd let me know none of the customers *remembered* seeing Bambi. Which would nicely cover their not knowing anything about Bambi at all.

Brian had visited Grumpy's regularly, but he knew nothing about Bambi. Macintosh had never met Bambi.

Bambi was a mystery, but that didn't mean she was Sal's mystery girl.

Sal's mystery girl had worn pantsuits. She had driven a "classic" car.

Roxy's brother owned a classic car. Roxy wore pantsuits.

All those clues and I'd missed them. Fine amateur detective I was.

As I opened the door to my loft, I thought of something else we only had Roxy's word for. That she hadn't known Malena was dead when she and Vic left Texas.

She was still looking out the window. Zack was standing next to her. He was telling her about the Acura Legend he'd owned for a while and what had happened to it. A gruesome story.

I apologized for taking time out, and made some lame excuse about something I'd forgotten. Benny had emerged from beneath the sofa. When he saw me, he squatted like a little garden statue of a rabbit for a couple of minutes, then stretched out on his side, twitched violently a couple of times and flung himself over on his other side. First time I saw him do that, I thought he was having a stroke, but I learned it was just one of his ritual stretching exercises.

Roxy had turned away from the window and had watched the whole maneuver, a small smile tugging at the corner of her mouth. "What kind of rabbit is that?" she asked, returning to her seat and making tutting noises at Benny, who ignored her. "He sure is small."

"He's a Netherland Dwarf," I said. "That's as big as he gets."

As if he knew we were talking about him, Benny made one of his sudden hurtling runs around the room, then disappeared under the sofa again, probably with intent to continue disemboweling it.

I took a deep breath. "My getting hit by that rock isn't what's important here," I said.

Roxy let out a breath.

Zack's eyebrows slanted up and he returned to the sofa.

I made my voice as casual as possible. "We're mainly interested in establishing exactly what happened in what order when you and Vicenzo left Texas all those years ago."

This statement was not in the script Zack and I had worked out, and he continued to look at me quizzically, but he had the sense not to comment.

Roxy frowned for a minute, then shrugged and began talking. "Well, I met Vicenzo like I told you, at a church dance in Houston. We hit it off and started . . . seeing each other. My name was Roxanne Spangler then. I was seventeen years old. Still struggling through St. Joseph's High School. God, I hated school. But I loved Vicenzo. I always did like older men."

I remembered most of these details from when we'd questioned her before, and something about the way she was presenting them was striking me as extremely peculiar. She was using what seemed to be the same words she'd used when telling Zack and me this story in the restaurant on the other side of Adobe Plaza. As though she'd rehearsed it. More than once.

"All Vicenzo told me was that he and Malena had this big fight and she threw everything he owned into garbage bags, so he left. He went back the next day to get something, he said, a watch that meant a lot to him. Malena wasn't home, so he went in and got it. Everything looked all right then, he said. We left Houston, and Texas, that same day."

She bit down on her lower lip. "He told me Malena might try to get revenge on me for him leaving her, and she had some mean friends, so we should go somewhere else to live. I was surprised he'd leave his boys like that, but he seemed to think it was better to make a clean break."

Her large eyes looked very sad. "I swear to you, Vicenzo didn't know Malena was dead. It was a week or so later that he called Mr. Sterling—Long John—and found out Malena had been murdered the day we left the state. Long John told Vic there was a warrant out for his arrest and he should get himself a new name and not come back to Texas ever again."

I was sitting forward now and Zack was looking at me questioningly. We hadn't rehearsed any of this. But I wanted to keep it going. It was as if she'd taped her previous responses somewhere in her memory and was playing them over, chapter and verse.

"Did you ever meet Bambi?" I asked, just as I had asked her before.

She shook her head. "Sal did, though. I called him up and asked him after Vic left. Sal said Bambi had come to see Vic at work several times, which he hadn't liked a bit. He said she was a perky little thing. Wore too much makeup. Smudgy stuff around the eyes. Blusher on her cheekbones."

Word for word.

"Does it seem funny to you that nobody else has met Bambi?" I asked.

Zack was frowning. He can manage to look very wise when he's completely at sea, so I wasn't sure if he was catching on.,

Roxy blinked. "You mean nobody *remembers* Bambi, nobody paid any *attention* to her."

"Doesn't that seem odd, when Vic supposedly met her at Grumpy's and supposedly she also came to where he was working on houses a few times. Doesn't it seem odd that the police haven't been able to turn up any trace of Bambi?"

She shrugged, but she was beginning to look uncomfortable. "So maybe *she* killed Vic," she said. "Maybe she hightailed it out of town after."

She paused. "Sal met her," she added. "He told me so."

"Did he have a thing goin' with her?" Zack asked. He must have finally remembered what I'd told him about Willie's comments.

Her eyes narrowed. With an obvious effort, she gave another shrug. "How would I know? I already told you I didn't like him and he didn't like me. We had nothing to do with each other."

She was getting on the defensive. Interesting. I flashed Zack an encouraging glance.

"I was thinkin' about this story we did on *Prescott's Landin'*," Zack said, sitting back on the sofa.

Roxy mirrored his position, relaxing back herself. *Way to go, Zack*, I thought.

Zack bestowed his most charming and irresistible smile on her, compelling her to smile back. "Seems this one young lady had a love affair goin' with this much older dude. Man lived alone. Nobody was sure if he was a widower or what."

Zack was talking about Bambi, of course. He didn't know what I'd just learned from Willie, the conclusion I'd drawn. I could use his setup, change it to fit the new information.

"I remember that show," I said. "The young lady—the woman—was married. At least everybody *thought* she was married. She used to go see this man every day—not where he worked, of course, that would have been pretty dumb, because her so-called husband worked for the man, too. Nope, what the man did, he went home for lunch and she went to his house. Went on for a long time."

Somewhere in the middle of this tale, Roxy had realized I was talking about her rather than one of *Prescott's Landing*'s unbelievable plots. Her facial expression had become set. Her hands were clasped tightly, almost rigidly in her lap.

"Seems some neighbor saw this woman visiting the old guy. Didn't tell anyone, because nobody asked. Until one day, an investigator came to the door and . . ."

"What neighbor?" Roxy asked.

"Someone from way down the street," I said hastily. I had no idea where this was going, but I didn't want to put Willie in any danger. "He saw you, Roxy. The neighbor. Described you in detail. Pantsuits, old car. I guess you borrowed Hank's car. If we were to show that neighbor Hank's car, he could probably identify it. You didn't want to be recognized, did you? The neighbor said you always wore a large sun hat."

"I never visited Sal," she said flatly. "Sal didn't like me. I told you that. He didn't like Vic, either. He's probably the monster who killed Vic and ruined my life."

"Why didn't you just leave Vic and go live with Sal?" I asked. "You weren't married to Vic. Why stay with him?"

She gave me a look that was supposed to indicate confusion. But her eyes were clear and knowing.

"I guess you and Vic were tied together because of the pretend life you'd cooked up," Zack said, suddenly getting back into the act. "Vic was wanted for murder by that sheriff's department in Texas. You'd established this whole new identity; you couldn't jeopardize it. You'd be held accountable for leaving Texas with him. Made you an accessory. Made you feel you couldn't safely leave Vic."

"Sal rented that storage locker, not me," she said firmly. "If Sal killed him, he did it alone."

"Uhuh," said our wise lawman. Evidently he didn't know where to go now.

"Malena's the one I feel sorry for," I said.

Roxy flashed me an aggravated look. "Why would you feel sorry for *her?*"

"Her husband killed her. Isn't that enough?"

"Vic didn't kill her," she said flatly.

"Okay. Maybe he didn't," I said, fishing. I threw in a wild statement just to confuse the whole issue. "Did you know Sal when you lived in Texas? Did Sal have anything to do with Malena's killing? Were you having an affair with Sal as well as Vic? I heard that Malena called your father and told him you were having an affair. Was she talking about Vic or Sal?"

Roxy stared at me, obviously bewildered.

"I thought we were talking about Vic's murder," Zack said. Evidently he was confused, too. But out of confusion and bewilderment come clues. Sometimes.

Like this time.

"I don't know why you'd feel sorry for Malena," Roxy said stiffly, seizing on the only part of my tirade that had any real meaning. "She had no business calling my father and telling him about Vic and me and the stupid black eye Vic had given her. Getting my father all fired up . . ."

She broke off and looked down at her long perfect fingernails.

"You told me you didn't know Vic had hit Malena," I said slowly.

Her head drooped. There was a silence. Into it came Benny hopping across the floor to sniff at Roxy's shoes as though he'd just discovered she was there.

Scooping him up, she stood up and tossed him onto the sofa next to Zack. There was a clunk as he landed, and I jumped up, too, scared to death she'd killed him.

Next thing I knew I was on the floor with a raging pain radiating from the place at the back of my neck where Roxy had socked me with something hard.

She had a revolver. She must have pulled it out of her purse while my attention—and Zack's—was fixed on Benny.

I tried to raise my head to see if Benny was okay. For a minute I thought I had raised it, but I was evidently hallucinating. My nose was still firmly planted on the carpet. It felt as if a giant had his foot on my head, holding it down.

And then a shot reverberated loudly through my loft and Zack said a word I hadn't ever heard him say before. Come to think of it, Zack didn't ever cuss. Not in front of me at least.

CHAPTER 17

"Roxy," Zack chastised. So I guessed the shot had missed him. I hoped it had missed Benny. I hoped it had missed me. I was so numb I couldn't tell.

It seemed wisest to stay very still and pretend to be unconscious. For the moment, I wasn't able to move anyway. It occurred to me to wonder if Roxy had broken my neck. Maybe I was paralyzed. The whole rest of my life, to be spent in a wheelchair, flashed in front of my out-of-focus eyes.

"Don't come any closer," Roxy said.

"I won't," Zack said.

I rolled an eye cautiously and saw him standing facing Roxy with both hands held palms out and away from his body in the age-old gesture of unarmed nonresistance. Beyond him on the sofa Benny was stretched out, not moving a muscle.

Rabbits can stay motionless for hours when they perceive themselves to be in danger. Ben did it at the time of the earthquake when I discovered the skeleton in the flowerbed. I could only hope that's what he was doing now.

I continued to emulate him.

"Stay away from her," Roxy said abruptly, and I gathered Zack had made a move toward me. Dumb, Zack.

"Are you okay, Charlie?" he asked.

Sure Zack, peachy keen. I kept my lips zipped, my gaze fixed just in case Roxy was looking at me.

"Look, Roxy, let's talk about this," Zack said. From the way he dropped his voice I could imagine his expression—the wry smile, the slanted eyebrows. Irresistible.

"We can work something out here," he went on in that same coaxing voice. "Just tell me what happened and I can help you walk away from this."

Outrage zapped through me like a jolt of electricity, but it didn't alleviate the paralysis. So, okay, maybe Zack was *pretending* to be sympathetic. But there was no way for me to be sure.

"She'll go to the police."

"No, she won't. I can handle Charlie."

In your dreams.

"I bet it was you slugged Charlie with that rock, wasn't it?" There was a chuckle in his voice. If I could ever move my legs again, I was going to kick him where it would do the most harm.

"No," Roxy said. "I don't know anything about any rock." She was silent a moment, then said in a voice that had surprise in it. "It was probably Hank. He told me he'd sent some kind of E-mail to Charlie warning her off. I told him I thought that was a dumb thing to do and he said she'd never figure out who it was from. Later on, Brian called while I was gone and said Charlie was asking questions about me. Hank probably listened in on the answering machine. He does that. Bugs me a lot."

"Was it Hank who killed Vic?" Zack said coaxingly. "It's my guess Hank did it and you were there with him but you haven't dared speak out about it."

"He was my lover," Roxy said.

"Hank?" Disbelief raised Zack's voice an octave.

"Not Hank. Sal. A couple of years ago, I went to Sal's office to ask about some woman Vic was seeing. He was hardly coming home nights anymore."

"Bambi?" Zack asked.

Roxy made a sound somewhere between a laugh and a sob. "Bambi didn't exist. Sal made her up. Nobody questioned that Vic might run off with another woman. There were so many women. This one was called Kitty. She seemed to be lasting longer than most. So I asked Sal about her. He didn't know her, but he took me out for a drink because I was upset. We'd never really spent any time together. One thing led to another."

She sighed. "I was always heartsick about having to leave Texas and my daddy. I really missed my daddy. Sal was like him. Kind and generous. But I couldn't leave Vic. I had to make sure Vic never found out about Malena."

What? *What* about Malena?

"Did Vic find you together?" Zack asked.

Ask her about Malena, you dimwit.

"No, it wasn't like that at all. Vic called me from one of Sal's houses—one he was working on. In Mountain View. He told me some detective—it turned out to be that Timpkin guy—had taken him into the station for questioning. A private investigator had been around asking questions about him. He said we'd have to leave, go somewhere else, start over. He was in a panic. I went to see him."

There was a silence. I didn't want to risk rolling my eye again, so I stayed put and pretended I wasn't breathing. I hoped to God I wouldn't sneeze—the carpet smelled dusty. I needed to clean more often. Maybe I could get the CHAPS janitorial crew to sweep through once in a while.

"Sit," Roxy said suddenly.

I heard the creak of my thrift-store sofa and surmised Zack had obeyed. I hoped he hadn't sat on Benny.

In the little slit of vision I had, I saw Roxy sit back down in the rocker. She wanted to talk. I was paralyzed on the floor, Benny on the sofa, and she wanted to confess. I remembered Bristow telling me there's an enormous internal pressure on a killer to talk about what he's done. Evidently Zack had tapped into that. I didn't remember if Bristow had mentioned whether the criminal type who felt all this pressure to confess would then kill all witnesses. That's the way it seemed to go down at the movies. At least the threat was usually there. Only ingenuity could save the good guys. I hoped Zack was capable of some ingenuity. I sure wasn't.

Roxy didn't confess.

Sal had killed Vic, she said. Sal had come in while Roxy was arguing with Vic that she wasn't going to run away with him. Sal was already ill with cancer and not thinking straight at all. He'd gotten mad at Vic and hit him over the head with an iron skillet. They were in the kitchen of the house. It was one that was about to be opened as a model and it had been furnished that day. Vic was there putting knobs on the kitchen cabinets, just as Otis had said.

So Sal simply grabbed a skillet and knocked Vic to the floor. Then he stabbed him and wrapped him in a tarp and fastened it with duct tape.

"He told me he'd take care of disposing of . . . the body," Roxy said. "I had no idea what he'd done with it. He said it was better I didn't know. Until it showed up in that storage locker, I thought it was probably at the bottom of the bay."

"Accordin' to the police, the person who wrapped the tarp around Vic didn't kill him," Zack said.

Way to go, Zack. That'll make her much more kindly disposed toward you.

I thought I was maybe beginning to get some feeling back in my toes. I risked wiggling them, but couldn't tell if they actually moved inside my cowboy boots or just seemed to. People who had limbs amputated could often feel as if they were still attached, I'd read.

"Okay," Roxy said with a sigh. "So *I* wrapped him up. Sal was running out of breath. Vic was already dead. I couldn't do anything about that, and I was scared. So I found the tarp in the garage and wrapped the . . . wrapped Vic in it."

"The police say the person who stabbed Vic was right-handed," Zack said.

There was an even longer silence this time.

"Why don't you tell me what really happened?" Zack said.

I risked an eye roll. Roxy was still holding the gun

on him. *Keep her talking, Zack,* I tried to send telepath-
ically. *Soon as I can move, I'll . . .*

Do what?

To my surprise, Roxy went back to talking about
Malena. I thought maybe her brain was running a fever
after all the excitement. Whatever the reason, it was
soon evident she wanted to let it all out.

And in the meantime I was beginning to get some
feeling back in my legs.

Malena had threatened to tell Warren Spangler
about her husband having an affair with his daughter.
Malena and Vicenzo had fought over that. Vicenzo had
refused to end the affair, so Malena bagged Vicenzo's
belongings and told him to leave. He got mad and hit
Malena, blackening her eye. He told Roxy what had
happened and warned her Malena would probably
carry out her threat. Roxy went to see Malena to beg
her not to tell Warren Spangler. Malena laughed and
said she already had. Roxy got mad and went to hit
her. Malena ran in the bedroom and brought out a gun
and chased Roxy back into the kitchen. Roxy grabbed
the gun and it went off, killing Malena.

That still wasn't the whole truth, I knew. Malena
had been shot from some distance away, Bristow had
told me. Roxy must have deliberately shot Malena. She
was still trying to cover her tracks.

She had wiped the gun in case of fingerprints, she
went on; then she'd called her father. He'd told her to
hightail it out of there. Later, Vic came back to his
house to get the watch John Sterling had given him
and had found Malena dead. He freaked out, taking
Roxy with him to Warren for advice on what to do.

Without telling him what Roxy had done, Warren had helped them get out of Texas and had passed out enough large-scale bribes that nobody got too serious about looking for Vicenzo.

Vic had never known what had really happened and had always been grateful that Roxy had stood by him and believed he was innocent.

But that day in Sal's house, when Roxy told Vic she wasn't going to run away with him again, Vic had decided that, in that case, *he* wasn't going to run, either. He would tell Timpkin the truth, and if the sheriff's department where he'd lived in Texas decided they wanted him to return and stand trial, he would go. He was innocent and would be found innocent, he said.

There was no way Roxy could let him do that. She had argued with him and blurted out in her anger that there couldn't be a trial or someone might find out *she* had killed Malena.

"I can still see his face," she said. "He was horrified. In that instant, any love he'd ever had for me turned to hatred. I could see it in his face. He must have really loved Malena. After all I'd put up with from him, I couldn't stand to see him look at me like that. And I knew right away I should never have told him. He would have turned me in."

The skillet had been right there on the kitchen counter. Someone was going to be cooking a meal when people came to the open house.

After she bashed his head in with the skillet and he fell to the floor, she grabbed a knife from a drawer, turned him over and kept stabbing him until she ran out of steam. "I loved that man in the beginning," she said to Zack. "But there was *always* another woman. One after the other. Each one younger than the one before. I thought of that when I stabbed him. I gave him a cut for each woman. I was out of my mind, I guess. It was just like it was when Malena brought out that gun. I don't know what came over me. It was like adrenaline cut in and took over. Like I was someone else. Some madwoman with inhuman strength."

Was she preparing an insanity defense now?

My whole body had warmed up a bit during this recital. I thought I was maybe going to be able to move soon. Evidently the paralysis had been temporary. Along with all the other returning sensations I really wanted to go to the bathroom, but this hardly seemed a convenient time.

"When I came to myself I tried to get hold of Hank," Roxy continued. "Apparently he was playing hookey from work, just as he often did—but he wasn't at home, either. So I called Sal. He came over right away and wrapped Vic in the rug he'd gone down on and then with the tarp. Then he sent me home, just like I said. A couple of days later, he came up with the idea of telling people Vic had run off with a teenager. I thought of the name Bambi because it could have been a nickname so it wouldn't be surprising if it wasn't traceable. Nobody was surprised to hear Vic had gone off with another woman," she added bitterly. "They didn't suspect a thing."

She was quiet again. "I guess Vic saying he was going back to Texas was the last straw for me," she said after a while.

Oh, yeah, sure, it was Vic's fault he got himself killed.

"There was always all kinds of stuff going on between us," she went on, as if she was thinking out loud. "Because Vic was always catting around, he figured I had to be doing the same. He was always jealous, controlling, always interrogating me about where I'd been and who I'd seen. And as long as I lived with him, I never went with anyone else until Sal. As for my father—he helped us get out of Texas after Malena died, but whenever I called him he kept saying I'd ruined my life and his."

She sighed dramatically. "Nobody except Hank ever really loved me," she said. "My father used to, but he stopped after the Malena thing. I thought Hank had, too, when he started blackmailing Vic. Long before he moved out here he kept threatening to report our whereabouts to the authorities and he knew that wouldn't be good for me."

"Hank knew you'd killed Malena?" Zack said softly.

"He and my father. Nobody else. He explained to me that he was blackmailing Vic so Vic would never suspect me of killing Malena, but he would never really turn us in."

Another sigh. "Vic always said he loved me, but he was too busy chasing other women to even think about what it was doing to me. And Sal—well, he just wanted to feel young again. He was already over sixty when we got together. He just wanted the sex. He never really loved me, either."

"*I* love you," Zack said.

What?

"I've loved you from the minute I met you," he said, his voice deep with sincerity and yearning. "When I first looked into your eyes, I felt that we were soul-mates. You have the most remarkable eyes."

"Vic used to like my eyes," Roxy said listlessly.

"You have a beautiful body, too," Zack said. "You probably thought I hadn't noticed, but I haven't stopped thinkin' about it since I met you, wonderin' what you looked like without your clothes, fantasizin' about makin' love to you."

I heard the sofa creak. From the sounds I thought Zack had stood up and was coming toward Roxy. Then she stood up. I hoped he remembered she still had the gun.

"The eyes are the windows of the soul," Zack said with great feeling.

Oldest cliché in the world, I thought. And then I thought, Wait a minute . . .

"You are such an old soul," Zack said. "I am, too. We are both old souls."

Where else could you find such deathless dialog? Prescott's Landing, *of course.*

I could even remember the scene. Molly Carstairs standing there droopily in front of Sheriff Lazarro, just as Roxy was standing now.

I raised my head. For real this time. Roxy's back was toward me. Zack had his arms around her. He saw me looking and glanced sharply from me to the gun which was dangling from Roxy's limp right hand.

I'd like to say I leaped to my feet and took the gun away from her in one mighty motion, but the truth is, not all the feeling had returned to my body after all.

There were parts that still felt as if they were dead, and one of those parts was my left leg, which let me down as I tried to propel myself upward. What happened was that I stumbled awkwardly into Roxy, almost knocking her and Zack over, and she dropped the gun.

I threw myself backward, afraid it would explode. What do I know about guns? When it didn't explode, I threw myself at it and scooted it across the floor and under the armchair. I noted at the same time that Benny was no longer flat out on the sofa. He had disappeared. Which would seem to indicate he had moved. In which case he was probably alive.

Zack was still holding on to Roxy, who was sobbing hysterically. I ran for the bathroom, did what I had to do, then came back and picked up the telephone.

At the same moment I heard Bristow's voice echoing up the stairs to my loft. "Are you up there, Charlie?"

I put the phone back down.

CHAPTER 18

Monday night, a couple of weeks later, Angel and Miguel brought take-out Mexican food from Casa Blanca; Savanna and Bristow brought a chocolate cake. Zack uncorked a really good Cabernet Sauvignon and set out some of his special beers. I used my security guard key to enter Dorscheimer's and borrow plates and cutlery. (Theirs were better-looking than mine.) Benny brought along his cage, complete with T-shirt blankie, cardboard box, and a sprig of parsley to chew blissfully on.

Ben hadn't suffered any ill effects from Roxy's cruelty. I had found him after the law arrived, hunkered down under the sofa in a nest of cotton batting big enough to house half a dozen rabbits.

We'd kept up with news accounts of the aftermath, of course. And Bristow had hauled Zack and me in to take statements, but this get-together was designed to bring everyone up to speed on the whole story.

"According to his bank records, Hank Spangler had been receiving regular payments from Vic Smith aka Vicenzo Cervantes for many years," Bristow said as soon as everyone except me was supplied with tacos and refried beans. I was having a taco salad.

I gave an exaggerated shudder. "I knew all along that man was sleazy," I said.

"Unfortunately, Charlie, sleaze isn't against the law. Nor is receiving an 'allowance' from your supposed brother-in-law."

"He says it was an allowance!" I exclaimed, outraged.

"He says and Roxy says. There is no evidence to prove otherwise."

"So Roxy is protecting her baby brother," I commented. "Good thing she didn't deny everything she told Zack. Even with me listening, his word probably wouldn't have been enough to convict her."

"Possibly not," Bristow said. "However, she's now insisting we coerced her confession, so your word is going to be pretty important."

"She says she's innocent?" Miguel exclaimed.

Bristow sighed. "Her lawyer says she's innocent. She just smiles and *looks* innocent. Her confession contains details of the murder that weren't released publicly, of course. A description of the rug wrapped around the body, the place where he was killed, which we didn't know before that, what happened to the knife she used. If we get to use the confession, we'll have her nailed."

"Roxy's father knew she was the guilty party," I said.

"He insists Vicenzo killed Malena. But yes, he had to know all along. That's why he got them both out of the state right away and paid off as needed. Protecting his baby girl. Hank knew, too, of course. He *says,* however, that he never knew anything about the murder and his brother-in-law gave him money out of the goodness of his heart."

He looked at me kindly. "I don't think we can prove he threw that rock at you, or that he set up those E-mails."

I shrugged. "Even if he doesn't get convicted of anything, I doubt he'd have another go at me without reason. He was just trying to frighten me off so I wouldn't find out that Roxy was the guilty party in both murders."

"Charlie told us Roxy killed our father at some house he was working on," Miguel said to Bristow.

"Because he'd suddenly decided to turn himself in and stand trial," I added hastily. "Roxy was so horrified at the idea that she blurted out she'd killed Malena to make him understand they couldn't go back to Texas. So then it was Vic's turn to be horrified and he was going to turn *her* in."

Zack, Bristow, and I had decided it wasn't necessary to let Angel and Miguel know their hiring of the private detective had been the triggering event. It would probably come out in the trial, but some time would have passed and maybe that would help ease any guilt they might feel. "What did happen to the knife?" I asked.

Bristow frowned. "Roxy washed it and put it back in the flatware drawer she took it from."

My stomach lurched in protest. "Someone might have used the knife afterward? On food?"

"Someone *did.* The couple who bought the model house made a deal with Sal Migliatore to keep the contents that had been arranged for display. Both had full-time jobs. No time to shop around, they said. They'd been living in a furnished apartment. The arrangement probably suited Sal very well."

"Ick," Savanna said. "Imagine cutting food with a knife someone was stabbed with."

She hadn't had much to say so far and she wasn't making inroads into her Mexican food. And Savanna *loved* Mexican food.

I studied her face. She looked okay, but without her usual shine. Normally there was a luster about her, but it seemed to have gone missing. She caught me looking and shook her head slightly. *Okay*, I mouthed, understanding she didn't want any comment made.

"Soon as we got the address from Roxy we sent in a lab team," Bristow said. "The couple who bought the house were very cooperative. Too cooperative. I've had to threaten them with all kinds of dire consequences if they talk to the tabloids or go on any talk shows until after the trial. The wife already has a book deal with a major publisher. No doubt there'll soon be a movie in the making."

Zack's eyebrows had slanted up. "They live in Mountain View?" he asked.

Probably he was wondering if there was a part in it for him. He could even play himself. To my considerable relief, he'd told me his friend the director had nixed the country-western tavern series idea after talking it over with some money men. I was willing to bet he'd be on the couple's doorstep offering his services the very next day.

"Anyhow," Bristow continued, after a puzzled

glance at Zack, "the blue-light special turned up some old blood that had trickled under the kitchen cabinets. It matches the blood on the rug Vic was wrapped in and that of Vic himself."

"Fingerprints?" Zack asked. He always made a big deal about fingerprints. *Prescott's Landing*'s writers must have been hot on the topic.

Bristow's grin was without joy. "This pair had one of the most thorough cleaning crews in the history of California. We were lucky their mops couldn't get between the floorboards and the cabinets."

"So does Roxy now deny Sal was there?" I asked.

"Not at all," Bristow said. *"She* wasn't there, so she has no idea if Sal was there or not. That's her story and she's sticking to it."

"He must have loved her to dispose of Vic's body like that," I said. "All the same, he didn't do a very good job."

Bristow nodded. "He was pretty sick by then, by all accounts. Possibly he hoped the treatments he was receiving were going to do some good and he'd be able to dispose of the body more sensibly later. Or maybe he just wasn't thinking straight at all."

"Do you think Roxy will be convicted?" Angel asked. His bronze complexion had gone almost blue-white around the eyes and mouth. Miguel looked strained, but Angel was the one who was suffering most. He was, of course, more sensitive than his brother.

He was sitting next to me, not eating. He'd pushed his plate away as Bristow talked. Now his hands were clasped on the table. I put my hands over them and pressed lightly and he looked at me and attempted a smile that didn't come off at all. The expression in his eyes made me want to cry.

Bristow looked at him kindly. "It's not going to be easy, but we'll do all we can to make sure she's convicted of both murders," he said.

He looked at Miguel. "You'll be going back to Salinas?"

"That's where I make my living," Miguel said. "Getting back on a bull is going to seem a lot easier compared to almost being accused of murdering both my parents."

"The worst part," Angel blurted out, then stopped. We all looked at him and he took a swig of beer before going on. There was a hectic slash of red across his cheekbones. "The worst part of all of this is that for the last twenty-three years I believed my father killed my mother. And he didn't. We should have known he didn't."

"How could we know?" Miguel said. "We saw them fight. We saw her body. He took off. What else were we going to think?"

"But he didn't do it. All those years we hated him. And he didn't do it."

Great. Angel was going to be the casualty here. Once someone decides to suffer from guilt, it's not easy to change their minds. I know from experience. I almost starved myself to death because I thought I should have died with my parents. They'd wanted me to go on the Tahoe trip with them in their Cessna, but I'd had a date with a high school jock and had pleaded to be allowed to stay home. It had taken a lot of therapy, arranged for by my ex-husband, for which I would be forever grateful, to get me out of the downward spiral guilt had put me into.

I held on to Angel's hands. Angel was a gentle man, but there was a lot of macho posturing about him also. I doubted he would take kindly to any suggestions of therapy.

We chewed over the rest of the details as we finished the meal. Or at least some of us finished the meal. Neither Savanna nor Angel appeared to have any appetite. Every once in a while I saw Bristow look longingly at Savanna, but she appeared to be avoiding eye contact.

When they left, I saw Bristow put his hand to her elbow as they went through the door. Savanna shrugged it off. The marriage I had expected to sail on effortlessly throughout their lives was in trouble, through no fault of their own.

Miguel was the next to leave. "I'm sorry we never had that date, Charlie," he said, then leaned over and kissed my cheek very gently. "It's not that far to Salinas," he added, his lips brushing the hair over my ear. "You could come watch me perform."

"I just might do that," I said.

Zack was giving me his amused eyebrow expression. I ignored him. I had truly become impervious to him again since the Roxy incident. Somehow the shock of the pistol-whipping Roxy had inflicted on me had either redirected my hormone activity or had totally killed off my libido. Whatever the cause, I'd been without reaction in Zack's presence ever since. Though he hadn't seemed to notice, which was a little irritating.

Just as I was hugging Angel and telling him we needed to have a good long talk real soon, Gina Giacomini walked into the main corral. "What are you doing here?" she asked us. "I came in to do some bookkeeping and saw the lights on. It made me nervous."

Good timing, Gina, I thought. She was looking at Angel adoringly. She never had been one to cover up her feelings. She'd also toned down her usual punk look, I noted. Though her ears were still surrounded by earrings and her clothing looked like thrift-shop chic, her hair was all one color, might even be her own natural chestnut brown. And her lips and nails were pink, rather than black or blue.

"Hi, Angel," she said tentatively. "How are you?"

"Okay," he said. For a moment I thought he was going to soften, but then he straightened his posture, picked up his white straw cowboy hat and put it on, gestured with his head to Miguel and said, "I have to be going. Sorry," to Gina.

"Hang in there," I told her as she stood, disconsolately watching him walk away.

"Sure, Charlie," she said flatly, then left herself.

"How about I open up another bottle of Cabernet?" Zack said from behind me.

I turned to look at him. It always amazed me that he could wear a cowboy hat for hours, then take it off to reveal attractively tousled dark hair. The warmth of my cowboy hat, though my relatively new white one had more ventilation than my previous one, was enough to make my hair crinkle into a million tight spirals. For the hundredth time, I wished Maisie Ridley—the hair stylist who was the only person to ever tame my hair into submission—hadn't married her long-lost boyfriend and gone to live in Vancouver, B.C.

But heck, did I really care what I looked like? As long as I was over whatever had been affecting me where Zack was concerned, there was no reason for me to worry about my appearance.

I took my hat off and put it on a neighboring table, then sat down again, ignoring the feeling of hair springing into curlicues all over my head.

We talked for a long time. About Bristow and Savanna, Angel and Gina. About the past few weeks and how sad it was that Angel and Miguel hadn't had the benefit of their father's company for so many years. Though Zack thought Vicenzo must have been something of a wimp to go running off when he hadn't actually done anything wrong.

He didn't, of course, consider Vicenzo's seduction of a seventeen-year-old to be anything to get upset about.

After a couple of hours, we thought we'd like some coffee, so I invited him up to my loft, which, of course, was a perfectly safe thing to do, all things considered.

I was wrong. We'd both had a few glasses of a rich and supple wine. Not enough to make us tipsy, but enough to give us a pleasant glow, a feeling, on my part at least, of complete contentment and relaxation.

"My hair must be a sight," I said, as I put the coffee makings together.

"I like your hair, Charlie," Zack said. "It's one of the many parts of you that I really admire. It has so much energy. Electricity."

Somehow during this discourse, he'd managed to come up behind me. He put a hand on either side of me on the sink edge, trapping me against it. His body wasn't touching mine, but there was a layer of heat between us that was almost like a touch. Glands were calling to glands—I could hear them through the pulse throbbing in my ears.

"You're all woman, Charlie," he said softly. "I have very special feelings for you. Would you like me to tell you what kind of feelings?"

I backed up, intending to push him away, but somehow that didn't quite happen. Somehow I got turned around instead and he was holding me very close indeed.

"I love you, Charlie," he said.

And then he started kissing me.

I think I've mentioned before that this man is a world-class kisser. There never was anybody in my entire life who kissed me as gently, smoothly, wonderfully as Zack Hunter.

So, did I kiss him back? Of course I did. What did you think? You didn't actually believe all that stuff I said about being cured, did you? The brain sets up neural highways and synapses to receive and analyze data. The body just reacts.

I must admit, it occurred to me that Zack had sounded just as convincing when he told Roxy he loved her. I also realized that you never really could believe anything an actor said, because he was used to saying things that weren't true in a very convincing way.

But there must be times when an actor is offstage, mustn't there? Times when he really is telling the truth?

Don't you think?